C000300113

Novels

The Lords of Xibalba
The Oil Eater
Blocking Paris
Edge of the Pit
The Catalina Cabal
Exodus from Orion
Quick Read
Legend of the Broken Paddle
Poets and Philosophers
The Island Classic
Scottish Roots

Novellas
A Present for Kainani

Middle Grade Books

Hunt for the Wild Honu
Hunt for the Wild Taro
Hunt for the Wild Pueo

Scottish Roots

Bill Thesken

KOLOA PUBLISHING

What though on hamely fare we dine,
Wear hoddin grey, an' a that;
Gie fools their silks, and knaves their
wine;
A Man's a Man for a' that:
For a' that, and a' that,
Their tinsel show, an' a' that;
The honest man, tho' e'er sae poor,
Is king o' men for a' that.

Robert Burns

BILL THESKEN

1.

It was half past three in the afternoon on the north shore of Oahu when Callum Maclean got the phone call and he was still stunned by it, walking as though in a haze.

The restaurant was bound to be busy that night. It was too late in the day to call anyone else in to cover his shift, and he couldn't leave his friends in the weeds, so he rolled up his sleeves and punched in at the time clock.

He shook his head while standing there, trying to shake the fog with it.

The day had started fair enough, light trade winds, passing showers, surf gribbly and pathetically small, barely shoulder high but the tropical salt water good enough to wash off the left-over grease that wafted from the fat fryers in the Mexican food restaurant where he worked the night shift.

Keeping to his regular schedule after the morning surf, he stopped at the liquor store near the beach to pick up a bag of poi and a tin of pineapples for breakfast. Tires crunching into the gravel parking lot he spotted his buddy Tavita standing near the side by the bushes so he wandered over to see what was happening.

Tavita, Polynesian for David was a strapping muscle-bound Tongan Hawaiian, mixed martial arts, rugby player, tougher than most and a world class rascal to boot.

"Check it out Callum."

He leaned down and pointed into the bushes.

A grubby white and brown spotted chicken was pacing nervously nearby, while hidden in the grass were two eggs, age indeterminable. It was impossible to tell whether they'd just been laid or were ready to hatch, smudged with dirt or something.

Tavita pulled out a crisp twenty-dollar bill from his pocket and held it shoulder high between them.

"I'll give you twenty bucks you eat one of those eggs, raw, right now."

Callum looked at the crisp twenty, down to the eggs, back to the twenty, shrugged his shoulders, reached down, grabbed one of the eggs, cracked it on a rock, swallowed the contents in one gulp and grabbed the twenty.

It happened so quickly that Tavita didn't have time to hold onto the bill.

"Hey! You gotta let me have a chance to win it back!"

"Right there cuz," said Callum pointing to the remaining dirty egg on the ground.

Tavita winced. He obviously didn't expect this turn of events. Hissing through gritted teeth. Reluctantly leaning over, grabbing the egg, muscles tensing along his neck as he took a deep breath, steeling his nerves, cracked the egg on a rock and tried to gulp the slimy contents but there was something else in the muck, he gagged, tried to chew and swallow, then barfed into the bushes, face red, veins bulging, sweat pouring from his cheeks.

"Ka-ching," said Callum with a smile, and pocketed the twenty.

"Damn you Callum," he whispered wiping his mouth with the side of his shirt.

"I was going to get some poi and pineapple for breakfast, but now I'm kind of full," said Callum with a grin. It was good fun to battle with the locals, and they admired his grit.

"I'll get that twenty back some day."

"Maybe."

"I got some new boards coming in next week if you're interested."

"Naw, I'm strapped out from my last trip to Indo. In fact, this twenty bucks is gonna put gas in my car."

He led the life of a nomad, working and saving his money for months at a time, then spending it all on exotic trips to faraway lands. All-in, no holds barred.

"How much did that last trip cost?"

"Ten grand. Six weeks. Private boat to all the islands."

Tavita whistled.

"I'd do it again," said Callum.

"You still renting that room from that crazy old lady?"

"Fifteen hundred dollar a month rat trap. You hear of anything better?"

"Naw, this place is packed. You know how it is this time of year. All the surf stars and wannabes coming over for the show, winter on the north shore, whoopee."

"Yeah, whoopee. At least I have a good job working nights, make enough money to pay the rent, buy some boards now and then, free food all night while I'm working."

"See you this Saturday for our match against Kaneohe," said Tavita with a serious face. "They kicked our ass last time. We want revenge."

Island style rugby. Saturday at the park. Grudge match. Kahuku against Kaneohe. Callum nodded.

"We'll get 'em this time."

"I gotta go," said Tavita. He reached over and swatted Callum on the shoulder, but he was no slouch either, six three, a hundred and ninety pounds, swirling black hair, smattering of freckles across a large, angled nose. Tavita's sizeable mitt didn't budge Callum.

"I'll get that twenty back someday," he promised.

When Callum got back to his little room on the side of the house with his pineapple and poi, he could hear the TV blaring from the living room and the crazy old lady Mrs. Harkins laughing, then cursing and talking to herself and the TV. Sometimes yelling and whimpering, then bouts of singing. This was her up time, midday before the meds kicked in. Callum had a couple of bites of poi and pineapple, put the rest in the little fridge, laid down on the cot, put the pillow over his head and fell asleep.

And then just as he was deep in REM land the cell phone rang. He looked at the screen. A mainland number.

"Hello?"

The voice on the other end was steady, the tone official, a businessman.

"I'm calling for Callum Maclean."

"Speaking."

"This is Winston Feldman, I'm your father, Archibald Maclean's attorney."

Callum had seen the name Feldman many times on documents over the years. He sat up and rubbed his eyes.

"Why are you calling me?"

"Your father passed away this morning."

Silence.

"What happened?"

"Old age. He was eighty-five you know."

Callum didn't respond. He knew how old his father was. Exactly sixty-two years older than him, nearly to the day. He heard the story many times while growing up. Three wives and no children, then with his third wife he struck gold so to speak. When he told one of his friends he was going to be a dad, the friend asked if he was crazy. Sixty-two years old with a baby. Bit of an age gap and maybe in the end that was the problem.

"How did he go?" asked Callum again, asking the same question with different words maybe he'd get a straight answer from the lawyer.

"He passed away peacefully in the middle of the night in his bed. The maid found him in the morning."

Bullshit thought Callum. No one passed away peacefully, even in the middle of the night in their own bed. It was a fairy tale.

"Now what?"

"You can come home and pay your last respects if you want. I have a copy of the will for your review. If you don't want to come home, I can mail the will to you. Part of the arrangement is to leave a ticket at the airport for your travel back to the mainland for the occasion."

"I can pay my own way," Callum lied, his face flushing red with a sudden rush of emotion. The hell they'd pay. He wouldn't let 'em. He'd have to scrape up the money. Sell the car and the surfboards.

"Have it your way."

"Was he still working?"

"Fourteen hours a day. Right up until last night in fact."

"What's the empire worth now?" asked Callum. "Ballpark."

Silence on the other end wasn't the attorney calculating the net worth. He knew to the penny and was just stalling. Maybe he was under no obligation to disclose.

"Somewhere in the range of fifty-two million. We'll need to audit the books and the accounts receivable, rents due, land appraisals. With the shopping centers, gas stations, car washes, restaurants, apartment buildings, vacant land, there's a lot of loose ends that need to be tied up. It might take a while."

Sure it will, thought Callum, and that whole while billing time as attorney's tend to do. Fifty-two million. The old man was busy. And that was one of the other problems. He was always too busy.

"I'll be there," said Callum and hung up the phone.

As far as Callum knew, he was the only heir to his father's empire, to his fortune. The two previous wives and even his own mom passed away long ago, and he was all that was left.

That thought sobered him, even as the crazy old lady next door cackled at the TV.

No brothers or sisters, aunts or uncles, niece's nephews, or cousins. It was just him and his dad for the longest time. And maybe that was the biggest problem of them all. Now that problem was gone and he was alone.

That's when the fog swept over him. As he stood by the time clock ready to punch in for his shift, the manager, Randy, came around the corner.

"Hey Callum, you're early today. That's good I think it's gonna be a busy night."

In that split second, just the formality of business, the things that needed to be said, messages that needed to be conveyed, the simple task of punching a timeclock and talking to a co-worker cleared the fog.

"Say, Randy, my dad passed away this morning. I'm gonna have to go to the mainland tomorrow."

Randy was a softie at heart and gave Callum a hug, patting him on the back for a moment.

"I'm sorry to hear about that buddy, you take as much time as you need. We'll handle it without you. No worries. Just let me know when you're coming back."

Callum shook his head.

"I'm not coming back."

With fifty-two million in his pocket, he figured he didn't need to work on a line anymore. That thought while standing at the time clock was the most sobering of all. Even though he didn't lift a finger to make that pile of money, it was there.

2.

The flight to California from Hawaii took exactly five hours and twenty-nine minutes from the moment the wheels left the tarmac in Honolulu till they touched down with a screech in LAX, the brakes and thrust reverse slowing the giant plane down, pressing the guests forward in their seats. In those five plus hours the sky had turned from bright aqua blue with low riding fluffy white clouds to dull grey strata cirrus at twenty thousand feet covering the world with a monotonous color.

The last plane ride Callum took was to Indonesia and that was a twenty-hour marathon each way, so this little hop was like going to the corner store on his bike.

The night before he dropped off his car and surfboards at Tavita's house, signing over the title to the little old truck.

"When I come back don't be surprised if I buy one of those oceanfront homes down by Pipeline."

He thought about renting a car at the airport in Los Angeles but decided to take up the attorney's offer to send his dad's chauffeur to give him a ride. He hadn't seen old Willie in about five years and he hadn't changed much.

Thin as a wire, chain smoking teetotaler, ragged hair, crooked teeth, wild look in his eyes but the guy could drive. He could do a five-lane merge on the freeway going eighty-five in a limo the size of a small caboose.

Callum tossed his bag in the back and sat up front. Willie squinted his sharp black eyes at him.

'You got any I.D.? You sure don't look like the kid I saw five years ago, heading out the front door swearing never to come back."

The great thing about Willie was he stayed above the fray and never BS'd you.

"How you been Willie? You sure as hell look the same. Maybe your hair got a little longer."

"Longer in the tooth too. See?"

He grinned nicotine-stained bicuspids. Callum grimaced.

The last time Callum saw Willie, he was standing next to the limo at the porte-cochere in front of the mansion, waiting for the old man, ready and waiting to take him anywhere he wanted to go. That was his job, to wait by the car in case something happened somewhere at one of the businesses, and the old man needed to take care of a problem. Callum walked by the front bumper with a backpack stuffed with clothes, murmuring: "I'll never come back here as long as I live."

Five years ago.

Willie whistled and shook his head, truly saddened by the past.

"It's a heck of a thing. A father and a son."

"Nothing we can do about it now," said Callum.

A car horn blared behind them. Someone was getting a little anxious. Willie put the limo in reverse to give them something to really be anxious about, then put the long car into drive and eased out into traffic, the glint in his eye peripheral, all business, weaving through traffic towards Bel Air.

The mansion was all lit up, red glowing sunset in the deepening sky to the west. It seemed as though there was a light in every room of the house, and there was at least a hundred different spaces, bedrooms, hallways, bathrooms, living rooms, dens, there was even a small theatre on the ground floor.

Moving vans were parked outside. Workers were wheeling furniture on dollies up ramps and into those vans.

"What's going on?" asked Callum.

"Didn't they tell you? It's time to move out," said Willie.

Callum looked over and it was the first time he'd ever seen a twinge of worry on the driver's face.

"You moving out too?"

"Afraid so."

They pulled under the roof next to the long sidewalk that led to the front door which itself was the size of a small house. Who had a front door fifteen feet high and twenty feet wide?

Callum started to reach for the bag in the back, then thought twice. Something made him leave it for the time being. He walked through the front door as a giant couch was being wheeled out, the edges wrapped with thick brown moving paper taped snug.

Giant foyer, crisp white marble tile under a round chandelier with a thousand diamond cut glasses lit the entrance. Callum remembered when his dad bought it from a palace in France and shipped it back to the states. Rumor had it that Beethoven played piano under it one night for some king or prince. To the left and right, sweeping stairways wide enough for a herd of elephants to climb to the second story with the bedrooms and spas. Straight through on the ground floor was the great room, with pillared columns from Rome, tapestries from Alexandria, and huge pots from ancient Greece painted with stiff looking animals and warriors battling with spears and shields.

Solid dark mahogany doors to the right of the great room led to the library with ten thousand books, thick leather chairs, wide desks, and a piano in the corner. A small bespeckled man stood at that doorway and waved towards Callum, who walked the long distance across the marble floor towards the man. This must be Winston Feldman the attorney.

The small man reached out his hand and Callum shook it politely.

"Thank you for flying over on such short notice, and again I'm very sorry for your loss."

Callum didn't reply, he just nodded and walked past him to stand in the center of the library. Rows and rows of books filled the walls twenty feet high around the room. Each wall had its own ladder on sturdy rollers to access the high shelves. He reminisced, in a split second just being in this place, the musky smell of the wood, leather, and paper balled up into a heady mixture, all the hours of homework and tutoring, the pain and torture of striving to be better, always better, have to get to the top of the class Callum, nothing less than straight A's would ever do.

If a room could somehow retain a bit of a person's spirit, it seemed to Callum that some of his remained here, entrenched in these paper-filled walls. One thing that always struck him was how quiet it was in here when the doors were closed. You could hear your eyelashes when you blinked, and your heartbeat was clear as a bell. How could anyone think and study with such an oppressive, overwhelming lack of sound. The thick books packed together, paper and ink, leather bound perfect soundproofing insulation. You could have a rock band perform in the center of the room and no one in the rest of the house would hear a single note. Callum knew that for a fact since when he was fifteen, he brought in a band for him and his buddies around midnight and the old man didn't hear a peep and slept through the night.

"What's going on out there?" asked Callum, rising out of his daydream and back to reality. "Why are all the furnishings going out the door? Isn't there normally a reading of the will before all the stuff is parceled out?"

"Yes," said Winston. "About that. Readings of the will are for TV, and movies. There's no set procedure. I have the will right here on the desk for you, and as the estate attorney it's my obligation to give you a copy for review. There will be no official reading of the will."

He motioned to the desk next to the south wall. There was a single sheet of paper sitting on the smooth wood, and a TV set up in front.

Callum sat down and looked at the paper. On top was letterhead in bold black letters:

LAST WILL AND TESTAMENT OF ARCHIBALD MURPHY MACLEAN.

At the bottom were three signatures, his dad's, a witness, and a notary public embossed stamp with a signature and date from last year.

In the middle were three short sentences, surely not enough information to convey a fifty-two-million-dollar empire, and yet he read:

To my beloved son Callum Murphy Maclean, I leave the family home in Oban, Scotland.

To my personal residence: driver, maids, cooks, cleaners, handymen and gardeners I leave Fifty Thousand American Dollars each.

The remainder of my estate will be sold at auction in accordance with the provisions of the recorded Trust documents, and the entire proceeds donated to Saint Jude Children's Hospital.

Callum looked up at Winston.

"Is this some kind of a joke?"

"I'm afraid not Callum."

"I'll challenge this. I'll contest this in court. The old man must have been senile when he wrote this. He was eighty-five years old for crying out loud. He must have had dementia. I'll prove it."

"He left you a video."

The blank TV was staring Callum right in the face. He could see his reflection in it. The old man left him a video.

"Alright let's see it."

Winston turned on the set and stepped to the side. There were two chairs nearby but he did not sit down, probably getting ready to run for his life in case the jilted beneficiary got rowdy.

His father's face came on the screen. He was sitting in a chair right across from where Callum was sitting now. In fact, the rows of books on the screen mirrored the ones in real life. The old man liked to put on a realistic show and was most concerned with minute details. At the bottom of the screen with the date nearly one year ago. His dad's face was long and full, deep wrinkles under his ears and eyes, and around his neck, the top of his head a mat of black tangled hair tinged with a sprinkle of grey.

"Well Callum, if you're watching this video then I'm long gone. Hopefully to a better place. You've probably seen the last will and testament and aren't in agreement, or maybe you are. It's been so long since we've spoken that I don't know what you might be thinking, and I blame myself for that. I know I've been a hard driving man most all of my life and I, in the end drove you away. It was probably for the best. A man must learn how to live on his own. You've heard this story before a few times, and you're going to have to listen to it one more time. As you know, my parents brought me to this country in ninety thirty-nine when I was two years old. Right at the end of the depression and things couldn't have been worse. You might think that a two-year-old would have no recollection of tough times, but you'd be wrong about that. I grew up poorer than the dirt we walked on and saw my parents suffer mightily. I promised myself at a young age to prosper and with the opportunity this great country offered, the freedom to build an empire, I did just that to some extent. I think at this point in time with all the businesses together I have a net worth north of sixty million."

Callum looked over at Winston who shrugged. Back on the screen his dad sat back in his chair and sighed.

"The problem might be for you, and hopefully it's not, is that this particular net worth I'm talking about is mine, not yours. I found out a long time ago that you can't give someone money or property and expect them to be grateful or truly happy. Only things that are earned are worthy. The greatest inheritance one man or woman can give to their offspring is never money. It's the grit and determination, the wherewithal, the drive, to make it on their own."

"The house in Scotland where I was born has remained in our family for the past two hundred years. It's yours. You can do with it what you want. Sell it. Bulldoze it. Give it away. Or do nothing. It's your choice. It was the one thing in my life that was actually given to me, and so I'm handing it down to you as well. My trust will provide a round trip ticket there and back and a stipend of one thousand dollars to see you through while you decide what to do with it."

"You'll note from the will that I'm providing some money for the people who I've employed over the years as severance pay. I've also helped each and every one of them invest their paychecks over the years wisely so that none of them should be in the poor house. They've worked faithfully for me all these years and they deserve it."

"The shopping centers, restaurants, gas stations, car washes, apartment buildings, houses, land, cars, boats, equipment, furniture, clothes, every last bit of it will be sold and the proceeds go to those who truly need it, the children and their families struggling with health issues in a hospital."

"I tried my best not to spoil you while you were growing up. It might not have been exactly a Spartan upbringing where you had to battle your peers and steal food to survive, but maybe it seemed like it at times."

His dad was silent for a moment staring out from the screen. Then with a solemn nod he said one word.

"Goodbye."

The TV went blank and Callum still watched it. Mesmerized. Where a moment ago his dad's face lit up the screen, now the reflection of his own took its place. An empty hollow feeling swept over him, emotions boiling up from deep within some pit at the bottom where his chest met his stomach, and he struggled to hold them back, steeling his will.

'Not now,' he told himself. 'Not with Winston standing right next to me.'

He stood up and took a deep breath.

"When's the funeral?"

"Yesterday. He left specific instructions that he was to be buried no later than twenty-four hours after his passing, and we followed his orders."

Callum shook his head. "The old man sure was efficient, wasn't he?"

"Precise."

Winston handed Callum an envelope. Inside were ten crisp hundred-dollar bills, a map with directions to the house from the train station in Oban, a key to the front door, and a name on a piece of stationery. Tom Gillam – caretaker.

"Tom works at the Glencruitten golf course and you can ask him any questions you might have about the house. He's been taking care of it for the past twenty years since your grandpa passed away. He knows that you might be coming for a visit."

"Mind if I take a look around? Just for old times' sake?"

Winston managed a bit of a sympathetic wrinkle of a smile on his face.

"Help yourself, I'll be with the movers."

Callum walked up the stairs to the second floor and opened the door to his old bedroom.

It was empty. Cavernous, silent. The walk-in closet was also bare and he wondered if the movers had just finished clearing it out, or if it had been cleared out five years ago on the day he walked out.

He looked carefully at the floor. The carpet was smooth, no foot tracks or furniture impressions. He checked the walls. No pin holes where he hung his rock n roll and sports posters. No glue where he pressed the little stars that glowed in the night when he was a child and afraid of the dark. The paint was a different color than he remembered and it was well cured. This room, he decided, had been empty for half a decade.

He thought about looking in the old man's room, then put that thought out of his head.

Standing at the top of the stairs, getting ready to walk down it for the last time, again, he smiled, hopped the seat of his pants up on the banister, one hand forward, one hand back for stability, gave a rebel yell, and slid down it.

He could almost hear the echo of his dad's voice yelling at him to knock it off. The movers stopped what they were doing when they heard the yell and applauded him when he landed on the ground floor and slid a few feet on the slick marble.

Riding down on his butt was easy. Over the years when he was young and reckless, he tried a skateboard, a snow saucer, and even a bike that nearly ended in disaster. Good times.

Outside and to the right was the ten-car garage, all the doors wide open, lights shining bright on the shiny grey epoxy floor. Lined up, front bumpers facing out, ready to rumble down the highway at a moment's notice, every one of them looked like they were washed and waxed every day; a black colored Bentley, a red Ferrari, three Mercedes, one of them a convertible, an ice silver colored Hummer, a black 1923 Ford model-T in mint condition, a 1961 Jaguar type E, a 1967 Camaro, and there on the end, the lime green 1969 Ford Mach 1 with the 428 Cobra Jet engine. The one he crashed when he was sixteen and got grounded for nearly a year.

Callum sauntered past all the cars, like a moth attracted to the green light shining from the low-slung hood of the muscle car at the end.

There was a large man with a bald head hiding it with a trucker hat and reflective sunglasses watching him from the outside corner of the garage. Security guard. These cars alone were probably worth over a million.

Callum nodded at him, but the man did not nod back, or move a single muscle. He just watched in silence. He was a big guy probably around two fifty, two seventy-five, and carried a serious attitude like most of them do at that size.

The bigger they are, the harder they fall.

Calculating weight speed inertia, Callum figured he could do a shoulder feint, get a head start, two, three steps at most, leap into a ninja spear tackle feet first into his ankles, get him sprawled on the ground nullifying his weight advantage, put him into a sleeper hold then drive off in the Mach 1.

Callum walked next to the lime green car, gazing at the magnificence of it, the perfect lines. Looking through crystal-clear windshield glass, he could see that the doors were unlocked. A long time ago before he wrecked it the first time, he hid a key under the seat on the driver's side, wedged it in between the tuck and roll leather and the metal support bar.

"Mind if I take it for a spin?" asked Callum, eyeing the guard carefully for a reaction.

"I'm sorry sir, everything has to stay put."

Sir. From a guy twice his age.

"You know who I am?"

"Yes sir, you're Callum Maclean. I was told you might stop by. I have specific instructions to make sure everything in this garage stays put."

Callum nodded. Specific instructions. What other kind was there in this house. He left the Mach 1 behind and wandered around the garage. It was lined with tools and supplies for maintaining the cars, everything had a place and everything was exactly in the place it was supposed to be, and not a single drop of oil or grease or dirt to be found. All ship-shape. Floor jacks, and compressors, air guns and hoses, waxes, washes, polishes all with their labels facing straight out, microfiber towels folded neatly and stacked in straight columns. A show room.

And yet there in the corner, tucked behind a tall compressor, he spotted something out of the ordinary and walked over to it. Hidden in the only shadow in this brightly lit garage were two golf bags wedged next to each other, while leaning against the wall in tandem.

"Well, what do we have here?" he whispered.

Two identical golf bags, matte black, with bold white names on each of them. Archibald Maclean on the left, and Callum Maclean on the right.

The bag on the left had a large silver tag hanging off the handle. In the middle was a quote in black letters: "Dig it out of the dirt like I did." A quote from Ben Hogan. It was his dad's favorite quote: "Dig it out of the dirt like I did, that's where you'll find your swing." His dad didn't only use it as an analogy for golf, he used it for life and his endless pursuit of business success.

In some ways Callum hated that saying. He opened the rain cover on top of the bag on the right. He could see the security guard watching him carefully in the corner of his eye.

Lined up neatly, forged irons glinted in the first light they'd seen in over five years. Three iron though sand wedge and putter. They looked brand new, not a hint of dust, except for the sand wedge which had a thin coat of rust on the face, and that was done on purpose long ago, the theory being that a bit of rust gave the ball a little more spin out of the sand. He took the head cover off the driver and lifted it out of the bag. There was a little strip of lead weight on the back of the head, something he tried to give him a little more umph off the tee. The grip had hairline cracks, probably from the dehumidifier in the garage sapping the moisture from the rubber.

He took a small slow practice swing with the big club. Envisioned driving a golf ball way down the fairway, following through with the club high over his head, watching the ball race through the sky.

He left his dad's clubs alone, not wanting to take off the rain cover to see if they were in the same mint condition. Put the head cover back on the driver and slipped it back in the bag. Nodded his head once in resolve. Took the silver tag with Ben Hogans quote from his dad's bag, and latched it onto his own, hefted the bag over his shoulder and walked towards the open garage door.

The big guy with the attitude took a step towards Callum with his hand stretched out.

He took his sunglasses off with his other hand and put them into his top pocket, as though he was getting ready for some action.

"I'm sorry but I have my orders, everything has to stay."

Callum stood the bag up right in front of the big guy. There was no way he was leaving without this bag, so if there was going to be trouble, they might as well get into it quick.

"You see that name right there? This is my bag, these are my clubs, and I'm taking them with me right now."

Callum took a half step back and watched the big guy. This was one of those deciding moments that came along every once in a while, and he got ready for whatever decision the guy made. One thing that was crystal clear in Callum's mind though, he was leaving with these clubs regardless of any specific instructions anyone on this whole estate might have.

The big guy squinted in the bright lights while studying Callum, sizing him up, then decided that he wasn't getting paid enough to get into a scrap with *this* guy over some golf clubs that belonged to him anyways. Besides, with an experienced eye, he could tell that there was no guaranteed outcome judging from his attitude and balanced stance.

"Go ahead man, take the clubs. Like you said, they're yours."

Callum nodded. Good choice.

"What about the Mach 1?"

"Don't push it man."

Callum grinned. "Guy's gotta try right?" He hefted the bag over his shoulder and headed for the limo parked in the porte-cochere, Willie standing faithfully next to it.

"Got your clubs back I see. You spending the night Callum?" he asked hopefully.

"Take me to the airport Willie." He stopped himself as he placed the golf bag in the back seat and looked over the limo at the old driver.

"Please."

As they pulled out of the long driveway back to the highway Callum did not turn to look back at the house, but he did manage one quick glance in the side view mirror next to the passenger window as they turned the corner, and it was gone.

3.

"So the old man cut you out of the will?"

It was kind of funny hearing Willie call his employer 'the old man'. He would never let Mr. Maclean hear him say that. He wouldn't even slip and call him Archibald, or Archie, that might be cause for termination, or worse.

In a way Callum and Willie were compatriots over the years as Callum was growing up, somehow, someway withstanding the withering overwhelming industriousness of the man who ran the iron-clad castle. They were like the pillars of Hercules holding up the temple walls upon which rested a mighty city.

"He gave me a thousand dollars and a house in Scotland."

Willie whistled. "That's a heck of a lot more than most people have in this world."

"Don't lie, I know he gave you fifty."

"Yeah, but a house."

"Have you seen the house?"

Willie couldn't lie. "I've seen a picture of the house."

"Me too," said Callum. "He took me there when I was three years old. I don't remember the trip, but I've seen the photo. He gave me a copy of it one day when I made the mistake of questioning his upbringing compared to mine. He showed me the picture and said this could have been the house I grew up in if he was a worse father."

"He showed me that picture too Callum. Not long after you walked out. Maybe a year or two. No one heard a word, not a peep from you. He finally hired a private investigator to search for you. The guy had a friend in the state department and got your passport records. Found out you were living in Indonesia, on the beach. Selling trinkets to tourists for enough money to eat rice, climbing coconut trees for water. Nearly killed him. He was supposed to go to an awards dinner and I went to look for him. In the library, hunched over the desk, he was a wreck, just staring at that picture. To be honest with you it's the last time I ever saw any emotion on his face and he would never admit it. After that it was all business. But that was fine too, business was his natural element and he was happiest, most content I should say, when he was plowing forward, merging this, selling that, building something else."

"He was pretty hardheaded."

Willie laughed. "Well dang if that coconut didn't fall too from *that* tree. Huh? You don't think you're a little hardheaded? Sheeeet...."

"Maybe a little. Jun kan po for a dollar?"

Switching the subject.

"Rock paper scissors? You're on," said Willie. Their favorite game while driving somewhere as long as the old man wasn't in the car. He would never approve. Willie kept his left hand on the wheel and his eyes forward on the road, and with his peripheral vision he could see Callum's hand and his eyes to make sure he wasn't delaying his motion.

"Junk Ana Po, I Canna Show" A shake of the fist with each word, then the player either opened the palm in shape of a sheet of paper, two fingers like scissors, or kept it in a fist like a rock.

Rock smashed the scissors, scissors cut the paper and paper covered the rock.

Simple. Except the two combatants would get into heated battles sometimes while hurtling through the streets to a soccer or a baseball game, or to school when Callum missed the bus.

It was a quarter a game, and Callum used it to his advantage since the old man didn't believe in giving a kid an allowance and Willie liked to bet. By the time they got to the airport Willie was up by a quarter and as they pulled in next to the curb Callum told him okay, double or nothing till the end of the world.

Willie put the limo in park, turned to face Callum and it was on.

"Junk Ana Po, I Canna Show"

They tied over and over, rock to rock, scissor to scissor, no one went to the paper since that took an extra millisecond of motion and was easy to spot. Finally, Callum could see a slight nuance in Willies' motion, he was going for the scissors again so he stayed with the rock, then at the last microsecond Willie extended all fingers from scissors to paper to cover the rock.

"Hey!" shouted Callum. "You watched my hand!"

"No way," laughed Willie. "Pay up."

And that was that. Callum dug deep in his pocket, handed the two quarters to the crafty old driver, reached into the back seat and placed his two bags on the curb. Willie stayed in the driver's seat. There was too much traffic next to the driver's side door, and the whole ordeal was suddenly too overwhelming. He reached towards the passenger window and in his hand was a business card.

"I bought the limo from the estate. Winston gave me a good deal. So, I guess I'm going into business for myself."

Callum smiled. "Best news I've heard all day."

"Call me up if you ever get back here. I'll give you a good rate."

"I'll never come back here," said Callum.

"That's what you said the last time I saw you."

"Well, I think this time it's for real. There's never going to be a reason for me to come back to this town."

They were silent for a moment, the implication settling in.

"Since I'm never going to see you again, I got a favor to ask," said Willie.

"What's that."

"When you left, you had a reason, and I always wondered just exactly what that reason was."

Callum shook his head.

"There was no one reason. I guess in the end I just got pushed too hard, you know? He was always pushing me. The tutoring, languages, art, music lessons, I was always on the go, he was always in full tilt attack mode, the pressure to succeed, always pushing me, like I was a horse he was training for a race, as though everything was a competition. He flew off the handle when I got a B in science. Can you believe it, a lousy B. The only B I had through *all* of high school. With one semester to go, I left. I thought about coming back a couple of times, but never could bring myself to actually do it. The longer I stayed away, the easier it was."

"You ever think about finishing that last semester and getting your high school degree?"

"Why? I wouldn't be valedictorian. What's the point?"

"So that was it. The straw that broke the old man's back. You weren't going to be valedictorian. All or nothing huh?"

"Nothing less."

"So now what?"

"Now I go to Scotland and sell the family house and move on with my life. Into the unknown." He made a gesture with his palm like a wing taking off.

"I'd like to give you some advice Callum if that's okay."

"Fire away."

"My dad told me life was like a long rut filled

country road. You needed to pick the right rut to drive in because you were going to be in it for a while."

"You were in this rut for a while."

"Forty years."

"That's a long time to be in a rut."

"It wasn't so bad. I had a steady job, nice house to live in. All the food I could eat. Brand new cars to drive. None of it was mine, but it seemed like it was. I remember the day they brought you home. You were the size of a loaf of bread from the store and wrapped tight as a sandwich from the deli."

"You remember that day?"

"Like it was this morning."

"Who carried me into the house?"

"Both of them. I pulled up into the porte-cochere and they walked through the front door with you in the little basket, both their hands on the handle in between them."

Willie stopped for a moment trying to decide if what he wanted to say was appropriate. It was now or never.

"You know Callum, your mother was a wonderful woman, she was like a beaming light in this house, and I know she'd be very happy with the way you turned out. Your father too. He might not have said it very often or maybe never, but I know he'd be proud. You take care out there."

He winked, rolled up the window, revved the engine, honked his horn twice, pulled out into traffic and was gone.

4.

"I'm sorry Mr. Maclean, it's airline policy."

"A hundred dollars for a golf bag?"

"Yes."

"Can you check again? I'm supposed to have a paid ticket to New York."

"Yes sir, but with one bag. You have two and the golf bag is considered an oversized bag."

Callum sighed and looked behind him. The people in line were not pleased with the delay. One lady rolled her eyes, while another tapped her toe impatiently on the floor.

The clubs were over five years old and even though they were in good condition were probably only worth about a hundred. But they were *his* clubs, one of the last items that he could call his own, and he wasn't ready to part with them. Not on someone else's terms. He thought about the money he could have gotten for his car and his surfboards on Oahu if he only knew he'd be in this pickle.

"Okay," he said and pulled out his wallet. The thousand-dollar stipend was being diminished pretty quickly. Ten percent gone and he hadn't left the city yet. He wandered by the convenience store and looked at the sandwiches. Ten dollars. A cookie, four dollars. Small bag of chips. Four dollars. Double checked his ticket. There was a meal on the flight, he'd tough it out.

Two hours later he was in the air. The jet went west over the ocean, ten thirty at night, the red eye to the east coast. Banked over the giant sprawling city, square webs of lights stretching from one end of the basin to the next, then they were over the Sierra Nevada mountains and a vast dark continent was all they saw with some spattering of lights along the way.

As soon as they hit cruising altitude the meal service began and ended fairly quickly. Most people were tired, and a lot of them skipped the meal altogether and bundled into pillows and blankets, pulled the shades down, turned the lights off and went to sleep.

Callum was on the aisle seat, and the two people next to him were fast asleep by the time the meal wagon came around.

He winked at the stewardess. She was sharp with her hair pulled into a bun and a bright smile.

"They said I could have their meals," said Callum. And so the journey continued.

At JFK there was a six-hour layover till the flight across the pond so he found an unused gate with ample seating and made a little camp in a corner. The British airline to London also charged a hundred for the golf bag, limey bastards, so now he was down to seven hundred and fifty but had some leftover sandwiches from the red-eye to gribble on. A quarter inch black stubble had formed on his face and he knew from experience that it was easier getting through customs with a shiny mug so a half hour before lift-off went into the bathroom and shaved.

Seven hours later at Heathrow the customs agent took a close look at his passport and flipped through the pages. Jakarta, Bali, Fiji, Tonga, Tahiti, Seol, Tokyo, Singapore, Manila.

He motioned to the chief and they took an extra look at Callum's backpack and gave him a pat down. Guaranteed they were looking through the golf bag as well somewhere downstairs, but he had that covered, he'd gone through every pocket and hiding place he knew while at LAX to make sure no contraband or speck of a leaf or seed was anywhere to be found.

You couldn't get a direct flight from New York to Glasgow so good 'ol Winston set him up with an eight-and-a-half-hour train ride from London to Central Station in Glasgow, the dear green place, and from there a three-hour train ride to Oban, arriving at around eleven in the morning.

Stepping out into the city at the train station he gave the taxi driver a twenty and pulled out the golf clubs that cost him a quarter of his stipend to get this far, the only wonder now was what the train charged.

Callum had been in over two dozen foreign cities in the past couple of years and this was by far the strangest of them all, since over half the people in the crowd looked just like him.

By his estimation since the wheels left the ground in Honolulu, he'd been on the move for exactly thirty-seven hours and twenty-seven minutes when he lined up in the queue as they called it to pick up his ticket on the train north.

A strange hyper-exhaustion enveloped him, an aura of relaxed meditated glow. Almost like he was floating while the weight of gravity was slowly gaining the upper hand.

It was a four and half hour, five hundred thirty-three-kilometer distance to Glasgow, and it soon became apparent that he needed to brush up on his metrics. Three hundred and thirty-one miles. At least they still counted time in hours and minutes. The trains left London every half hour and the cheapest one was the last one that left the station ten minutes before midnight, and the ticket was fifty bucks paid in advance. No charge for the golf bag so he counted that as a saving grace, and yet the stipend was dripping away. As luck would have it, late at night the passenger count was on the low side and he found an empty row and laid his head on a pillow by the window.

Even with the bumping and rolling, clicking and clacking, tracks curving this way and that, climbing and falling, through tunnels over bridges, horn blowing now and then forlorn through the dark night he slept. He might have had a dream, one or two but so fleeting and overwhelmed by utter physical exhaustion that he couldn't remember a single disturbance through the night. The last thing he remembered before falling down a deep well of unconsciousness was the clickety clack of wheels on the track, and that's the sound that woke him from the silent depths.

He must have slept on his right side the entire night and it ached from his shoulder down to his toes. His hip was stuck in a crack between the seats and he took a deep breath and sat up. The window faced east, while the sky was black a tinge of orange lit the horizon that came in and out of view as trees and hills flew by. He thought about his dad then. Three days passed now on his way to heaven probably, left his only son a pauper and rightfully so. How it must have been to be sixty two years older than a rambunctious boy.

Fifteen was a tough year, thought Callum, that's when everything changed in his life as he got stronger, more independent minded, and it got tougher for the next three years till he finally left home to the rugged outdoors to find his own way in the world. Imagine how it must have been for the old man being seventy-seven years old, an ultra-conservative workaholic with a wild teenager under his roof.

Maybe it would have been easier if his mother had survived to help smooth things out, even the keel of the ship so to speak. But she passed away when he was three. He barely got to know her, and the grace and humility that came with the fairer side of humanity.

As the train horn blared far ahead wafting through the night sky, he pulled out the picture in his shirt pocket. There she was, standing next to his father with young Callum cradled in his arms on their last trip as a family. In the background a small stone house with a grass roof. It was a simple house, square in shape, whitewashed walls, a single door in the middle and a small window on the corner. Rounded hills and mountains draped in dark ominous clouds lifted into the sky behind the house.

The Highlands.

5.

Glasgow at dawn on the first day of December can be described in one word: cold.

To the people walking alongside Callum, they had different opinions. It was Baltic dreich, with a coorse approaching from the north and drookit expected by nightfall.

Callum figured they were just saying what was obvious, it was cold and wet and miserable, and there was a storm approaching from the north and drenching rain tonight.

He wrapped his jacket up around the back of his neck and shivered into the mist that rose from the ground like ancient spirits come to life. Hefted the golf bag over one shoulder, backpack on the other and looked for the sign pointing to the train to Oban.

He actually felt a little rested from sleeping on the train, but still out of sorts with all the noise and jostling. He sat down on a long bench and it felt as though he were still moving. There was a half hour wait time before boarding the next train, and as he sat there listening to the people as they passed by, their conversations and banter, he realized that he could barely understand a word they were saying. It was a type of English, the King's English, royal and rich in tone, but foreign to his ears, vowels and syllables rounded out and scrunched into strange sounds, a robust guttural language that seemed to take great effort to speak. And even greater effort for him to understand.

Glasgow Central Station spread out in front of him. The hub of transportation to the edges of Scotland.

Someone, in great wisdom, placed a piano against a wall, free for anyone to play. A young boy with his mother standing by his side was playing a version of chopsticks, then she looked at her watch and pulled him off the bench.

Callum stood up and strolled over. Fifteen years of piano lessons, grilled into him over the course of his young life since he was three years old. Recitals, competitions, in the end he came to despise it since he was never actually good enough to win, which to his father was the only important thing in life. By Callum's estimation he had well over five thousand hours of instruction. Some things in life you never forgot and a few of the songs he'd learned could never be unlearned, woven into his DNA, into the very structure of his hand mind coordination, from the inner synapses of his brain to the tiny sinews at the tips of his fingers. He set his bags down and stretched his hands, loosening up knuckles, pressing palms together, thought about what song he might remember the best, sat down and began slowly.

Frédéric Chopin. Polonaise in A-flat major, Opus 53. His fifty-third work. The Heroic

Polonaise. Arthur Rubenstein called it the song closest to his heart, and Callum couldn't disagree.

Technically difficult with a myriad of broken chords, trills, arpeggios, quick ascending perfect fourths, rapid octave scaling, the composition was a miracle of music, a beautiful uplifting song that brought forth visions of Polish men and women dancing at court.

Ascending and descending crescendos of notes and chords, one hundred eighty-one measures blending perfectly into a six-and-a-half-minute song that ended in a flourish with two powerful yet subdued chords echoing throughout the station.

When Callum first started the song no one was nearby, and when he finished, completely entranced by the melody he was playing, fully committed to the performance, channeling Chopin, he was startled to hear applause and see a few dozen people gathered around.

Someone put a pound note on the keyboard, and a few other people followed suit, some others held back to see if he would play another song, but it was apparent when Callum stood up and thanked them, that it was a one song performance, and they all moved on. He gathered up the notes, five pounds, enough for a cup of coffee and a donut.

"Well, if things get rough," he thought, "I can always make money as a busker."

6.

Oban.

The name didn't roll or slide past your lips off the tongue, it billowed, like a cloud of cumulous mist billowing in the airy sky, or a bubble oozing out of the primordial past, the name itself sounded round at first, a two-syllable smooth edged sound, starting out like that mystical eastern mantra with an open flowing mouth full of air, then ending with tongue against the top of the tooth ridge preventing air from exiting.

Try as you might to make it sound light and airy, it was anything but that. It was a low tone with a drawn-out ending, in some ways like you were saying open but with the subtle b sound at the end, saying oh ben.

Oban. In Scottish Gaelic An t-Òban; the little bay. A rounded craggy harbor a thousand meters wide facing west northwest protected by the Isle of Kerrara that stretched along the western horizon, a mile from the center of the cove. The city ranging around the shoreline and edging up into the hillsides.

Humans lived in this very spot since at least twelve thousand years ago, during the Mesolithic, the middle stone age, coming across the land bridge connecting the islands to continental Europe during the waning years of the last ice age when the ocean levels were four hundred feet lower, the English channel a dry low running hill before the glaciers melted and the tsunami from collapsing ice shelves off Greenland smashed the dyke, emptying the Rhine into the Atlantic, filling the English Channel, and making the islands.

For thousands of years following that, the people left behind in the new islands, the hunter/ gatherer/foragers were on their own until the long boats came from Iceland and Scandinavia, before the Vikings and the Normans arrived.

Up until the 1800's the town of Oban was sparsely populated with just a few homes scattered here and there. Sustenance farmers and fishermen. Fishing boats pulled into the harbor to escape the winter storms.

Then in the year seventeen ninety-four, when France and Britain were hard at war; while British troops captured Martinique, Port au Prince, and Corsica, and the year Robert Burns published the song Scots Wa Hae in the Morning Chronicle in London, a distillery was built near the shoreline in Oban, and that small feat would change the landscape forever.

With malt barley grown in the fertile countryside creating jobs, the town began to grow.

Sir Walter Scott, the great writer of poetry and novels, such as Ivanhoe, traveled by horseback in eighteen fourteen, and that prompted more people to visit the area and it soon became a popular tourist spot. A rail line was proposed around eighteen sixty-four and was finally finished twenty years later.

It was a winding track from Glasgow, past Milton and Dumbarton over the crack in the earth that separated Lowland Scotland from the Highlands, over mountains and rushing streams, next to lochs, and hidden glens, through the Argyll Forest, heading northeast and when parallel with Ben More, The Great Mountain, the route hooked around to the west and headed back and through the Crianlarich Hills.

Over, around, and running along the Loch Awe, through the trees a quick glimpse of Kilchurn Castle, home to the powerful Campbell clan in the dangerous 1400's.

Damaged by lightning and completely abandoned in 1760, standing alone on the peninsula that stretched out into the loch, lonely and forlorn like the mountains surrounding it.

Running east to west along a long cold loch, turning southwest at Connel then though uninhabited farmland and woods, past the Railway Cottage, and MacKay's Pond, through the woods a glimpse of a golf course, Glencruitten, over a rise then past low running hills and between homes, then by the Fire Station a right turn and north into the city.

The train pulled slowly into the station and they disembarked right at eleven twenty-seven in the morning. He spotted one of the train attendants look at his watch and smile. Right on time, to the button.

Callum slung the backpack over one shoulder, the golf bag over the other and trudged slowly towards the town. Most people ignored him, but a few nodded politely. A taxi driver asked if he needed a ride and he respectfully declined. From the map he'd memorized, it was about a mile walk to the house, past the harbor, up the hill to Laurel Road, then down a side lane towards the east.

7.

The house was square and plain with whitewashed walls, set off the road by about a hundred feet connected to the asphalt highway by a thin gravel driveway.

There were a lot of other houses nearby, but this one was tucked into the woods with a few empty acres behind it.

It looked different from the picture in his pocket and he pulled it out to compare; the photo with him at three years old standing between his mother and father, and he held it up at arm's length.

The structure itself was the same general shape, but the one in the picture had a grass type roof and this one had a new modern roof with asphalt shingles. The front door was in the same position to the right of center, and the window to the left of center, a small wooden shed connected to the house on the side past the front door. He would find out later that it housed the wood burning hot water heater, but for now he wanted to make certain that he was at the right house and wasn't about to trespass on some crazy Scotsman's turf.

"Hello!," he shouted out and silence was the reply so he walked up the front door.

The wall at the front of the house was not flat but covered in round bumps. He patted the surface, it was solid, like rock, covered with plaster and paint and then he saw a small area where the plaster had cracked off, exposing a dark black stone, a river rock smooth and worn.

The house was built with stone. He knew that it was built around eighteen fifty by his great, great, great, great grandfather and it certainly looked that old. It was a wonder it was still standing. The walls were solid though and he patted them with the palm of his hand.

To the side of the front door was a small metal plaque, copper that had turned turquoise over the years, and etched into the middle in black letters: MACLEAN. Certain that this was the house he pulled out the key from his pocket and opened the door.

It was empty and dark. There was an old folding cot next to the front window, a fireplace with neatly stacked wood and that was it. Didn't look like the fireplace had been used for years, no telling if the flume was working and even though it was cold, he left it alone.

There was a bedroom at the back of the house on the left side and he popped his head into a small dark room with curtains on the back window. The open kitchen was on the right side of the house with some kind of stove and a sink. There was no refrigerator. There was a single light in the center of the ceiling in the kitchen, he found a switch by the wall and flipped it. Nothing. He went over to the sink and turned the single valve on the side of the spout, a gurgling noise from pipes somewhere under the cabinets, a burst of air mixed with bubbles out the spout, then a steady stream of greenish water that slowly turned clear. It was ice cold. He cupped his hands and filled them, studying the clarity, it looked clean, he smelled it, fresh, decided to try his luck and bent down and tasted it, sipping cautiously out of his cupped hands. It was good.

Well at least he had running water. He wouldn't need it for long. Went back into the bedroom and found the door to the bathroom.

There was a sink and a toilet and a little shower and a small window that looked towards the back yard. He flushed the toilet and it worked, the sink and shower also gurgled at first then ran with a steady stream of clear cold water. The whole set-up was the size of the trunk of a small car but it would do for now.

He went back over to the front and studied the walls at the doorway. They were just about a foot thick, rocks covered with plaster and paint, the doorframe bolted into the rock with rusty bolts. The door itself was solid and looked like it'd been sawn whole from a two and half foot wide log. He shut the door from the inside and checked the edges, they seemed to fit tight.

It was starting to get dark so he walked around outside. There was a clearing out back behind the house, the nearest bushes and trees a hundred yards away. The ground felt soft and boggy. There was an old plastic chair leaning against the back wall, so he sat in it and listened to the world around him. It was quiet.

Off in the distance he could hear a car approaching on the road out front, it whooshed by and all was quiet again. He saw a movement in the corner of his eye and stayed completely still while searching for the source. There it was again, scurrying in the treetops then dropping down to the forest floor, a little red tinted squirrel. It darted around under one of the larger trees then zipped back up it again.

At least he wouldn't be alone in this strange place. Off in the distance a dog barked long and eerie, the echoes of its howling drifting through the darkening landscape.

That's when he realized that there were no shadows and he hadn't seen one the entire short afternoon on his walk to the house. The diffused light through the thick high clouds afforded no sharp light to effect an outline against shapes. Even the colors were muted, making everything a dull shade of grey. He sat there pondering the events that brought him to this place.

"This is my inheritance," he thought and sat there until it was nearly pitch black, then felt his way around the house to the front door, locked it, shuffled with shoes till they met cot, laid down and fell into a restless sleep.

8.

The next day at dawn Callum woke up with a cold nose. Dim grey light filtered in through the kitchen window as he looked at the ceiling and remembered where he was. Tucked into the wool blanket wrapped tight around him from the top of his head to the tip of his toe, still bundled with layered shirts and jacket, socks and shoes, he peeked out from his igloo and covered his nose with the blanket for a moment to try and warm it before venturing out.

He yawned, deep and long and his breath fogged in the cold air. There was no getting around it, he had to get up and use the loo.

Looked at the fireplace with the cords of wood stacked neatly next to it and decided to give it a try that nigh. He sat on the edge of the bed with the blanket wrapped around his shoulders and looked at his watch.

Eight thirty. He'd slept for fourteen hours straight, like a bear in hibernation. He shuffled across wood floors to the bathroom, then over to the kitchen window and looked outside. It was a gloomy day with high overcast clouds that didn't look like they were moving. The front door opened with a creak and startled the squirrels nearby that scampered quickly away.

It was quiet. There was a bit more light than when he got there last night and he took a walk around the house. It looked solid enough, four walls set on a concrete foundation and a simple roof with a chimney.

Hunger, the driving force of life, made its sudden painful growling appearance in the empty pit of his stomach. He went back in the house, pulled out the last soggy sandwich, tried to take a bite and couldn't do it, went back outside and flung it into the bushes nearby for the squirrels, emptied his backpack on the cot and put it over his shoulders, grabbed his wallet and started walking back to the city.

It felt good to stretch his legs and as he walked his spirits lifted. The air was fresh, the day was young, and he was in Scotland. In the Highlands. It had taken so long to get here.

Forget about the fifteen hours in the air, and the nine hour train ride after leaving Los Angeles. It took twenty years since the last time he was here, and he didn't remember a single thing about that trip when he was three years old. Might as well spend a couple of days looking around before selling the house. Not one to shop for the best deal when he was hungry, he stopped at the first store he came to.

With backpack full of bread, sliced meats, cheese and fruit, and a donut in hand ready to eat, he began to feel better, checked the map and headed over the hill to the golf course and asked the first person he saw if they knew Tom.

"He's down at the buggy barn."

"The what?"

"The maintenance shed."

He was an old lean man, but sturdy in stature, changing a tire on a golf cart. For some strange reason he seemed to know exactly who it was that had come to pay him a visit.

"Well, well, well, Callum Maclean, in the flesh. How you doing lad?"

He reached out to shake his hand and it was a hearty shake indeed from the old man.

"Just wanted to say hello, I just got in last night. Wanted to see if there was anything I needed to know about the place."

"I was sure sorry to hear about your dad. He was a nice man and came back to visit just about every year for the past four or five. You found the house alright. Glad to hear it. Did you catch a ride with a taxi, or have another friend of the family pick you up?"

"I walked. It's not too far from the train station."

"I could have given you a ride but no one gave me a phone number, or a time that you were arriving. Are you staying at a hotel nearby?"

Callum looked at him with a quizzical eye.

"I'm staying at the house. I slept there last night."

"That drafty old house?"

"Wasn't so bad. There's a cot with blankets and a pillow."

The old man narrowed his eyes.

"You sure that you're Callum Maclean, son

of Archibald Maclean?"

"Positive."

"And you stayed in that house rather than a hotel?"

It suddenly became clear to Callum. Tom Gillam thought he was rich like his dad.

"That house is all I have. My dad left his entire fortune to charity and gave me a round trip ticket to Oban to take possession of the family heirloom and do with it what I want. That's why I'm here."

Tom settled back on his heels. "You don't say. Now that's a lump to digest. No family fortune?"

"Maybe there's a bag of jewels hidden in one of the walls." Callum shrugged his shoulders. "Figured I'd stay a few days and take a look around. Might never come this way again."

Tom nodded. "So that's why they gave me specific instructions..."

"Who gave you instructions?"

"Your dad's attorney, Winston Feldman. Told me you were coming to Oban and to leave a cot with blankets and a pillow at the house. Nothing more, nothing less. Said it came directly from the top, from your dad."

"After traveling for two days on planes and trains, that simple cot made me feel like the richest man in the world."

"Is there anything I can do for you lad?"

"I need a recommendation for someone to help me sell the house."

"Oh," said Tom visibly surprised.

"I'll never live here, and I don't have the

funds for the upkeep."

Tom nodded, eyes studying Callum.

"I understand lad, and I know just the person. Let's go right away if that's your choice.

I'll give you a ride back to town, and we'll go to her office."

9.

They parked at the back of the alley behind the Oban Distillery and walked by the entrance on the side. The looming building itself was constructed mainly of rough-cut granite blocks, while large square black stones, polished with bright white grout formed an arch over the heavy wood double doors.

They could smell the wafting aroma of single malt flowing out into the air, mixing with salt seaweed fish fragrance of the port town at low tide. Small boats lay on their side in the muck waiting for the tide to turn and refloat them again. Tom promised Callum an authentic plate of fish and chips from his favorite cart down by the bay. They could hear the distant fluting of a bagpipe somewhere down by the water and were just about to round the corner by the shoe store and head south along the tourist traps.

"Penny's a good lass," said Tom. "She'll take good care of you. I can help ya fix the place up a bit, make it easier to sell."

"I don't want to put you out anymore. You've been a great help to me already. I can't pay you any money, I'm just about tapped out."

"I'll make a deal with you. I'll work for free, and when you sell the place you can pay me a fair wage from the profit. Eight pounds an hour, what do you say?"

Callum got out his phone and punched the calculator.

"It's a buck twenty-three cents to the pound lad. It's the equivalent of ten dollars. With my skill level and work ethic, I don't think you'll be disappointed."

Callum was still looking down at his calculator while walking around the corner and didn't see the three girls walking around the corner towards him. Tom tried to pull his arm but it was too late, Callum plowed right into one of the girls, nearly knocking her to the ground.

She barely caught herself from going splat in the mud and had a fiery look of anger in her eyes.

"Watch where you're going, ya big ooff!" she shouted.

In that split second, everything in the world changed.

Callum took one look at her as she was bouncing away from him. He juggled his phone from one hand to the other, nearly dropping it on the ground, finally latching onto it with two nervous hands, then standing still watching the person he nearly knocked into the street.

She was about five foot two, with dark auburn hair down past her shoulders, a pert figure dressed in a jumpsuit and faux leather jacket with black felt boots up past her well-shaped calves.

Callum had seen his share of beautiful women on his trek through the southern oceans, all around the balmy seas and maybe it was the physical act of bouncing off of her, or maybe her spicey perfume, or the look in her eyes, or the shock of being physically out of control, nearly dropping his phone in an uncharacteristic moment of klutziness, or maybe it was the way her mouth set perfectly on her face, or maybe it was everything all rolled into one, he was stunned.

"Sorry Margaret," said Tom, removing his hat in respect, "We weren't paying attention to where we were walking."

She looked to be about twenty or twenty-one, and the two other girls she was with looked about the same age. She put her two hands on her hips and nodded.

"I should say so. I nearly get knocked into the mud, and here with me new boots and all."

She looked at Callum, tilted her head, waiting for him, the giant offensive bloke, to apologize.

He stood there, mouth slightly open, eyes wide, glazing over, immobilized. The proverbial deer in the headlights.

"Well, what about it?" she asked him again.

"Uh..." was all he could manage. His brain was frozen jelly, his voice nonexistent. He blinked.

"Does he talk?"" she asked Tom.

The two girls with her giggled.

Tom looked over at Callum and chuckled,

shaking his head. He thought about poking the young man in the ribs to bring him back to life.

"Well, I'll be damned. Margaret, I'd like you to meet the honorable Callum Maclean. He's here for a short stay, he inherited the Maclean house up on the hill. You're practically neighbors."

She looked back at Callum with renewed interest.

"So, you're Callum Maclean? I've heard about you."

In that moment he thawed. The iceberg that was his brain came suddenly back to life. There was hope after all.

"You have?"

"You're the boy who ran away from home five years ago."

He frowned, his temperature now on the other end of the spectrum, cheeks turning red. He turned towards Tom with an inquisitive look on his face. Tom shrugged his shoulders.

"This is Scotland lad. We're a clannish people for the most part, and yet when times are slow, we catch up on the neighborhood so to speak. Your father, bless his soul, told me the details a few years ago, and I might have let it slip over some beers at the pub."

Callum turned his attention back to the attractive tormentor. He did his best to hold back a scowl.

"I was eighteen and not quite a boy. And I didn't run away. I walked, at my own pace and on my own terms."

"Well, I usually walk around this corner at

about this time of day, at my own pace and my own terms, during the week. And I hardly expect to be knocked down by a..." And then she was at a loss for words while looking at him.

"A big oof?" Callum finished for her.

Her face softened a bit.

"Well, yes. I'm on my lunch break and I like the sandwiches down at the Deli. These are my friends, Coraline and Tammy."

He shook both their hands politely.

"You can call me Maggie." She reached out and placed the palm of her hand in his while they looked at each other, her hand much smaller and he was careful not to crush it. "Well, I've got to get back to work," she said as she pried her hand away. "Have a nice day."

She turned efficiently on her heels, gathering her two friends with her and off down the sidewalk they went and crossed the street.

Tom put the hat back on his head and looked over at Callum who was dumbstruck again, standing still, watching Maggie as she walked away. He was waiting to see if she looked back. The most important question in the entire history of humanity itself hinged on the next few moments. If she didn't look back then it was over for him, there was no hope in the world. And might never be again. She'd already taken about twenty-five or thirty steps, and with each additional step got incrementally farther away from that mystical glance back.

"Best forget about that one," said Tom. "Let's get moving again. C'mon lad." He reached and pulled on his elbow.

Then, just as Callum was about to turn and walk in the other direction for the rest of his life she turned her head back over her left shoulder, quickly, without her two friends noticing, and locked eyes with Callum for a split second then just as quickly turned looking forward again.

That's all it took. A slight wrinkle of a smile formed on Callum's face as he turned, then shrugged his shoulders.

"Nice little neighborhood you've got here."

"Yeah sure," said Tom. "Well, really gonna miss you even though I just met you Callum. Actually, gonna miss taking care of the Maclean house. I won't lie, that fifty pounds a month came in handy. Oh well, that's life. Let's get you on over to Penny's real estate office."

He reached over, patted Callum gently on the back and tried to nudge him forward. But Callum did not tend to budge easily. His feet remained planted firmly on the sidewalk.

"I'm startin' to be thinking what's the rush," he said. "I mean after all I did just get here. That old house has been in the family for a couple hundred years, what's a couple extra days to give it a good send off. Besides, to be honest I kind of like the look in that girl's eyes. Feisty. Kind of wouldn't mind seeing them again, just to see if it was an illusion, some sort of magic trick she played on me."

"Now hold on Callum Maclean. Out of all the girls in Scotland, out of all the girls in the world for that matter, Margaret MacQuarrie." He shook his head woefully.

"So that's her last name."

"Yeah, that's her last name and that's the reason you'd be best off forgetting all about doing the two step with her."

"She seems nice enough, what's the problem?"

"Are you daft man? It's her namesake, her kinfolk. The problem isn't with her. It's with her father."

"Mean dad syndrome huh?"

"Not to her he isn't. Dotes over her like she was the princess of the entire world. But he can be one of the meanest orneriest bastards this side of Argyll forest to everyone else. Especially outsiders like yourself. Most especially Yanks."

"How old is she?"

"Well, I figure she's probably twenty-one by now."

"What's the age of consent in this country?"

"I'm sure it's sixteen."

"Well, there you go."

"It doesn't matter what the age of consent is lad, not in all situations and in this one in particular. The consent of the father is the law of the land with that clan. He may relent someday to his daughter getting married, but there is no way in hell on God's green earth that he'd allow her to marry anyone but a Scotsman."

"I didn't say I wanted to *marry* her, I just wanted to take another look at her."

"Well, that's fine then Callum Maclean. You can look all you want. Talk to her all day long on the corner. Gaze at her to your heart's content. Have a sandwich with her down by the Deli. Keep her picture by your pillow while you sleep at night. But I'm telling you straight, if you think you're going to play footsies under the table or hold hands walking through a meadow on the moor, you're going to find yourself in a world of trouble."

"What's he got against outsiders? And I'm a Maclean you know. I have roots here. I'm a Scotsman. Well sort of."

Tom shook his head. "No, you're not. You weren't born and raised here. You're an outsider and you always will be. Even if you live here till you're old and grey and a hundred years old, you'll always be an outsider. It doesn't matter if your dad was born here, you weren't. You're a blow-in as we call them. They come all the time, blowing in on the winds from all around the world. Some of them stay, but most of them leave, the weather is too harsh, and they're not connected to the land enough to withstand it, and they blow right on out of here the way they came in. True Scottish roots are in the feet of the people who've walked this land barefoot from the cradle. It's just the way it is. No offense."

"Nothing new to me," said Callum with a shrug. "I've had to live with this attitude everywhere I've gone in my short twenty-three years. I've always been an outsider. Never thought I'd be an outsider here, where for once nearly everyone kind of looks like me. It's okay, I can handle it."

10.

The next day around ten in the morning Callum took a stroll towards town and got there just around eleven fifteen. He picked wildflowers along the way, and by the time he got to the edge of the town he had a fist full of blooms and a bouquet the size of a soccer ball.

He waited by the corner by the shoe store with one eye on the Deli, and the other down the street where he'd caught the back glance.

At exactly eleven thirty the three girls came strolling down the street, laughing, and giggling at something or other, like girls normally do when they're young and full of life.

He held the bouquet behind his back, stood straight, feet planted firm and swore to himself that he wouldn't freeze up this time when he saw her. Control. That was the key word. In life, in martial arts, in surfing, rugby, control was everything, even when things were spiraling out of control around you, within was calm.

They spotted him and their demeanor changed. His eyes latched on Maggie's and he could almost see her whisper, "What the..."

As they got closer, he smiled to take the pressure off his face, and lighten his mood, but inside his heart was pounding, and his breathing was becoming short and shallow.

Looking at her for the second time was making him feel very uncomfortable. On edge.

She raised her eyebrows as they stood in front of him.

"Well, well, well. Callum Maclean. Two days in a row. This is becoming quite the regular event. Have you knocked anyone down yet?"

He frowned.

"Not yet, but the day's still young. I might get lucky again."

Her friends giggled while her eyes sparkled. The ice was broken for good. He pulled the bouquet from behind his back.

"I brought you these flowers, sort of an apology for yesterday."

Then it was her turn for short shallow breaths, palpitating pounding heart, and an uncomfortable feeling sweeping from head to toe. She tried to hide it with Scottish toughness but failed miserably.

"I don't know what to say." Her nearest friend poked her in the shoulder.

"Maybe say thank you?"

Maggie reached out and accepted the bouquet, obligingly taking a sniff with a petite nose. People walking by smiled knowingly.

"Would you like to join us for lunch?"

He shook his head. "No, thank you for the offer, but I've got to get back to the house, got a lot of work to get it in shape."

"We heard you might be selling it."

"Thinking about it. Haven't made up my mind. Never owned a house before. It's a burden in some ways, wondering if the roof's going to blow off, or this constant rain leaks through the windows, yet there's a bit of freedom, knowing I have a place to stay. It's comforting, in a way."

"Sure you won't join us?"

"Maybe some other time." He winked at them, tipped his hat and walked down the sidewalk and across the street. Just about the same spot where Maggie turned to glance back yesterday, he kept walking and did not turn his head back, but in the reflection of the window of the store that he passed, he could see the three of them watching him walk away.

"'That's how you do it,' he said to himself. 'Pay all the attention in the world, then ignore them.' Girls hated to be ignored.

The next day he was waiting at the corner again, and this time she was walking down the street alone. They watched each other warily like two prize fighters approaching the center of the ring, getting ready to do battle, then he smiled broadly, tipping his hat as she walked across the street.

"Good morning Maggie. A fine day wouldn't you say? You're looking bonnie also I might add."

She laughed. "Bonnie? So you're picking up on the slang are ya? Well, you're looking mighty braw yourself Mr. Maclean."

He frowned. "Mister? I think we're both

about the same age, I'm twenty-three. Not quite a mister yet."

"That's an old man around here."

"And you?"

"I'll be twenty-one in few weeks."

"I hope you'll be having a party."

"I'm thinking about it. Are you still going to be around?"

"I'm thinking about it."

"If I do have a party, I'll let you know."

Bobbing, weaving, jabbing.

He stated the obvious.

"I see you're travelling alone today."

"You, Callum Maclean, are a veritable master of perception."

"Heading to the Deli?"

"It's an obsession."

"Care if I join you? I'll buy you lunch."

"You can join me if you'd like. Dutch treat, I barely know you and it wouldn't be proper."

He nodded, she knew how to play the game, and try as he might, his face beamed in a giant smile. It was a date. He wanted to reach out, throw her over his shoulder and carry her to the Deli cave man style, but held himself in check.

As they walked, the people they passed nodded their heads and smiled, most of them acknowledging Maggie by name, with inquisitive looks on their faces at her companion.

"It seems the whole town knows you."

"They should. I grew up here."

He stopped. He almost forgot the cardinal

rule. The question he needed to ask before taking another step.

"You don't have a jealous boyfriend, do you?"

"No boyfriend. At the moment."

Jabbing, feinting in the ring.

"And you? A jealous girlfriend? Hiding in the bushes, ready to pounce on me."

He shook his head. Tried to say the right thing. "No girlfriend. They're too much trouble."

"Oh? So you've had trouble with girls?"

Digging himself into a hole.

He scoffed, trying for a rebound. "Naw, I do alright, just never met anyone that I really liked." He wanted to kick himself in his own ass for a stupid answer.

They walked slow and steady now..

"That was nice of you to bring me those flowers yesterday. Were you waiting for me to walk by today?"

"Naw, I just like to hang around that corner for some reason. It seems to have a lot of action."

She frowned. Their conversation seemed to hit a brick wall with a dull thud, and he knew it was time to get serious, so he spoke clear and concise.

"I'll be honest. I liked the look in your eyes the first time I saw you, and I wanted to look at them again, to see if you were real or just a figment of my imagination. Ever since I got here to Scotland it's seemed sort of strange. This place has some kind of a mystical vibe to it. Everything's different, the air, the clouds, the people. The way the sun rises and sets so low on the horizon and it's dark about twenty hours at night. I haven't slept this much in my entire life. I was afraid that maybe I just saw you in a daydream. Or an apparition that came out of the mist."

"Be careful Callum Maclean, you must know that we Scots are very superstitious. We believe in ghosts, fairies, leprechauns..."

"I thought that was the Irish."

"...the loch ness monster." She punched him lightly before continuing in a solemn voice as though she was telling a ghost story. "If you lived by the misty bogs all your life, with the silent clouds drifting by just above the ground, shivering you to your bones day after day, the whistling of the wind, strange shadows from a colorless sky, invisible animals howling from the mountains in the Highlands, you'd be superstitious too."

She reached out quickly, put her hand on his shoulder, made a scary face and yelled loudly.

"BOO!"

He nearly jumped out of his shoes and barely avoided crashing into a lamppost.

As they laughed while walking it was almost as though they'd known each other for a very long time.

The deli was crowded and they found a table towards the back along the window, facing each other.

The busy waitress was a gum smacking tart woman with big blonde hair and a lot of rouge and lipstick with a nametag that said Darlene. She spoke fast.

"Halo Maggie, where's the girls? You trading up today are ya?" She eyed Callum up and down. "You'll do in a pinch I reckon. Got any brothers?"

"This is Callum Maclean."

She looked at him carefully with curiosity.

"I've heard about you. The boy who ran away."

He sighed and shook his head, sagging into the palm of his hand while Maggie giggled and thought about hiding under the table.

"Well," said Darlene. "I've thought about running away from this place as well, most of my life actually, but never could think of a place to go."

"How about Bora Bora?" asked Callum and pulled a picture out of his pocket with him standing with his arm around a surfboard next to a grass hut while a bright blue sapphire lagoon spread out in the background.

"Ah, now you went and did it," she lamented. "My poor aching feet schlepping soup and sandwiches while I could be sipping rum from a coconut on a beach in Bora Bora."

Her eyes glazed over like a movie star on the set, dreaming of the southern seas.

"Hey Darlene!" someone shouted with a grizzled voice over the noise in the room. "More coffee!"

And just like that she snapped out of her dream and back into reality.

"You want a menu sugar?" asked Darlene to

Callum.

"You can order for me," he said to Maggie.

"Be careful or she'll order you a little Scottish delight."

"Oh yeah, such as?"

"Savory pudding."

He shrugged his shoulders.

"Sounds great."

Marlene smiled broadly, they had a green horn sitting in front of them, a rookie from abroad. "Haggis," she said with a glint in her eye.

Maggie looked at Callum mischievously.

"What's haggis?" he asked innocently enough while looking from one to the other, and Maggie was more than obliged to tell him the exact details. Happy to do so actually.

"Sure, and it's a little puddin' made from a sheep's heart, liver and lungs, mixed with onion, oatmeal, fat, salt and spices, cooked while encased in the animal's stomach."

Trying to scare a guy who just a few days ago ate a raw dirty egg from the side of a parking lot on a bet.

"Haggis sound great to me," he said with a smile. "I once ate a whole chicken raw, feathers, beak, feet and all in one bite for breakfast. Haggis sounds like dessert."

Darlene and Maggie both looked at him sideways, scrunching their faces and squinting their eyes with suspicion.

"Eww," said Maggie.

Exaggerating a story was a time-honored Scottish tradition, it some ways it was a

national sport, but it had its limits and usually
called for a swift rebuttal.

"Sure, and you ate a whole cow, hooves and
all for dinner that night," said Darlene.

"Now you're talking fantasy," said Callum,
shaking his head in disappointment.

He pounded the palm of his hand on the
table and said loudly for all to hear.

"One plate of haggis here, please!"

Maggie narrowed her eyes. "A whole
chicken, beak and all?"

"And I never lie," he said, eyes steady on her.

"Make that two," she said unwavering.

"Two what?"

"Two plates of haggis, please."

She did not elaborate on whether she ever
lied and he did not press her on it. With eyes
like that she could lie to him all day, and he'd
be a happy man.

Darlene smiled, whirled on her feet,
snapping gum, big hair bouncing, past the
cook's window, shouting:

"Two Hags!" Then in one swift motion
picked up the coffee pot to deliver a hot dose to
the squeaky wheel at the end of the bar.

"There's something else I need to tell you,"
said Callum.

Her eyes lit up.

"Tom told me flat out that I should stay
away from you."

Her face scrunched and her mouth dropped
open.

"Why?"

"Because of your father."

"Oh, that."

"Well?"

"Nothing to worry about. We're just having lunch after all. This isn't even a date. It's Dutch treat."

"So he's a bad-ass?"

She chuckled.

"More like a big teddy bear."

"Not what I heard. Protective of his little daughter?"

"I can handle myself." She sighed and shook her head. "Okay, he's a little protective. Just a wee bit. You see my mom passed away when I was five years old."

"I'm sorry."

"That's okay it was about sixteen years ago now. I've gotten over it, learned to deal with it, but he, in some ways, never really has."

"She must have been beautiful."

He wanted to tell her that he knew that it was a fact just by looking across the table at her.

"Oh, she was a knock-out, no doubt about it. Kindhearted. Hard worker. She volunteered everywhere, for any occasion, no questions asked even if she didn't have the time. When people find out you're a volunteer, you get every job in the book thrown at you. We were always on the move. And then when she passed, we came to a complete shocking halt. It took a few months to get back to some sort of normalcy. In some ways those few months when I was five years old are a distant blur, and in other ways seems like it lasted a hundred years. My father said he would never get married again. His job in life was to raise their little girl. I think it's hard for him to realize that his job is done."

"Does he have an actual job? Does he work?"

"Foreman down at the docks. Twelve hours a day, six days a week. He's a workaholic."

"I know the type."

"Is your mom still alive?"

"She passed away when I was three. I never really knew her. My father and I had a bit of a different life than you and your dad after that happened. When I was growing up I thought my name was 'DAMMIT CALLUM!'"

He smiled, taking the seriousness out of the statement.

"I exaggerate sometimes, but I try to never lie, even just a little. It's easy to remember the truth, but hard to remember a lie."

"Chicken in one bite?"

"Truth."

She shook her head.

"That's disgusting."

"So you come here on your lunch break. What do you do for work?"

"I work at the bank. I'm a teller most days. It's terribly boring, but it's a steady job and I do get to see just about everyone in town." She leaned over. "And I know how much money they have in the bank. There're some rich ones that you'd never even guess."

Darlene set two piping hot plates in front of them. They looked like giant white sausages bursting at the seams, the size of a fist. Maggie showed him how it was done, slicing the sausage on the side, exposing the steaming puddin' as she called it, then with fork in hand, lifted a bite up to her mouth and down the hatch it went.

Darlene waited patiently until Callum followed suit, took a bite, swallowed, smiled, rubbed his belly and looked towards the kitchen and gave a universal thumbs up. The cook was leaning out the little window watching the whole show along with most of the rest of the patrons in the dining room. This must be a ritual that they got to participate quite often, and they all clapped and cheered as Callum took another bite.

Apple pie with vanilla ice cream was the dessert, then a cup of tea to finish them off.

The people at the table next to them were speaking Italian, not loudly but with just enough volume for both Maggie and Callum to hear them.

"I wonder what they're saying," said Maggie.

"He's asking her if she wants apple pie and ice cream. She said that it looked pretty good."

"You're making that up."

"Oh really?"

"You don't speak Italian do you?"

Callum smiled wryly and leaned towards the other table and spoke for a while in Italian to them, and they responded in kind, smiling widely, happy to be conversing in their native language.

Callum turned back to Maggie and winked.

"They said they're having a great time here,

even though it rains a lot, and they're hoping to come back again for a visit in the summer."

Maggie was intrigued.

"How many languages do you speak?"

"I don't know." He looked down at his hand and counted on his fingers. "English, Italian, French, Spanish, German, a little Hawaiian, Tongan."

"Say something in Tongan."

Testing him.

He patted his stomach. "'Oku ou fonu. I'm full."

"Full *of* it," she smiled. "You don't speak Gaelic do you?"

"Not a bit."

"Tha sùilean math agad," she said.

"What? Say it again," he asked her.

"I will not," she said.

His face stoic, mind recorder on rewind he tried to repeat the sentence. "The suilean math gad."

She giggled, and he realized it was the wrong pronunciation and tried again.

"Tha sùilean math a-gad. What does it mean?"

Maggie's face and eyes turned haughty; her chin lifted. "I will nae tell you."

"Oh, you won't eh?"

Marlene was walking by and Callum held up his hand for her to stop for a moment.

"Excuse me Marlene?"

"Yes?"

"Tha sùilean math agad."

She blushed. "Why thank you."

"Do you even know what I just said?" he asked.

"You said I have nice eyes."

Now it was Maggie's turn to blush. "You pronounced it wrong Callum Maclean. I said tha suilean cath agad. Suilean *cath*."

Callum looked at Marlene and shrugged.

"I have battle eyes?" she asked, raising her eyebrows. "Well, it's been a busy morning."

Maggie looked at her watch. It seemed to both of them that the time had flown by. Half an hour was as though half a minute.

Marlene gave them each their own check per Maggie's instructions. Dutch treat, and they paid the exact same amount for the meal and the exact same amount for the tip. Callum tried to up the ante by adding an extra pound to his tip, but Maggie put her hand out on his and shook her head silently.

"She won't like it."

"An extra tip?"

"Dutch treat is supposed to be exact. If you add more, then you might think you're entitled to something."

Outside, walking along the sidewalk, they were suddenly silent as though everything they needed to say had already been said.

He stopped walking and she looked over at him in wonder as he leaned forward and gave her a light kiss on her lips.

11.

Some people might say that things move fast in the Highlands. But it's not a trait exclusive to the geographic area and the people that live there. Human nature being disorganized chaos within individuals on opposing sides of a wheel, opposite sides of the spectrum so to speak, man and woman, yin and yang, when they come together in harmony, suddenly, magically, out of the blue, unexpected and yet seemingly destined from the beginning of time.

Like a wheel broken in half coming together that can travel the road of life. You can't bottle or analyze it. It's not visible, but no one can deny that it's real. If you could figure out the magnetic force that attracts two individuals, you'd have the key to the universe.

Try to deny it all you want but when things are going well, it's what the entire world is made of.

As though angels on high were playing a game, putting moving pieces on a board, then rolling the dice to see what the next move would be. Put this person here, and that person there. Time it just right, and bingo.

What started as a chance encounter on a

street corner, then a simple kiss, turned into everything. The big oof and the girl in the Highlands melded together, two peas in the proverbial pod, and bloomed quickly into a whirl wind affair.

Maggie's friends noticed it immediately, the far-off look in her eyes and the glow on her cheeks and they pumped her for all the info and juicy details. She wasn't aloof, but just a bit secretive, they kissed and decided to go steady and meet every day, but that was all she would tell them.

Callum for his part was happy on the outside when she was around, he couldn't help it. Just the sight of her gave him pause, not the kind that took away his ability to talk, like the first time they met, but the kind of pause that made everything else in the entire world take a back seat, as though nothing else even came close to mattering.

But on the inside, there was a growing, nagging fear. He was running out of money and was down to his last hundred pounds. He was in a foreign country, even though the land of his ancestors where his father was born, he was an outsider and unable to work, legally.

He never had a problem finding work anywhere in the world he went, but this town so far was impossible.

If he was utterly frugal, he could make his last few pounds last a month, buy some flour and canned meats, pull wild roots from the ground.

He had no electric bill to worry about and

relied on the wood burning stove to cook his food, the wood burning hot water heater outside for showers. Candles to read by. He called the airline to see if he could sell his ticket to someone else but found out it was illegal. The best they could do was give him a voucher for future use.

He found out that he was eligible for an ancestor visa if he could prove that one of his grandparents was born in the UK. That wasn't a problem. The problem was that it might take three weeks to get a decision and it cost five hundred thirty-one pounds.

They met every day after Maggie got off work, taking long walks around the city. She showed him the whole town from the Kilbowie house on the south to the Dunollie castle on the north, and every bit in between. He declined her offers to have a bite to eat at restaurants and cafes, saying that he preferred to be outside where the air was fresh.

One evening the weather turned pleasant, it was the second sunny day of the month so far after twenty days of rain, and rather warm around forty-nine degrees. Callum joked that they should get their bathing suits and go for a swim in the bay.

They decided to take a walk up to McCaig's tower and count the one hundred forty-four steps up Jacob's ladder.

"Why a hundred and forty-four?" asked Callum.

"Have you been living under a rock all this time Callum Maclean? Jacob's ladder is the pathway used by angels to pass from earth to heaven. There are seventy-two names for God, and this gives you the opportunity to say each of them twice."

He frowned. "You made that up."

She poked him in the ribs with her free hand. "I have it on great authority."

At the top of the hill, they nearly got run over by a band of hooligans, kids of all shapes and sizes, ranging in age from five to fifteen hooting and hollering chasing after a ball rolling on the ground with weapons that looked like hockey sticks.

"Watch out!" shouted Callum, pulling Maggie safely to the side of a large bush, as the mob tumbled by in a cloud of dust, oblivious to anyone around them except for the little round ball and their nearest combatants.

"What in the heck was that?" he asked.

She laughed. "Shinty."

"Is that slang for street hockey in Scotland?"

"It's an old Gaelic game, thousands of years old. The stick is a caman, cam means bent in Gaelic. Most of them are hickory these days and can leave quite a welt. The ball is cork with a leather stitched cover like a baseball, sort of bouncy but can also leave a scar if you catch one in the chin." She lifted her chin and showed him a small old scar. "Shinty. It's usually played in the winter."

They sat by the side of the wall facing west and watched the sun set slowly into the sea south of Mull. He seemed to be sullen, brooding almost and she leaned against his shoulder.

"I might need to leave for a while."

"Leave Oban?" she asked worriedly.

He shook his head and looked at her with steady eyes. "Leave Scotland."

Her heart began to sink, but she tried not to show it.

His face was steady. He had a plan.

"I can't legally work here in Scotland without a visa and it'll take three weeks to get one. I'll apply for one and in the meantime go back to the States for a month, find a couple of odd jobs and be back before you know it."

All good things must come to an end and their happy-go-lucky carefree love affair was about to meet the realities of life.

"I made a mistake," he said. "Maybe a few on my journey here. My dad told me a long time ago to never assume anything, I remember him telling me that and never really knew what he meant, till the day I found out he left the family fortune to charity and to me a rusty old house. I never should have assumed that he'd leave me a penny, and I gave away all my possessions thinking I was going to inherit the old man's riches. I was an idiot. So, I figured that I'd come over here, sell the house and be on my way. I never thought I'd meet you."

She smiled.

"You've run out of money, and that's why you've declined stopping in a restaurant even for a cup of coffee. Tell me the truth Callum Maclean, are you broke?"

He nodded. "Flat."

She punched him in the shoulder.

"I have money you know. Loads and loads of it sitting in the bank with nothing to do."

"I don't need your money."

"I've been working since I was about fourteen years old and saved nearly every penny of it. I'm fairly rich you know."

"Congratulations wealthy madam, hold onto your money. You'll need it when you're old and grey."

"I don't want you to leave."

"I might not have a choice."

She narrowed her eyes at him.

"I've got an idea," she said.

"What's that?"

"We'll get married."

He chuckled wholeheartedly, a glint in his eye, and she clenched a fist in case he said no.

"Are you asking me to marry you, Maggie McQuarrie?"

She nodded and smiled.

"Yes, I believe I am."

"Don't you think that's the man's job?"

"Why is it? Because you're superior? You're the king, and I'm a lowly servant without a voice?"

"I'm not the king. I'm a pauper at best."

"You're a prince among men," she said. "And I've thought it over quite thoroughly over the past couple of weeks. I am the princess McQuarrie and as such have the right to choose my spouse, and I hereby choose you, prince Maclean."

He frowned and shook his head.

"You don't want to marry me?" She pouted.

"Of course I do. I wouldn't even need to think about it for a single split second. It's just that *I'm* supposed to be the one doing the asking. Not you."

Her eyes smoldered.

"Then I withdraw my proposal," she said and lifted her chin haughtily, looking away from him.

"I don't even have a ring," he muttered, then with a spark of inspiration broke a section of a green stem from a bush, bit it to length with his teeth, rolled and twisted it into a makeshift ring, and got down on his knee in front of her.

She turned her haughty chin and smoldering eyes towards him.

"Princess McQuarrie, would you be my wife?"

She threw her arms around him.

"I thought you'd never ask."

She admired the ring on her finger.

"There's just one thing left to do," he said.

"What's that?"

"Ask your father's permission."

"Oh no you don't," she shook her head seriously. "There's no need for that."

"Oh yes there is," he countered.

"Oh no there's NOT!" she shouted and punched her two open palms into his chest for emphasis. "This ring from a bush is enough. We'll jump in my car right this moment and get down to Gretna Green and get married tonight."

"After your father's permission."

Her voice swerved into a mix of Scots Gaelic and English. "Ya do nae know what you're talking!"

He shook his head.

"I can't do it Maggie. You have to trust me on this."

She sighed and hung her head, then placed it gently on his chest before looking at him seriously.

"When he tells you no, and he will say that exact word to you, I want you to take it with a grain of salt, rub in on your wound right here over your heart and on your lips for daring to ask him for permission. This is Scotland and I am of age and can marry whoever I choose without consent. I could marry without consent even when I was sixteen. So, when he tells you no, I want you to promise me that we'll pick up and go straight to Gretna Green. It's a Scottish tradition. Promise me."

He nodded. "Okay, it's a deal. But only if he says no. That still doesn't solve my problem. I still have to leave Scotland for a few weeks. I'm not taking a dime from you Maggie. I've got a bit of pride you know."

She knocked on his head with her knuckles. "You've got a bit of a hard head is what you have." Her eyes lit up. "Hey, I know someone who needs help down at the docks."

"I don't have a work visa."

She laughed. "Descended from a Scottish warrior clan, living on Scottish land, I think you can bend the rules a bit. You wouldn't be the only one, believe me. Time to give a Scots rebel yell Callum, it's in your blood."

She was silent for a moment looking at him and squinting her eyes.

"Say, wait a minute. Wasn't your dad born here in Oban?"

"Yes."

She slapped her hands together.

"That's it. He was born on Scottish soil. That means he was automatically a British citizen."

"Why not a Scottish citizen."

"We don't have independence yet. Not yet. Maybe next year. Maybe never."

She pulled out her phone, pulled up a web browser and punched at the keyboard, and smiled when she saw the gov.uk page with details on applying for citizenship if you have a British parent.

"There it is. You are automatically a British citizen if you were born outside the United Kingdom between January 1, 1983 and June 30, 2006, your mother or father was a British citizen when you were born, and they must have been married if your mother was not a British citizen. Was she?"

"She was from Pasadena."

"Were they married?"

"Yes."

She slapped her hands together again.

"You're in."

"That's it? That's all there is?"

"Well, says here you need a letter from the Home Office confirming your status."

"A letter. How long will that take?"

"It doesn't say on this website." She punched

at the keyboard, then frowned. "Maybe up to six months."

"Back to square one. Okay. What about that friend of yours that needs help on the docks?"

"Follow me."

She led him down the hill, one hundred forty-four steps from heaven back to earth, down a couple of side streets to the wharf where the pop-up seafood huts by the ferry terminal lined the sides, catering to the tourists and locals alike, then to the side door of a little blue building with billowing steam coming out the door. She popped her head in, shouted a name, and out walked a young man with sweat on his cheeks wearing a cook's apron and hat. He looked tired, but when he saw Callum he smiled broadly and held out his hand.

"This the bloke?"

"I'm Callum."

He talked fast, he was in a hurry to get back to the kitchen.

"Curtis. Heard from Maggie here that you're looking for work."

"I don't have a visa yet." Might as well be upfront about it.

"Doesn't matter to me mate. I can't find anyone to work, visa or not, resident, alien. I'm in a bit of a bind here. I've got another worker but he's an older guy and needs two days off. I can pay you cash, ten pounds an hour and all the fish and chips you can eat, you ever work in a kitchen?"

"My last job actually."

"I won't lie to you Callum. You'd be helping

me out. Maggie knows our family; my wife is home with the new baby. I'm doing everything I can to keep this place going. I can use you two days a week to start. Twelve-hour shifts."

Callum did a quick calculation, that was two hundred forty pounds per week and he nodded. "I'm in."

The look on Curtis' face was total relief with a tinge of hopefulness in the next question.

"You can start right now if you want?"

"Let's go."

Maggie kissed him on the cheek, patted his bum and watched as he went through the side door into the hot steaming kitchen, and just like that Callum went from being a line cook on the north shore of Oahu, to a line cook on the shores of Oban in the space of a few weeks.

He jumped right in; Curtis showed him the workspace. They mostly sold fish and chips, seafood chowder, shellfish, oysters, raw with a sauce. There was a cutting table, breading station, hot stove and two deep fryers.

Callum was in charge of cleaning the fish, cutting them to size, breading and deep frying, all in one conveyor belt of action. The line of hungry people out the door never let up till around nine o'clock that night and they started cleaning up and closing down.

True to his word, Curtis handed Callum five ten-pound notes.

"I only worked four hours. You gave me five."

"Signing bonus. Cash on the barrel, no paperwork, and probably best to keep this on the hush-hush if you know what I mean."

Callum walked home in the light rain with his jacket up tight against the back of his neck, fifty pounds of freedom in his pocket.

When he finally got home it was after ten at night and he was so tired he laid on the cot without taking a shower or lighting a candle and went straight to sleep.

The next day he went into town and stopped in at the bank five minutes after the doors were unlocked and opened up a savings account with the manager at his desk set to the side of the tellers. He really wanted to get a look at Maggie at her window all prim and proper and businesslike.

"How much would you like to deposit?" the manager asked.

"We'll start with fifty pounds," said Callum and put the notes on the desk. "There'll be a lot more of that in the future, I just want to test your establishment out before I go all in."

Paperwork in hand while heading to the front door, he turned and winked at Maggie.

She was busy with a customer but managed a bit of a smile, while her friends Coraline and Tammy working at adjoining windows nodded their approval.

12.

Tom was just finishing work, clearing out a culvert with a shovel, when he spotted Callum waiting by the parking lot.

"How are you doing there lad, care for a couple of holes before it gets dark? The rain's let up for a bit."

"Naw, I'm just here to see you. Got something I want to tell you."

Tom nodded. Must be something serious by the look on his face. "Alright, let's have it."

"I've decided to marry her."

"Marry who?"

"You know damn well who. Maggie McQuarrie."

"The girl you've known for about two weeks?"

'Going on three. Twenty days and fifteen hours exactly."

Tom set the shovel on its point and leaned on the long handle with a sigh.

"Are you daft man?"

Callum nodded.

"Probably. Well, some people might say it's

an absolute guarantee that I have rocks for brains. I won't change my mind."

"She's a fine girl. Does she know about this?"

"Yes of course, we've come to a decision."

"What about her father, does he know?"

"Not yet. I'm planning on asking for his permission two days from now."

"On Christmas day?"

"It's her birthday."

"I know that lad, he gives her a birthday party every year on that blessed day. Opens his house to one and all. And for one day out of the year he's a pleasurable man, reasonable, well behaved. So, you're thinking of asking him on that day because it'll give you some protection? The sanctity of the day of our lord will clothe you in goodwill? This is Scotland lad; you don't need the parents' permission to get married and the legal age is sixteen. She's well within her rights to marry whoever she chooses without any permission given."

"Just seems like a good thing to do."

"Seems like a good thing and actually being a good thing are often times at odds with each other young man. Icarus thought it was a good idea to fly close to the sun and look where that got him. Splattered all over the ground. Evel Knievel thought it was a good idea to jump over the fountains at Caesar's Palace. Same result."

"She didn't think it was a good idea either."

"So, you're going to start off your life with her by *not* listening to her advice? I think you might want to talk with my wife on that subject to see how far it'll get you lad. She'll have some words of wisdom."

"It might not be a tradition in her country, in your country, but it's a tradition in mine."

"America?"

"Yes, and well, some of the other countries I've lived in the past couple of years. Fiji, Tonga, New Zealand. It seems to work well in those places."

"Malcom McQuarrie lives in his own little country lad. It's not a republic, or a democracy or even a fiefdom, it's a dictatorship, and if you give him the decision, I'm guaranteeing you disaster. Take me advice and take your future bride by the hand, there's no need for crying the banns, announcing the wedding, just get on down to Gretna Green on the border, find the first priest you see and have it done. Asking permission from that man to marry his daughter would be like asking the Duke of Wellington to hand over all his treasure no questions asked."

"It's a done deal Tom. I'm not standing here asking for your advice; I'm just telling you what I'm going to do since we're friends and I don't really know anyone else in this blasted country."

"Well, it's been nice knowing you lad."

Tom reached out and shook Callum's hand.

"C'mon, jump in the car and I'll give you a ride home.

"Thanks, I'll walk. I need the fresh air."

"What time are you proposing to the father? I usually go to the Christmas party with the wife, just for a few minutes to pay respects.

This is something I don't want to miss."

"High noon."

Tom nodded.

"Didn't a couple of cowboys think it was a good idea to battle with Wyatt Earp and Doc Holliday at high noon at the O.K. corral? How'd that end up?"

13.

Callum walked up to the house at exactly eleven thirty in the morning on Christmas day carrying chocolates in a silver wrapped box for Maggie in one hand and a bottle of champagne to celebrate the announcement in the other.

The air was freezing cold, with a mist of light snow heading their way from the west. You could see the sheets angled in the wind and he just made it to the edge of the porch before the first flakes hit the pavement. The temperature hadn't gotten over forty-five degrees the whole month that he'd been there and was usually hovering around forty with a semi-miserable light misting rain. Thankfully the temperature was dipping down on this morning and with it the light snow. Rain, snow, it didn't matter to Callum, he was heading to the most important meeting in his life up to that moment. Asking Maggie's father for permission to marry her.

It was a lively event, the big house lit up from top to bottom, people streaming in and out of the front door. There was a piano and singing, a wafting aroma of simmering food filling the air every time the door opened.

"I'd like to ask your permission to marry your daughter," whispered Callum as he walked. "I'd like to ask permission to marry your daughter. Sir, I'd like to ask your permission to marry your daughter." His face was turning red as he practiced the sentence over and over. It didn't sound right, and then it was too late to practice any more since he was walking up the steps and through the front door.

Her father was a bear of a man, thick black hair on top of a massive head, bright black eyes shining with the glint of the chandelier over the center of the room, wearing a long sleeve shirt with the collar open at the top and curly black hair pushing up from a barrel chest, and wearing a kilt the size of a small tent spread out past his knees to hairy legs. He was standing next to the fireplace mantle that had a long double-blade sword hanging over it, glinting like his eyes.

There were probably thirty or forty people in the room all talking at once, and the moment Callum walked in the front door, the massive man squinted his eyes, stifled a frown, and managed a slight savage grin as he walked across the room.

"Welcome young man," he said, reaching out a hand the size of a catcher's mitt and shook Callum's hand. It was a firm handshake, the kind you would never want around your neck, and Callum tried to give back as well as he was getting but it was no use and when the bear finally let free Callum flexed his hand to get the blood circulating again.

"Nice handshake you have there."

"That was only half. Welcome lad, you must be a friend of Maggie's. She's in the kitchen getting more food. It's her birthday you know and we still put her to work."

He put the mitt on Callum's shoulder and maneuvered him to the makeshift bar next to the fireplace under the tip of the sword. It was almost as though he were standing now under the sword of Damocles and an imminent threat of catastrophic doom. The big man smiled broadly, aware of the implications.

"Drams on the house lad. It's a tradition."

He poured two small shot glasses full of scotch from a large square bottle, handed one to Callum, picked up the other, clinked the two glasses together and shouted.

"A toast to our new guest."

Then he took a small sip and watched Callum out of the corner of his eye.

"Thank you, sir," said Callum politely and took a mirror image sip. The liquid was smooth like gasoline and took everything he had to keep a straight face while every inch of his body wanted to gag, and he wondered if he would ever be able to use his voice again, holding back a cough while swallowing mightily. "Very distinctive."

"Special family recipe lad. It'll grow hair on your chest."

"That's why I don't drink it," said Maggie as she swept in from the side carrying a tray of small sandwiches that she placed on the table.

Wearing a bright yellow dress with her hair bunched up at the back, cheeks glowing, Callum was surprised to see her, and even though the firewater didn't make him cough, the sight of her did.

"I see you've met my father. Dad, I'd like you to meet Callum Maclean. Callum, I'd like to meet my father, Malcolm MacQuarrie." She leaned over and kissed Callum on the cheek and put his hand firmly in the palm of her own intertwining their fingers and arms as she watched for her father's reaction.

The room grew quieter as all the people noticed something different in the atmosphere, as though an electric shock went through the room. Perhaps more like a bolt of lightning on an otherwise calm summer day.

The giant magnanimous man looked at both of them and suddenly realized that he'd been ambushed. He drank the rest of the scotch in one gulp and set the glass firmly on the bar. All eyes were now set tight on them.

"So, this is how it is. Callum Maclean. You're Archibald Maclean's son, are you?"

"Yes sir."

The big man nodded.

"I was sorry to hear about his passing. So, you've come from the States to sell the family home and move back."

"I've decided to stay sir."

"Have you now." It was a calm drawn out statement with the gravity of the entire planet pulling them all down with it.

"Yes sir."

Maggie squeezed his hand ever so slightly, and Callum lifted the glass to his lips and drank the scotch in one gulp. It seemed like the right thing to do at that very moment if he wanted to stand on equal ground with the giant man who had just done the same, before he dropped the hammer, or had it dropped on him. He tapped the glass back on the bar like her father had, eyes watering slightly, then took a deep breath.

No sense in waiting any longer.

"I've come to ask permission to marry your daughter sir."

Malcolm's face grew hot red while his eyes turned icy cold, his right fist clenched and they could all hear the sinews and knuckles cracking loudly as he made a fist. His left hand stroked his black beard as though in a feint, drawing Callum's eyes upward while the fist was about to make an uppercut into his jaw.

"MAC GALLA THA THU BASTARD!" he yelled as he slammed his fist onto the bar.

Callum flinched a bit but held his ground, while Maggie tightened her grip on his hand.

The room went silent at the sudden outburst the moment the big man slammed his fist like a stick of dynamite exploding in a coal mine.

All the air in the room went flat. The once lively party was now dread silent as everyone with both ears heard the statement clearly, and all eyes were on the three of them.

Malcolm took a deep breath. Steadied himself.

"So, you want to marry my daughter, do you?" Calm now, measured, even toned. As though he were asking a normal question, in a normal quiet conversation with a friend. And yet the words hovered in the air menacingly like the tip of the sword hovering over Callum's head.

"Yes sir."

"A Yank?"

Callum gulped slightly. Even though he was warned by Tom, the anger that was building in Malcolm MacQuarrie's eyes was terrifying and real.

"Dad," said Maggie, almost pleading. "He's a Maclean."

"Sure, and he could be the direct descendant of Robert the Bruce himself. It wouldn't matter one bit to me and you all know it." His voice was forceful and loud, not quite a yell, but coming close to a shout. "He was born and raised in America, and that makes him an American, nothing more, nothing less. He'll never be a Scotsman. You think it's cold today boy, a little Baltic? Well, it'll be a colder day in purgatory before I give my approval for anyone but a Scotsman to marry my only daughter."

"Malcolm!" blurted a woman from the side.

"Stay out of this," he warned. "You may be my sister, but this is a private family matter."

"You hardheaded fool, on Christmas Day of all."

"Give it a rest woman."

"I will not. Instead of holding your hand out in gratitude to that young man that you'd be gaining a son, you just might lose that only daughter that you cling to so tightly. And with her celebrating her birthday as well. Shame on you."

"Yes, and they've waylaid me, like thieves on the side of the road while an honest man, myself is happily riding along, enjoying the day. Jumping out from the bushes to rob me."

"Rob you of what?" said another woman standing nearby.

"Of my peace and tranquility in the sanctity of my own home is what."

"Like Robin Hood in Sherwood Forest?" chimed in another woman on the side. "And you, more like the evil Duke of Nottingham."

"Gang up on me all you'd like, my answer is the same, I can nae in good faith give my consent. You all know this is the truth."

He looked around the room with all their eyes on him, and he looked back at Callum and Maggie standing sullen in front of him. She looked so much like her mother when she was younger and still alive, he could not for a moment budge in his beliefs.

The room was silent while the crowd waited for him to make the next move.

He poured another two shot glasses full for himself and Callum and put the glass nearest to Callum closer to his hand while he spoke softly.

"On one condition."

They all waited while Malcolm and Callum looked at each other. One condition, he'd said. Maybe there was hope yet.

"You win The Open," he continued, while nodding his head slowly, "and I'll give my consent."

The crowd groaned as one.

"Dad," said Maggie.

"What's The Open?" asked Callum.

"Why lad, it's the most important golf tournament in the world. You win that and I'll take you as a Scotsman. And I'll give my consent to the marriage. Nothing less."

"Of all things, why that?" asked Callum.

Malcolm leaned menacingly closer.

"Because you can nae do it. That's why."

"A golf tournament?"

"Not just *a* golf tournament boy. *The* golf tournament."

Callum's eyes narrowed on Malcolm's bloodshot angry eyes. As though his own father had suddenly come back to life, an adversary, prodding him, rattling his cage, challenging him at every turn, irritating him, enraging him, ratcheting up the pressure until he finally picked up and left.

This time he wasn't leaving.

This time he was running straight through this bastard of a one-man gauntlet. He nodded his head and said simply.

"Okay."

A bit of a cruel grin edged into the corner of Malcolm's face. It was a bargain now, and bargains were not to be broken, not here in Scotland, and everyone around them including Maggie knew full well the implications.

He picked up the shot glass full of scotch and motioned to Callum who did the same.

They both brought the glasses to their lips, downed them in one chug, then slammed the glasses on the table, nearly breaking them in the process. The bargain was sealed.

Maggie had a tear in her eye and let go of Callum's hand and swept away through the crowd towards the door. It was snowing heavily outside and she didn't care, opened the door and went straight out into the semi-blizzard hoping it would wake her up from a bad dream, shutting the door firmly behind her.

Callum followed right behind her carrying his heavy jacket that he wrapped around her shoulders. She was crying now, tears streaming down her cheeks, and tried to hide her face from him.

"Hey, hey now," he said.

"Don't hey now me, you big oof. Do you know what you've done?"

"I do indeed," he said. "I stood up to my father."

"That's *my* father."

"Same thing, in a way."

"You don't understand."

"I do."

"No, you DON'T!" she shouted, then calmed down. "You're standing on Scottish soil and you just made a bargain, a promise with one of the most ruthless men in this entire country."

"He wasn't going to budge an inch. I could see that straight and true."

"He got you liquored up is what he did. We didn't need his bloody blessing until a few minutes ago. And now we do."

"You told me it was a bad idea."

"And you did nae listen to me."

"I had to do it Maggie. There was no getting away from it. Not for me anyways. It would have been like robbing the cradle."

"The cradle is it? I'm twenty-one years old Callum Maclean, hardly still in the cradle, and I didn't need his approval."

"You have to understand Maggie, that I do. I'm not running away from it. I couldn't stand at the altar with you thinking I might have missed a step. Looking over my shoulder the rest of our lives."

"Well, there's never going to be an altar to stand at unless we find a way to break that bargain. Do you even know how to golf?"

"I was the school division champ."

"All year?"

"One tournament."

"How old were you?"

"Sixteen."

She shook her head and punched him lightly in the stomach. Such a big oof. Her mom used to joke with her to marry a man who was dumb as a rock and keep him well fed. Well, here was a young man who was dumb as a rock you'd find on the side of the road.

She used to say that joke when her father was near enough to hear it, then laugh and laugh. She missed her mom and knew that her dad did also. In fact, she knew without a doubt that had her mom been in that room just now she would have shut down any notion of a bargain, a bet that would determine whether a young man such as Callum Maclean would have the right to marry her. It would have been a done deal at that very moment that he asked permission with singing and dancing and champagne flowing.

But what was done was done, and there was no going back now.

"We better get you back inside Mr. Maclean, before you catch your death of pneumonia."

"I feel great," he said and bellowed out a cloud of hot air that jelled into a cloud in the cold air.

"It's the whisky, believe me."

"I'm not going back in there," he said. "I've come here to do what I meant to."

"Put your foot in your mouth?"

"Ask your father for your hand in marriage. It had to be done Maggie."

She sighed and pulled his jacket closer around her neck.

"I have to go back inside. It's my birthday party tradition you know. Prime rib sandwiches and drams on the side. With a bit of a twist this year. Oh, but the tongues will be wagging over this around Oban, I can guarantee it. You'll be the talk of the town Callum Maclean. Making a wager with old man MacQuarrie for the right to marry his daughter. I still can't believe you did it."

He smiled goofily, and she punched him in the stomach again.

"You big ooff. Well, if you won't come back inside, what will you be doing?"

"I've got to learn how to play golf again. Remember? I've got a bet to win."

He leaned over and kissed her, pulling her

close. She opened one eye and tried to pull away.

"They're all watching," she said.

He looked over through the windows and smiled.

"Let 'em watch." Then kissed her once more lightly on the cheek, and once on the top of her hand, then bowed deeply at the waist, it seemed like the courtly thing to do here on the front porch of a house on the west coast of Scotland in the freezing cold.

She reluctantly took off the jacket and handed it to him, shivering as she did so. Then turned on her heels and went back into the house to wild applause. Everyone it seemed was clapping and whistling, patting her on the back and hugging her with congratulations.

Everyone except for Malcolm.

He stood at the bar with a sullen face that would not be broken. The Duke of his household and all that walked in his realm.

With an insurrection at hand, a rebellion. If this were a ship at sea it would be a mutiny and no one would blame him if the perpetrator was keel hauled and tied to the mainstay. He watched as the young man on the deck, the instigator of the mutiny, stubbornly folded the coat rather than put it on, draped it over his arm and walked down the steps and disappeared into the mist, the light wonderful snow turning into light miserable rain.

14.

At six feet four inches in height, and a quarter of a thousand pounds, a full eighteen stone in UK weight, Malcolm MacQuarrie was not a man to be taken lightly. He squashed normal sized men like bugs and was well suited on the docks where large boats, rough seas, and perilous conditions existed that would smash you to bits if you weren't quick and strong, and smart. Even the strongest man in the world couldn't stop a fifty-ton ship under power, but when that deck rope the size of mule's leg was tossed from the deck to the dock, you'd better be ready to tie it off quick and taut and keep all your extremities out of the way. Malcolm MacQuarrie ran a tight harbor and his word was law.

It was a busy working harbor that handled over thirteen thousand ferry crossings, and nearly five thousand large vessels per year, not counting small yachts, and sailboats, open around the clock in all types of weather, from dead calm seas to gale force winds, although navigating from the Firth of Lorne in the most extreme conditions was frowned upon, especially in the narrow channel between the Dunollie lighthouse and the Isle of Kerrara.

During the busy summer months there could be a giant ferry in the channel every fifteen minutes. It was a very dangerous place if weren't careful.

The day after Christmas was a tough one for everyone around Malcolm on the dock. Barking out orders right and left with more ferocity than normal, one of the young dock hands asked his partner what was up.

"Mr. McQuarrie seems a bit on the downside today. Maybe he got a lump of coal and a stick for Christmas?"

His friend shook his head in dismay.

"Some bloke asked him if it was okay to marry his daughter."

"Maggie?'

"That's his only daughter man, of course it's Maggie."

"So, what's the problem?"

"The blokes a Yank."

"Oh."

"Yeah, oh is right. I heard he read the guy the riot act, said he wasn't going to marry his daughter if he was the last eligible man in the world. I heard he picked the guy up with one hand on his ear and the other on the scruff of his pants and threw him out into the street. On Christmas Day no less."

"The bastard."

"Yeah."

Another dock hand nearby heard what was

said and laughed.

"You bloggers will believe anything you hear, won't you?"

"Well, what about it?"

"I was there, at Maggie's birthday party on Christmas Day. Mac was drinking quite a bit, having a good time with the whisky he was. When out of the blue Maggie's beau, a newbie from the States, ups and asks to marry her. Stands right there, toe to toe with Mac and a bottle of Scotch and asks for his permission. You could hear a pin drop. Mac was like a volcano ready to explode but kept the lid on fairly well I'd say. Only problem for that bloke was 'ol Mac told him the only way he was going to marry her was if he won The Open at Troon. And the bloke agreed."

"Damn fool."

"So why is Mac so pissed? That's never going to happen. Never in a million years. Some bloke from the States. Give me a break."

"That blokes last name is Maclean."

The other man scoffed.

"So what? That and two pounds will get you a cup of tea."

They both jumped at the sound of it. Malcolm standing above them, eyes flashing, hair on end. He didn't need a bullhorn; he *was* a bullhorn:

"GET BACK TO WORK!"

It wasn't' the full blast from a ship's horn but just as rattling and they scampered for a moment, feet slipping on wet dock and got right back to business.

15.

Also, on the day after Christmas, Tom took a ride up to Callum's house in the late afternoon after work and parked by the old rock wall out front.

He could hear a dull thumping noise as though someone was punching a heavy bag or digging a ditch with a pickax. It was methodical, a thump, then a pause, then another thump, in rhythm, the pause between thumps uniform, the timing even. As he walked around the corner of the house, he saw the cause of the disturbance.

Callum had a golf club in his hands and was swinging it down, punching it into the bog down by his feet. Tom noted that he had a nice wide stance, a good arc to his swing, shoulder turn, hip rotation textbook clean, but all he was doing was pounding the club into the ground and had dug a nice wedge into the grassy mud, like a starting block that a runner could use to sprint off the blocks.

Thump. Pause. Thump. On one of his full back swings Callum noticed Tom watching him, and as he turned to look him in the eye, his swing still came down perfectly, the club thumping precisely into the wedge cut mud.

'There's better tools about to dig a garden you know," said Tom with a wry grin. "I could loan you a shovel and show you how to use it if you'd like."

Callum frowned. "Shovels are too easy. A fancy man's digging tools. They'll make you soft like white bread dough. I'd rather take the hard road. It's better for you in the end."

"You'd rather take the hard road eh?" said Tom. "Well, I don't doubt that. I heard all about it. Thought I'd come have a word with you."

Callum was brooding. Sweat pouring down his face and beading up on his arms even in the cold weather.

"So he said you could marry her if you won The Open eh? It's the kiss of death."

Callum shook his head. There was fire in his eyes and he was silent for a moment as he looked at Tom.

"I'm gonna to win that tournament."

Now it was Tom's turn to be silent as he watched the young man for a tell-tale sign. He knew better than to question a person's determination. After all, who knew what resolve might lay under the surface of any human being. Just look at Mother Theresa's work in Calcutta, or David facing Goliath alone on the battlefield in between two opposing armies, with a couple of rocks and a sling. But sometimes resolve met reality, and miracles didn't always happen.

"You want to win The Open."

Callum shook his head.

"I don't want to win it. I *have* to win it."

And there it was, thought Tom. Want to and have to were two different motivators in any struggle. Want could be drained from a person. It was a fleeting emotion. Wanting a shiny toy, or an object of affection was a cerebral desire displaced simply by waving a different shiny toy in front of someone's eyes, it was a child-like desire.

Have to, on the other hand, was a primordial gut wrench not easily dislodged. Like having to breathe, or live.

"I see you have golf clubs. Do you know how to play golf?"

"I've had lessons since I was five years old. Played junior golf every year till high school, then played on that team till I left home."

"The high school team. Five years ago?"

"More like six. I skipped the last year."

"So you know how to play in tournaments."

"I've been in a few."

"Ever won?"

"A few times."

"In high school?"

"Junior golf. I never won in High School."

"Why not?"

"Probably didn't feel like it."

"You didn't feel like winning in High School, and now you're going to try to win The Open."

Callum shook his head as though he didn't want to get dragged any further into this conversation, but it needed to be said.

"I had golf lessons since I could walk. Had it drilled into me. It was my father's dream that I get a golf scholarship at one of the big colleges. Win an NCAA championship. Then maybe turn pro."

"But you didn't like that."

"It was his dream, not mine. I haven't touched a golf club in five years. I still remember how to hit the ball though."

Tom nodded. Time to put on the brake pedal, not with a little tippy tap, but slam them.

"The pros that play in The Open drive the ball over three hundred yards without breaking a sweat. They can hit the ball on the hood of a car from two fifty. And those are the ones that barely make the cut. The ones that actually win can do all that, plus hole out bunker shots and fifty-foot putts on a regular basis, and they rarely *ever* miss a four-footer. The ones that win, I believe, have that attitude that you just elucidated with your statement that you don't want to win, you *have* to win. They have that utter, complete desire, the will to win, and that's what separates them from the rest of the players in any given week. The only difference is, they have the game to do it lad."

Callum walked over to the golf bag leaning against the side of the house, lifted out a club and pulled the hood sock off the head. He showed the bottom of the club to Tom.

"Three wood."

He picked up a ball and a tee from the ground and stepped over to the gouge he'd made in the ground and teed up the ball on a flat area nearby.

"You see that old trash can out there?"

Tom stood up and peered into the distance with his old eyes in the dimming light. Far out on the bog he could see a rusted old can, it looked like an oil drum that was cut in half to water the cattle.

"I see it."

"How far do you think that is?"

Tom could tell where this was headed and shielded his eyes from the glare on the horizon to get a good estimate. It was about the distance of a drivable par four.

"It's at least two fifty, probably a bit more."

Callum nodded then took a couple of practice swings, set his feet square, brought the club back in a wide round arc, and with a ferocious down swing cracked the golf ball, nearly coming out of his shoes with the impact.

Tom swiveled his head tracking the high flight of the ball through the grey sky as it flew up and up, and over the bog then took a vicious turn to the right and disappeared. Overall, it looked like it travelled about three hundred yards and ended up around two hundred yards from its intended target.

"Bit of a slice," said Tom.

Callum grimaced. "Ah!" Then teed it up again. Another giant arc, another ferocious downswing and crack of the ball, and again it flew high and mighty, and yet this time took a turn to the left, a little closer to the trash can this time but still about a hundred fifty yards wide and short.

"Bit of a hook," said Tom.

"Gad," swore Callum, his face wrenched and turning red. Then he started spewing curse words shouting into the sky, slammed his club on the ground in frustration.

Tom remained silent. He'd seen this type of reaction in players and made a lot of money as they mentally imploded.

Callum didn't say another word, just teed up a third ball, got ready to hit, then backed off, stretched his neck one way then the other, lifted first one hand off the club shaking out the fingers, then the other hand, took a deep breath, closed his eyes for a moment, then stepped back in with his square stance, looked once down the bog at the can, taking aim, a mighty swing and a crack, then as both men watched, the ball had a slightly higher flight this time, straight for the rusted can and landed smack dab on top with a loud CLANG.

Callum beamed from ear to ear, shouted out, fist pumping as he looked over at Tom, who shrugged. The old man was un-impressed.

"Sure, but can you putt?"

Callum frowned.

"I only pulled these clubs out yesterday."

"Anyone can practice a circus shot and pull it off every now and again. What's the lowest score you ever shot?"

"Fifty-nine."

Tom scoffed. "For eighteen holes? Not a par three course?"

"Well, it was a fifty-nine and I was playing best ball."

"With a ringer? A professional golfer in a pro-am maybe?"

"Naw, just myself one day. Best ball with three balls."

Tom frowned. "What about with just one ball?"

"Seventy-one."

"May I?" asked Tom as he pointed to the bag of clubs.

"Be my guest," said Callum with a gallant wave.

Tom pulled out an eight iron and hefted it in his hands, feeling the weight, grabbed it lightly with an overlapping grip and swung it a few times, then studied the face of the iron.

"How old are these clubs?"

"Probably seven years old."

"Any good?"

"The best that money could buy at that point in time."

"They're still the best that money can buy."

"They're almost ten years old, I'll bet there's new equipment..."

Tom cut him off, he knew where this was going.

"Sure, and there's new clubs that are longer, stronger, more accurate, more forgiving. Buy these new clubs and your game will be transformed like magic. It's a gimmick, but a necessary one to keep the club manufacturers in business. If golfers weren't constantly upgrading and buying new clubs, they'd all go out of business."

"Doesn't matter one way or the other.

They're all I have and I'm going to make them work."

Tom nodded.

"Aye, put your clubs away and come with me, you'll be having dinner at my house."

Tom drove them down the hill to his house and parked in the garage. A big golden retriever raced around the yard as it was nearly dark and Tom threw a ball a few times to get the dog some exercise.

His wife was inside cooking stew and fresh bread, the aroma wafting out into the night air and stirring juices in both man and beast's stomachs. Tom poured dry food from a giant bag into a bowl for the dog by the front door and ushered Callum through and into the warm light.

Colleen was by the stove with a big yellow apron, beaming from ear to ear when she saw Callum.

"Oh Tom, I didn't know we were having company." She smoothed her hair and her apron and came out to greet them.

"Mrs. Gillam," said Callum putting out his hand. She brushed the hand away and put him in a bit of a bearhug, patting him on the back and kissing his cheek. "You call me Colleen and come any time you want for dinner. I was so sad to hear about your poor old dad passing."

"He had a good life. Eighty-five you know."

"Good Scottish genes," she nodded.

Tom waited patiently on the side.

"It's potato and onion soup for dinner tonight with a loaf of fresh bread. It'll be ready in about half an hour. Now you boys go down to the sports room, I'm sure Tom wants to show you his trophies."

"Ahk," said Tom waving his hand in mock annoyance.

"This way lad," said Tom and headed down the stairs to the basement. He turned on the lights as they went down into darkness.

It was a wood paneled basement about twenty feet by twenty feet with thin green carpet like a putting surface, thick leather chairs, a pool table, dart board, giant flat screen TV on the wall and a bar with shot glasses, bottles of whisky lining the back, and the tap of a keg hidden somewhere under the bar.

"Care for a nip? I'm just having a beer."

"Sure, I'll join you for a beer."

"I've got single malt too. Best in the land. I've got a bottle from Inverness, a hundred years old. A monk found it in a barrel in the dungeon of the castle, hidden behind a false wall."

"You're joking me."

"I never joke about whisky lad."

"I'll try a nip of that."

That made the old man smile and he got out two double sized shot glasses, pulled a dusty bottle from the back shelf. It was square and thick, unlike any bottle Callum had ever seen.

"Still has the dust from the dungeon. Carries a bit of the good luck with it, surviving all these years and all. He poured each glass half full of an amber colored liquid. Callum could smell the alcohol and almost had second thoughts.

"To your good health," said Tom and clinked his glass with Callum who watched the old man carefully to see how he did it. First, he sipped at the edge of the shot glass, prepping his lips, like he was warming up for a sporting event, then tipped the glass in one swift motion gulping the shot in one swallow. Scrunched one side of his face, hissing in, then out a quick breath, then swallowed again, a warm glow enveloping his face. Instant sunburn.

Callum did the same, the vapors from the alcohol burning his nose and eyelids while he prepped his lips, then down the hatch, hold on to your seat burning as the wretched fluid passed his surprised tongue and over the esophagus, nearly choking him, holding on, holding on, then keeping his composure, no scrunching of the face of hissing of breath, the warmth of the hundred-year-old dungeon whisky seeping into his system.

Tom reached over and popped him on his back.

"Good man."

Then he led the way over to the wall with some framed photos.

Most of them were of a much younger Tom and he was always surrounded by a small band of golfing companions, or competitors.

Someone was always holding a trophy, and in a lot of the pictures it was Tom. In one of the photos, he was holding a trophy in one hand and a scorecard in the other. In the frame next to that was the actual card. The date was forty years in the past, and the score in bold lettering was fifty-nine. One of the holes, a par three had a 1 in the box.

"Shot a fifty-nine in the last round to win the tourney at the Eden course outside St. Andrews. It's a par seventy run and not an easy play on a windy day. Nine birdies and an eagle hole in one on a par three. I started the day five strokes back and won the bloody thing. Pissed the hell out of the blokes who were in the lead at the beginning of the day and ended up trying to catch me. Check out the scowl on this one's face." He pointed to a sullen man on the end who looked like he just sucked on a sour lemon.

"Barnaby Larrabee. The sorest loser I've ever come across, and I thoroughly enjoyed putting the whooping on that one. The rest of the lads were happy to see me get the fifty-nine though, and most especially the hole in one since it meant free pints from yours truly at the pub after the round."

"Why wasn't 'ol Barnaby smiling on that account?"

Tom chuckled.

"He was a teetotaler."

He walked down the line to the last photo and stood in front of it, pondering in silence before tapping the wood paneling. It was the only photo on the wall where he was standing all by himself, just standing there, arms folded with a bit of a frown on his face, in the background was a white banner with blue letters stretched out between two flagpoles that read: The Open.

"Did you play in it?" asked Callum.

"Aye. If you can call it that. Missed the cut by ten strokes. Tore my rotator cuff on the first hole of the second round. Could barely swing the club but there was no way in hell I was going to withdraw. I've got this picture here at the end to remind me that pride is a lonely occupation. I was out of the game for over a year with that injury, and never really got it back. Maybe if I would have withdrawn on the first hole I could have healed quicker, but I guess I'll never know. I was hardheaded."

He tapped on the wall again then turned to Callum.

"When I saw you thumping the mud with your club it brought back memories of me swatting at the rough on that first hole and pulling my arm out of the socket for the effort. What genius told you that was a smart way to practice?"

"Ben Hogan."

Tom nodded. Of course. The old saying.

"He's been gone a long time."

"He said to dig it out of the dirt like I did, that's where you find your swing. Pretty sure he meant to hit a golf ball out of the dirt, but I'm in a hurry, and so modified it. He won the British Open you know."

Tom frowned.

"Take it easy there laddie boy. We do *not* refer to it as the British Open. It's just The Open. The British didn't give us anything good and they certainly didn't give us golf. Call it the British Open anywhere but here in this house

118

while you're in Scotland, and you might have a few blokes swinging for ya."

"Sorry, the guy who said dig it out of the dirt won *The Open*."

Tom nodded.

"Aye. July tenth, nineteen fifty-three, at Carnoustie. He won by four strokes, six under par. The first day he shot one over par, the second day one under par, the third day two under par, and the final round four under. He got better as the tournament progressed and squashed the competition on the final day."

"How do you know all that?"

"I know a lot about golf. I know a lot about the history, the etiquette, the equipment, the players, all the different techniques for hitting the ball and scoring. But there's one thing I know that's universal. Golf is more than a game about hitting a little ball. It's about controlling your emotions." He pointed with his forefinger to his head. "It's about controlling your mind. It's about gathering it all together, and then letting it go."

"What does that mean?" Callum was genuinely confused by the statement. "Gather it all together and let it go."

Tom chuckled. "You know back at your house; you were spraying the ball all over the countryside? Then when you calmed yourself down, you hit the ball pretty well?"

Callum sighed. "I'm an idiot sometimes."

"You're like a wild animal. Like a racehorse that's only used to racing other horses on the open range and has never set foot on a track.

You have a lot of raw talent, I can see that in your swing, you have a lot of fresh energy and strength. Maybe, just maybe if you can harness that power, bring it all together, gather up the loose ends, ball it all up and tame the wildness, you might be able to tame a golf course which in and of itself is the toughest test in sport. Seven thousand yards of twisting, undulating, divot filled, bunker peppered, shin high rough that takes a machete to hack it out. Power only gets you so far in this game. You still have to put the ball in the fairway and be able to make a four-foot putt where if one dimple on the ball hits a single blade of grass the wrong way you slide past the cup. A four-foot putt is the same stroke counted on the card as a three-hundred-yard drive smashed down the middle of the fairway. But a missed four-footer can be more devasting, if you let it."

Callum looked back at all the pictures lining the wall. The old man had been around.

"Maybe you can help me?" he asked hopefully.

Tom nodded and patted Callum on the shoulder.

"That's why I brought you here. But I must tell you straight out, I have no time to mollycoddle anyone, nurse a hurt pride that needs mending, or an ego that needs stroking. There's no money it in for me, no trophy at the end that I'm going to hold for a picture. I do, however, have a tremendous respect for the game, *and* I know a little secret that might help you. To be honest, call me selfish, I guess in a way, if we can pull this off, I can use you to get back to the Open."

"Thank you." Callum put out his hand for a shake, but Tom did not take his hand just yet.

"On one condition. You do exactly as I say, no question."

"I have a question."

"Already with the questions are ya?" Tom nearly shouted, the shot of whisky magnifying his crustiness.

"What is this a dictatorship?" Callum was incredulous.

"Ay, in a way."

"What if I don't understand what you're telling me to do, and ask for the reasoning behind it?"

Tom nodded.

"You're right lad. If you don't understand what I'm a telling ya, fill out a complaint form in triplicate, take it down to the post office, and address it to the old bastard who doesn't give a rat's ass if you don't understand it."

Callum shook his head.

"It's like talking to my dad again. Are all Scots like this?"

Tom smiled. Perhaps this would be fun after all. "Okay I'll give you an example. One time."

He went to a line of golf bags filled with clubs and pulled out an old persimmon fairway wood and handed it to Callum who looked at it with interest. There was a brass plate on the bottom and a little wedge of brass on the back for weight. While the wooden body of the club was nutmeg in color, the wooden face had a square about the size of a golf ball, painted red, with thin horizontal grooves. Callum tapped the face and it made a dull noise.

"It's an old club," said Callum. "What is it, fifty, sixty years old?"

Tom nodded. "At least. Back in the mid nineteen fifties, when your idol Ben Hogan won the Open at Carnoustie with a six under par, this was the type of club he won it with. It's also the exact club I shot the fifty-nine with."

"Nice club," said Callum and handed it back to Tom, who handed it right back to Callum.

"What gives? What do you want me to do with it?"

"I want you to learn how to play golf with it. In fact, I want you to use all these old clubs sitting here to learn the proper way to play the game. And I'll tell you why. These new clubs we have these days irons with perimeter weighted cavity backs, hollow lightweight drivers, and fairway metals with titanium and now carbon faces. Everything faster, lighter, bouncier, you can hit the ball much farther than ever before, but one critical thing has not changed. You still have to learn how to hit it straight, or when you need to cut a shot around the corner of a dogleg, or hook it around a tree, you need control."

"You want me to play with these old dinosaur bones."

"For a time. Believe me lad, I wouldn't steer you wrong. The clubs may have changed, but the courses are still the same. And the game is still the same. Stay out of trouble, get the ball on the green as fast as you can, and make that first putt, and if you don't make that first putt, get it close enough to just give it a wee tap in."

Callum looked over at the framed scorecard with the fifty-nine and sighed. "Okay you're the boss."

"There's one other thing," said Tom as he reached into one of the bags and pulled out what sort of looked like a baseball the size of a golf ball without dimples.

"What the hell is that?" asked Callum.

"That lad is a feathery." Tom handed it over. "And this one is over one hundred years old. This is the ball we'll start with."

Callum looked with interest at the ball and bounced it off the bar. "What the heck..."

"The gutty was invented in 1848. It was made from the rubber sap of the gutta percha tree. It could be made in a mold and took over the game, sort of resembling a modern golf ball with dimples and all. But before it came along, for about three hundred years from the 1500's to the mid 1800's it was the feathery. Three pieces of cow leather soaked and pliable, sewn into a ball inside out with a little hole left over, then the whole of it pushed through that little opening till it was outside in. Then you boil goose feathers, the downiest ones close in on the body in a vat, shove them with a stick into the hole, finish the stitch and when it dries, the elastic keratin from the goose feathers expand like a plastic, while the leather shrinks and it forms this hard yet bouncy ball, and you can paint it whatever color you want."

Callum bounced it on the bar a few more times. "You want me to play golf with this relic."

Tom nodded.

"It'll set you straight lad. I guarantee it. You'll be needing a golf course to practice on, and as luck would have it, I happen to be the greenskeeper on a fine run. We'll start tomorrow. Now here's the nuts and bolts of it. You want to be in The Open, you have to qualify. It's called The Open because it truly is open to any player. There's a hundred and fifty six spots available. A hundred forty of those are for the top professional players on tour, the guys that actually play in tournaments and win money, past Open champions under sixty, and the winners of various tournaments around the world. There's sixteen spots designed to give the everyman an opportunity to get in, and that's where we're going to take aim. They have the regional qualifying tournament at the end of June at thirteen courses scattered around Scotland and England, and the top players from those get into the final qualifier the first week of July at four courses. You have only two ways of getting into the qualifying tournaments, either by being a professional golfer, or an amateur with a handicap less than one, in other words a scratch golfer."

"I'll just enter a few tournaments as a pro golfer and I'm in."

"Costs money to enter. How much do you have to waste?"

That shut Callum up.

"You've got six months to get ready. Twenty-four weeks. A hundred and eighty days." Tom pulled out a calculator from the side and punched in some numbers. "If you played golf twenty-four hours a day for six months, that's four thousand three hundred and twenty hours. Even that might not be enough. I'll tell you what though. If you could manage about half a day of golf, every day for six months, throw in a couple rounds of competition every week, a thousand hours, and fifty competitive rounds should be enough if you're any good."

Callum was silent.

"It'll take about a thousand hours to see if you have what it takes to even get into The Open. Or if you're only good enough to watch from the sidelines like the rest of us mortals. You'll need to learn how to play in the cold and the rain and the wind because that's what we have here eighty percent of the time, and you'll need the clothing. You'll need waterproof and windproof pants, shoes and jacket, rain gloves so you can still grip the club when they're damp and wet, a good umbrella, waterproof golf bag and plenty of dry towels. We might see ten sunny days in the next four months, and it won't get to a balmy fifty degrees till May. I know you don't have much money so we'll set you up with everything you need from the thrift store in town. I know the owner. But there's something I have to ask you first."

"What's that?"

"Your bride to be and the dilemma you're in."

"What dilemma beside winning The Open?"

"Have a seat lad," said Tom while taking one of the barstools and settling into it gravely.

Callum did as he was asked, sitting down next to the bar again. He hoped this was going to be some sort of Scottish humor, before dinner.

"You know that her mother passed away when she was young?"

"Yes, she told me."

"Did she tell you the whole story?"

"No. She only showed me a picture of her and told me about how she was a champion volunteer. I didn't ask her for any details. I don't think I need to know any more than that, do you?"

"I think you do lad. I think you do."

Tom pulled the top off the whisky bottle and poured them each another shot, this time only half. He set his hand flat on the bar and did not take a sip as yet.

"Her mother was a beauty, that was for certain, and yet much more than that. Much, much more than that. She was the whole of Oban in one person if that was even possible. Gracious, humorous, giving, courageous."

Callum got a chill down his spine and asked the question more as a statement.

"What happened."

"Her one fault and it wasn't her own doing was that she married too young. Seventeen is too young."

Callum waited while Tom gathered himself.

"It was an American on vacation. A Yank,

and I say that with no disrespect to you. A Yank on a golf vacation. A rich Yank travelling up and down the coast playing golf at all the finest venues. Saint Andrew, Royal Troon, Inverness, Muirfield, Carnoustie. The usual run for that type. If only he stayed the course so to speak and played those courses and kept away from Oban. But he heard that we were the seafood capital of Scotland, and he wanted to go out to Mull and play Tobermory and Craignure."

Tom stopped for a moment, seeming to need a breath to compose himself. He took a small sip of the whisky either to calm himself or remind him of something.

"They were having a rough patch as happens now and again between a husband and a wife. She left him for a week, took the ferry to Mull and stayed with a friend when she met this Yank and went off to America with him. Some said she was doing it to teach Malcolm a lesson. She was twenty-two years old with an overbearing husband, a young rambunctious child, and as rebellious a streak of Scottish as you'll find in any woman. Malcolm took all her clothes, all her belongings into the middle of the street and set them on fire. Nearly set half the town on fire in the process. Went to jail for a few days for criminal property damage then released on his own recognizance. They reconciled after a couple of days, over the phone. She wanted to come home. Her wild streak was over. It took less than a week for her to get it out of her system, and she was on her way home, back to Oban. She was on a little boat travelling from a private island to the airport outside of New York when that little boat hit the wake from a cargo barge, capsized, and that was the end of it."

Tom was silent for a moment and pushed the shot glass away. Callum did not even look down at his own.

"Do you think he hit her," asked Callum. "Is that what drove her away?"

"Malcolm? Not a chance. He grew up with three older sisters, they would have pile driven him headfirst into the ground. No, that man has a great respect for the fairer species, out of necessity, that's for sure. He'll battle any man alive no doubt, but there's not a chance in hell he'd raise a hand against a woman. No chance. It wasn't battery, it was money, or the lack of it at that particular point in time for that family. A wild streak in a Scottish woman, and a couple of quarrels over money was the straw that broke the camel's back so to speak. A rich American tossing money around on Mull during the breakup didn't help matters."

"She never told me any of this," said Callum. "Seems it's something I should have known."

"I'm telling you this because you need to know the bit of prejudice that you'll be having with Mr. MacQuarrie. Maggie was five years old. Curls in her hair and heading to kindergarten. Seems like a long time ago."

"I didn't know," said Callum. "I'm an idiot. Now what do I do?"

"We're all a little surprised that he even gave you an option, even though an impossible one.

You're lucky he didn't grab that broadsword on the wall over the bar and chase you out of the house. One thing that probably saved you is that your family, the Maclean's, and their family the MacQuarrie's were friends at one time."

"We still are."

"Aye. I believe it. You know, it's even quite possible that you and Maggie met each other a long time ago. I recall that your father brought you here and I took a picture of you, your mom, and dad out in front of the house."

"I have that picture."

"Maggie would have been a year old. If we could just put the two of you together at that point in time."

Tom tapped his head, trying to dislodge a distant memory from the dusty cobwebs in the middle of his brain, but it was no use at that particular point in time with a couple of shots of whisky.

"Dammit man, I can't think what time of year it was when you were here. I'm sure we had a party for you. And they definitely had a party for her at Christmas, but I don't think you stayed around for that one. There were a lot of kids running around. I remember that."

He shook his head again. It was useless.

"Let's go up to dinner lad. Not sure if I can hear the kettle boiling over, but I can definitely smell it."

They headed up the stairs into the kitchen and there at the thick wooden table were three bowls of steaming goodness laid out, and a covered pot in the middle in reserve. On the side a loaf of bread, sliced, with a slab of butter on the waiting for the lathering.

Tom kissed Colleen lightly on the cheek before heading to the table. He pointed to Callum's seat of honor at the head, they all sat down, and he put his hands together, closed his eyes and said a prayer for one and all, and especially for Maggie's mother at the end of it.

"She was a beautiful soul," said Colleen, wiping a tear from her eye. She hadn't expected that prayer.

"I've got a question for you," said Tom. "You remember the last time we saw young Callum just out of diapers, when he was a wee lad around three years old?"

She nodded as she took a slice of bread and put it on a plate for Callum.

"Like it was yesterday."

"Do you remember by chance a party for all the kids at that time. Over by MacQuarrie's place. There was a tent, and music, a magician, a bagpipe, folk singers, I remember a quartet with a lute and a violin. It was a celebration of one type or another."

She smiled and winked at Callum.

"I've got half a mind to accidentally drop that special bottle of whisky he has in the basement while cleaning one day. It was Guy Fawkes Day; we had a party for the kids during the day and it extended into the night with a bonfire and fireworks. And yes, young Callum was here with his mom and dad. I remember it clear as day."

Tom snapped his fingers.

"That's it! I knew it! We were all there together. November fifth. How could I forget."

"How indeed," smiled Colleen.

"That's when I first got the job to take care of the Maclean mansion."

"Mansion?" winced Callum.

Tom pointed at him.

"You, and Maggie have laid eyes on each other in the distant past, here in the Highlands."

He looked out the window to make sure the sacred rowan tree was still standing guard by at the front of the house. The leaves gently swayed in the breeze.

"You know," said Tom conspiratorially while leaning over his bowl of soup. "There's something strange going on here."

16.

Two days after Christmas, Callum still had not ventured into town to see Maggie.

Like the pot of soup in Colleen's kitchen he decided to let it all cool down a bit after boiling over.

Tom brought him a few sets of golf rain gear, and he kept to himself around the house, painting and fixing, digging in the dirt with the four iron.

At around noon Maggie came by on her lunch break with a basket full of fish and chips from the docks.

Her father had calmed down she said, confident that what was done was done. A wager in the Highlands took on as much significance as an oath to the almighty at the pearly gates.

"I'm telling you it's a silly bet between two of the thickest headed blokes I've ever seen in me life," she said as he savored the fried fish with vinegar, the first real meal he'd had in days.

"No such thing as a silly bet," he countered when he came up for air. "Unless it's one that costs you your life. I'm not jumping over the fountain, or flying too close to the sun..."

She looked at him with bewilderment as he rambled on between bites. What in the heck was he talking about?

"...and I'm not having a gunfight at the OK corral."

She sighed and took a bite of fish herself. Couldn't understand a word he was saying.

"This is an honest bet, no, it's not even a bet, or a wager. This is a promise..."

He was rambling.

"...this is a promise to you and him, and this whole town of Oban, the whole country of Scotland, and every good man and woman in it that I will win The Open."

"And if you don't?"

"Don't say it Maggie. Don't say it."

"If you don't then we're off to Gretna Green the very next day. That's a promise you'll make to me."

"I'll travel north to Inverness. There's an old castle in the hills. I'll shroud myself with thick brown robes made from the hair of mules, shave my head and be a monk for the rest of me life."

"You do that and I'll shave my head and join you Callum. You're not getting rid of me that easy."

17.

Later that afternoon, Tom took him on a tour of Glencruitten, the golf course where he worked, introducing him to everyone from the head golf pro, front desk personnel, and everyone under his command out on the course, mechanics, weeders, mowers.

Since he wasn't a citizen, he couldn't officially be on the payroll, but with a wink and a nod, it was agreed upon that if he did a bit of light work around the course, painting, sweeping, taking out the trash, he could use the facilities.

Everyone around the town heard about the wager, and the people at the golf course were most curious about the type of game that Callum possessed. Wild rumors circulated that he was the best golfer on the west coast of America, exiled to Scotland by his evil father, but when they saw him hitting balls on the range on that very first day he ceased to be an object of curiosity, but one of pity.

His method of digging it out of the dirt in the bog behind his house the past few days had not miraculously created a precise swing, but an erratic one.

True to his word Tom came to the rescue and pulled Callum from the driving range and down to the little green from which to pitch and putt the feathery.

"Still want to win The Open do ya?"

"I have no choice."

"Well, I suppose the only truly worthy dreams are the impossible ones. The ones that everyone in the world says you can nae do, and then you still give it a go. Maybe it's the trying, the striving, the battle against all odds that makes a man a man. We'll start with the wee game, then work our way up. If you can nae chip and putt the ball, then hitting it far has no purpose."

He tossed an old grimy looking ball on the ground and handed Callum an ancient rusty wedge and thin putter, both with wooden shafts and grips wound with black tape.

"Did you use these when you scored fifty-nine?"

"Naw, I didn't have them at the time. I got these from the old clubhouse before they bulldozed it and built the new one over there. Nobody wanted 'em and they were going in the trash. Now I'm not entirely certain, and I could be wrong, but I believe that it was none other than young Tom Morris made these very clubs. He made a little etching mark. And they were headed for the trash."

"Was he a good golfer?"

"Was he good? Damn man, he won your Open four times, three in a row, eighteen sixty-eight, sixty-nine, seventy, and again in eighteen seventy-two."

"With these clubs?"

"We'll never know for sure. Hickory shaft, wrapped leather grip, forged iron head, waxed linen thread to hold the head tight to the shaft. This is a niblick, sort of a nine iron. Young Tom used this to hit high shots over hazards, sometimes with back spin."

"With this club?" Callum looked at it with skepticism while Tom continued.

"In eighteen sixty-nine at Prestwick, he scored the Open's first hole in one on the hundred sixty-six-yard eighth hole. In eighteen seventy-three they purchased the Claret Jug for the tournament and his name is the very first one on it. He died on Christmas day in eighteen seventy-five. He was twenty-four years old."

The implication was not lost on Callum. One year older than him and gone.

"What happened," asked Callum. "Why'd he die so young."

Tom grimaced.

"That's the pity of it. His wife and child died four months prior while he was trying to win a golf tournament."

Tom was silent for a moment while he gathered himself. Something seemed to bother him about it, and Callum let him be till he continued.

"On September 11, 1875, young Tom and his father were playing in a match in North Berwick, Bearaig a Tuath. A town on the coast twenty miles east of Edinburgh. They were in a heated match against Willie and Mungo Park, two hotshot Scottish golfers in their own right, and with two holes to go when young Tom got a telegram that said his wife went into early labor and it was not going well. For some stupid reason they decided to finish the match. Pride. Stubbornness. Maybe a little bit of greed. Thought they were invincible. They won the match, then took a ship across the firth and up the coast but got there too late. Both mother and baby were gone. Some people say he died of a broken heart, and I for one would not deny that. I don't think for a moment that he wouldn't have traded every penny he ever made from match play to be with his little family at the end. "

Callum held the club in his hands with more respect after hearing that. This damn old club I'm being forced to practice with suddenly became this wonderful club. It felt heavy, clumsy.

"I'm afraid to use it now."

"Naw! Golf clubs are made to be used, not put on a mantle to look at. Feel the magic."

And so, it began. Tom had but five featheries that were playable so he stood by the flag on the green and had Callum hit pitch shots from fifty yards, then he'd throw the balls back, over and over till they hit a hundred times.

Towards the end, he was getting the ball within a few feet of the pin every time and holed it out twice.

"That's the key, a hundred reps per shot. Hit it so many times from the same distance that it becomes second nature and you don't even think about it. Takes your mind out of it, engages the full eye hand coordination. No thinking, just action. Nothing more, nothing less. Now here's the gutty."

Tom had five of them in his pocket and tossed them on the ground then went back to the green next to the flag. The first few pitches were nowhere near the pin, the feel of the ball bouncier, lighter. By the fiftieth shot he was getting the hang of it, clipping the ball lightly for spin. A hundred reps and that was it.

Tom looked at his watch. It was half past three and the sun was setting somewhere behind a curtain of thick clouds. The first tee was wide open.

"Let's go, I'll caddie for you."

He picked out a driver, four iron, the rusty nine iron, thin putter and headed for the tee.

"Those are all the clubs you're bringing?" asked Callum.

"They're all you'll need. Five holes is all we have time for. Let's go."

They stood on the first tee and looked out over a wide stretch of land with a small creek running across the fairway about a hundred and fifty yards away.

"Where's the first hole?" asked Callum.

"Up on top of that hill about four hundred fifty yards away."

"I can't even see the flag."

"And you won't lad, until you're up on top."

"Is it a par five?"

Tom chuckled. "You wish. There's not a par

five on this course. Not from the men's tees anyways."

"Up on top of that hill that looks like it's about a mile away?"

"This is a highlands course lad, and one of the toughest you'll find. You need to be half mountain goat to walk it. Some of the older crew walk the first five holes and call it a day since that's about the equivalent hill climbing and distance of a mere mortal man's course."

The first feathery lasted all of one swing. With a massive crank of the driver, the ball split in two at the seam, still held together by one stitch and winged down and towards the creek like a wounded bird in flight.

"I'm sorry!" said Callum. "That's a hundred pounds."

Tom chuckled. "You didn't think I'd let you hit one of my old collectables did ya? I made that one myself. Aw well, that one was ready to split anyways. There's a few more where that one came from. We won't count that as a shot."

He pulled another out of his pocket, studied it for a moment, turning it in his hand, then tossed it Callum.

"You'll nae be able to split this one lad. Give it your best shot."

Tom was right. With a smooth back swing, cranking with all his might through the ball, Callum smashed the feathery all of a hundred and seventy yards just over the edge of the creek, then it curved to the right at the end of its flight into the edge of the rough and sat down in the tall grass. It was like hitting a little bean bag filled with hardened rubber. He could see a little wry smile on Tom's face as they started walking.

For his second shot, still a hundred fifty yards from the base of the hill, Callum tried to punch the ball out with the four iron and it scooted up in the air all of five feet and down the fairway about fifty yards.

"You're getting closer!" Tom shouted as he walked ahead of Callum whose face was turning red with anger.

"You ever use this teaching technique on other players?"

Tom shook his head. "No lad, I've only seen this used by one other person in my entire lifetime, and that was myself, way back when I was young. I'm not a teacher Callum, I'm a player. But for you I'll give you a little insight into what turned me from a very bad golfer to a manageable one. I'll work with you for a couple of days and then you're on your own. This is a game that's learned by doing, not telling."

Still about a hundred yards from the base of the hill and sitting two Callum hit the feathery again with the four iron and ended up right at the base of the upslope.

When they got to the ball it was sitting up on a tuft of grass on a good lie. The hill itself seemed to be a forty-five-degree angle about a five-story building high and at the top marking the center was a black and white striped pole about a hundred yards above them.

"Now what?" asked Callum.

"The green is about fifty yards past that

striped pole. Hit it right over the top of it and you'll be sitting pretty."

"This is my fourth shot and I can't even see the green," Callum muttered. With one foot on the upslope and one foot on level ground he pounded the feathery with a four iron and it flew high up and over the striped pole. "Yes," he whispered with a silent fist pump. But when they climbed the hill and saw the ball he was still fifty yards from the green that was sitting on the plateau.

Callum studied the distance.

"I feel like I should hit the four iron again."

Tom shook his head and handed him the nine iron.

"Just keep your eyes on the little feathery, head down through the ball and hit a high shot. Don't look up until your arms pull your head with them. I think you might be surprised."

The nine iron and feathery were made for each other and the ball thumped off the clubface high into the air, so high that when Callum's cranking arms lifted his head he couldn't see the ball at first, hidden in the misty background, then he saw it in the sky at its apex a perfect round trajectory like a rocket falling out of the clouds onto the green and bouncing lightly against the pin, then dropping out of sight into the cup.

"Blasted!" Tom yelled. "That's a scramble of a bogey five if I've ever seen one. Damnit man, I hope you didn't waste all your good luck on that one shot, because that's all it was, pure luck."

Callum smiled but did not yell out.

"No such thing as luck Tom, remember? That, my friend was all skill."

As it turned out though, perhaps luck did have a hand in that one shot. For the rest of the day over the next four holes Callum struggled mightily with the ancient clubs and featheries.

His drives were short and to the right, the four-iron clunky, and the putter stiff and awkward. The only club that worked fairly well was the nine iron. At the end of the five-hole round after starting out one over with the miracle shot, he ended up ten over par with three double bogeys and one triple. Double bogey golf.

"Keep your eyes on the ball, that's the most important thing in the game lad, you can't hit what you can't see. Intensify your sight, somehow. Bring all your senses to bear on striking that little round ball crisp and clean. Think about the shot before you set up and plant your feet, line up your body angles, square up the best you can and then clear your mind of all thoughts. Muscle memory is the key."

The next day he started hitting the ball better, not trying to kill it, since that didn't do anything except make it fly erratic, he tried to hit it square on the clubface, nothing more, nothing less. It still wasn't travelling very far, the bean bag filled with plastic, but was going straight down the fairway with a nice trajectory like a jet taking off low and rising towards an apex at the end.

On the fifth day after Christmas after playing fifty-four holes over three days with the old wooden clubs and the feathery, Tom showed up on the practice tee with Callum's bag of shiny clubs.

"Play time is over," said Tom. "I'm sure you've had a lot of fun with the feathery, but now it's time to get to work. You're on your own now Callum. I think you've come a long way in three short days. You can always come back to the feathery if your game gets out of sorts, it has a way of setting you straight, but for now it's time to play with the modern clubs, and balls."

He reached out to take the old clubs from the stand, but Callum held onto the nine iron.

"Mind if I keep this for a while? I want to see how it works with a modern golf ball."

Tom nodded with a serious face. It was like handing a cherished battle ax to the next generation of warriors to defend the land against invaders.

"Use it as long as you want. I'll walk with you one more round just to see how you do."

As they walked to the first tee, Tom whistled a tune, then said a rhyme.

"There was an old man named McGinty. He began to walk a little bit gimpy. As it turned out, he said with a shout, in his shoe was a little sharp flinty." Tom laughed at the look on Callum's face. "It was a wee rock, a pebble, a flinty."

"Alright," said Callum. "I'll play along. There was an old man named McGinty. His eyes were a little bit squinty. Upon further apprise, the townspeople surmised that the squint was from the glint of the sunrise."

"Hey," said Tom. "Not bad. Not good, but not bad either. I'll give you a middlin."

As they stood on tee, Tom reached out and shook Callum's hand.

"There's only one more thing I wanted to tell you before I set you off."

"What's that?"

Tom bent down and picked a bit of grass and held it in the palm of his hand.

"A golf course is not an inanimate object that you can impose your will upon. It's not a synthetic, artificial turf manufactured and assembled in a factory, then shipped to your door. It's a living breathing entity, all the roots deep in the ground, interweaving, interlocking, alive, communicating. Every blade of grass from the first tee to the eighteenth green is somehow connected. It has a spirit, and if you can connect to it somehow, someway, it will help you do magical things. Have you ever chipped in from fifty yards out, or made a hole in one from three times that length? Or maybe just a slippery putt that breaks four feet from right to left or left to right, the shape and undulations of the green like a Greek goddess in mythology. Ever had a putt that looked like it was going in, then stopped, inexplicably held up by a single tiny blade of grass? You can hit massive drives three hundred yards and more, approach shots from two twenty plus, and yet sometimes it's a single dimple on the golf ball, a single blade of grass at the rim of the cup that can make the difference between winning and losing."

Tom held out a new sleeve of golf balls.

"The feathery has a compression of around twenty. These are ninety. No practice swings, no practice tee, I want you to go from hitting the feathery to a modern ball designed to travel twice as far in one fell swoop."

It was like having a racehorse drag around a plow for a few days, then taking off the yoke and letting it run free. Like putting a parachute behind a dragster on the starting line, then cutting the cord.

"Use the same swing that you've grooved the past couple of days. Change nothing," advised Tom. "Pretend as though you were still hitting the feathery. Solid and true and let's see what happens."

What happened was Callum teed the shiny new ball high above the turf, envisioned in his mind that he was still hitting the bean bag that looked like a golf ball, took the driver smooth away from the ball in a high arc behind his head, kept his eyes on the ball well past impact, leaning on it, leveraging every sinew from the tip of his head to the tips of his feet, and when his arms swinging through parallel, clubhead above the horizon lifting his eyes towards the sky, the ball was already two hundred yards away and still climbing until it hit a gentle apex and descended into the middle of the fairway three hundred yards away.

"That went well," said Callum with a

surprised look on his face. Like a prize fighter training for a week in the deep sand at the beach with heavy Army boots and a trench coat, pockets filled with lead, suddenly in a bouncy air-conditioned boxing ring with light shoes and shorts.

Every shot seemed to have an extra punch, precise control that he'd never experienced before. The heavy old nine iron, hickory shafted, rusty faced beautiful club was turning into his favorite weapon. From ninety to a hundred thirty yards, it seemed like he was throwing darts in a pub with a laser sight. With every chip shot his confidence grew, until the eighth hole from a hundred and five yards out he hit a high pitch shot from the right side of the fairway, over a bunker with twenty feet of green to work with. The ball landed softly, rolled slowly up to the edge of the cup, sat there for a moment, then dropped out of sight.

Callum did not shout out in victory, it was surprising, and calming in a way how it unfolded. He looked over at Tom who merely nodded. The shot was well played, high over the bunker, but the way that it rolled towards the cup, hovering for a moment, and then dropping. It was almost as though the golf course had a hand in the outcome. Callum listened carefully, trying to envelope himself in the moment, trying to remember just what exactly he did, or didn't do, to make that shot.

It was surreal.

"And that's how it's done lad," said Tom. "That's the magic. Try as you might to figure it out, it's here, all around us. When I made that hole in one for fifty-nine and the championship long ago, I felt it. It was just as real as the air that we're breathing and just as visible. When you're playing on these golf courses, no matter where in the world you are, it's best to treat them with respect. Curse at yourself or your shot, but not the course. It may just give you the break you need when you least expect it."

18.

The last day of December, New Year's Eve brought a snowstorm roaring off the North Sea, down the Hebrides islands and through Argyll.

All the land was covered in a thin layer of snow a few inches high.

Tom went down to the course to check on the conditions. One person was out trudging the fairways, he could see the footprints in the snow heading in a straight line from where the first tee should be to where the flag stood in a field of white. Then the footprints headed off into the distance to the second tee and off into the winter wonderland.

Angus was up at the clubhouse tidying up. He had a pot of coffee on the hot plate and Tom helped himself to a cup.

"Got ourselves a player today."

"Aye," said Angus.

"Wonder who it is?"

"You know who it is. Damn fool was playing with a white ball as well. Should be playing with an orange ball in these conditions so he can see it on the snow."

"Orange balls now you're saying. How many

times has he been around?"

"This is his second trip around the course and it's not even lunch yet."

"Well," said Tom. "I would think in these conditions he'd be playing with blue balls after the first roundabout."

Angus laughed at that.

"He sure is a hardheaded bloke."

"Aye, that he is. Seems determined to prove himself a true Scotsman even if it kills him."

"He shoveled all the snow around the clubhouse before he went out. Said he was warming up for the round. Fixed the roof yesterday. Painted the deck and the railing all around the day before. He'll probably pave the parking lot with gilded stones and build an old folk's cabin out back after playing fifty-four holes this afternoon. He doesn't have to prove he's a Scotsman to me anymore."

"Malcolm MacQuarrie will never buy it. Not unless the lad wins The Open."

Angus spat in the snow. "Win The Open. Bah. How's he even going to get in The Open? Regional qualifier?"

"Aye."

"You have to be a scratch golfer to enter. He's nowhere near that."

"Not yet maybe. He can turn professional and enter. He's got that option. We have five months till June."

"Maybe five years."

"He's got the length; you've seen that yourself. Not many people can drive the green on sixteen."

"Sure, and like a wild beast, flying the ball all over the course."

"He's got potential. You must admit that at least."

"And what will potential get a man in this life. An official stamped copy of potential, and a pound will get you a cup of coffee at the local deli maybe."

"I'm telling you he's got a chance."

"I'm not sure now who's more hardheaded Thomas, you or him. And if you do get him down to a scratch player by June, what course will you be aiming for, you get to pick four out the thirteen courses."

"Goswick, Kilmarnock, Moor Park, and Kedleston Park."

"Kedleston eh?"

"It's seven thousand yards. Might even the field out a bit."

"Just make sure he doesn't get it in his head that he can drive for show *and* dough. There's a little thing called putting that comes into play you know."

"I've got a plan."

The next morning, New Years Day at seven thirty am, while the sun was still an hour away from rising and the freezing bog was covered in mist, Tom showed up on Callum's front door and knocked loudly. He could hear the echo inside the living room and a low groan as though a bear had been awakened from slumber. He knocked again, louder this time and fairly shouted.

"Let's go you lazy bastard, we've got miles to

go before we rest!"

Footsteps across the old wooden floor and the door open wide, Callum in his nightshirt and flannel trousers, thick socks and a wool cap, blinking cobwebs, a thin covering of stubble on cheeks rubbing his eyes, blubbering incoherently.

"Tom, what?.....It's New Years Day. I just got to bed a couple of hours ago."

"You can sleep on the boat, grab your game gear, change of clothes and one golf club, we're going to Mull."

Callum's face went blank.

"One club, what?"

"We're going to Tobermory on the isle of Mull. C'mon now or we'll be late for our ride."

Callum was suddenly sober and squinted his eyes. "Why one club?"

"It's New Years Day, and this is the day of the one club challenge at Tobermory, it's a small nine-hole course on the northeast shores of Mull and we're going to challenge them. You and me. Grab one club, be quick about it, if you had only one club to play an entire round of golf which one would you choose? I personally am taking a four iron, gets me off the tee, I can chip around the green, get out of bunkers if I de-loft the face, and it putts fairly well. So, what club will you be playing with? And choose wisely young Callum."

Callum rubbed the remaining sleep out of the corners of his eyes. "Six iron?" It was more of a question than a statement.

Tom went to the bag, pulled out the six iron,

and two golf balls from the pocket.

"Let's go. The boat leaves in half an hour, and it's not waiting for us."

"You didn't want to give me prior notice? Maybe yesterday, or even last night would have been nice?"

"This is part of the training lad. No questions, remember?"

Callum mumbled as he went back into the bedroom to grab his winter playing gear and came out still grumbling.

"Do I have time for a quick cup of coffee, or a biscuit?"

Tom led the way out the door into the dark. The streets of Oban were mostly empty at that time in the morning and especially on the first day of the new year. They passed by a few people standing on street corners with coffee, waiting for the bus, steam rising from the cups and their faces wrapped tight over thick jackets.

"Are we taking the ferry across?"

Tom shook his head. "Doesn't run on New Years Day. But I've got a friend with a boat. He doesn't talk much as you'll see, and the boat's a plodder at best, but he'll get us safely there and back."

They pulled up to the dock. Parked in an empty spot and headed down to the water to a rusty looking scow around twenty-five feet in length with a low rumbling diesel engine, the slight hint of black smoke from the exhaust and the rancid smell of burnt fuel. The captain was gruff and merely nodded to them while shaking their hands, welcoming them aboard, then untied the lines, headed to the helm, and they were underway.

The sea was choppy, grey, dimly lit by the rising sun through dark skies to the east as the boat rumbled slowly across the water.

Nearly three hours later they pulled into the dock at Craignure and tied up to the wharf.

Whereas the sky over Oban was dark and gloomy, here on the island the light was crisp and cracking. Tom shook hands with the captain. "Sure you won't join us for a round?

"Bah," he spat. "Waste of time. Hitting a little ball around the hills. The only round I'll be having is dragging lines 'round the south side of the island and reeling in some fish for dinner if I'm lucky."

They bade farewell, the two men with one club each headed to the roadway while the captain untied the boat and pulled away from the dock.

"Follow me," said Tom. "I've got a friend who loaned me their car for the day.

He led them to a little blue sedan and reached over the rear wheel to retrieve the hidden key.

"Pay attention lad," he told Callum as they settled into their seats and he started the engine and pulled away from the curb. "You'll be driving us home later this afternoon.

"Is that why you brought me? To be a designated driver?"

"One of the reasons. But not the only one. You'll see. I brought you here to witness a yearly ritual, practically like a Pagan event where the druids gathered 'round to watch the sunrise through Stonehenge. I grew up here lad, on this island. I graduated from Tobermory High School, class of seventy-five. There were thirty of us that year and now we're scattered all over the world like sand from a broken hourglass, but there's still a few that live here, and we're going to see one of the very best of the best. But be on your toes, it's a hardy bunch that live over here and for good reason, separated from the main, living like savages at times, they must be hardy just to survive."

Callum looked at Tom with a frown.

"Like pagans at Stonehenge? We just went by a donut shop and there was a line out the door."

Tom narrowed his eyes conspiratorially.

"Sure, and this is Craignure. The civilized part of the island. This is where the fancy people live in gilded houses and golden bannisters. We're going north to Tobermory. Baliscate lad. The scattered village. Coille Creag A'chait. There you'll find standing stones in a little quiet glen just outside the town. Where some type of people lived four thousand years ago."

Forty-five minutes later they went up over a hill and down into the city, then along Main Street next to the little harbor. Two- and three-story brick buildings, square faced neatly stacked neat and snug next to each other, colorfully painted with cheerful colors, blues, pinks, reds, yellows, some with natural stone, hotels, arts and crafts, bars, a single-story pink ice cream store right on the water.

"Hey Tom, is that a pagan ice cream store?"

"Pay attention Callum, don't be forgetting you'll be driving home after the golf match."

They passed a medieval church with a tall steeple, a tea-room, a museum, then as they were getting closer to the end of the wharf Tom slowed down and pulled in front of a cute store, three stories high, painted red on the first floor with white windows, and black with white windows on the second and third floors. Tilted to the left over a giant sign that read in bold letters TOBERMORY was a three-foot wide and tall mockup of a hardcover book with the title: TACKLE & BOOKS.

"Strange name for a store," said Callum.

"They sell fishing tackle and books," said Tom. "This storefront has a long history. It was once home to a butcher, a baker..."

"A candlestick maker?" said Callum with a wry smile.

"...a chemist and a grocer," continued Tom while frowning at Callum. "This current store was started sometime around nineteen seventy-five when I was still in high school. There were a few wild chickens that used to hang around this area and we nicknamed it 'Cackle and Books'. We thought it was pretty funny, but it got us in a bit of trouble one day. There was a group of old ladies that used to have a get-together, a reading club, and one day they heard a group of us boys joking around about cackle and books and thought we were talking about them. Got us all a flat purse to the side of the head."

"Fishing tackle and books," mused Callum. "They should call it hooks and books."

Tom turned to him with his perpetual frown, but suddenly on the edges, a bit of a smile.

"You're catching on lad."

They pulled back onto the road, took a sharp left turn, up the hill on a one lane road, behind all the buildings now, a little hand painted sign on a rusted metal fence between guardrails on the side that said golf course with an arrow pointing the way along Back Brae Road.

Winding up along a long stone wall, Callum looked back and could see the church steeple down below them now with the harbor in the background. Back Brae to Erray, then up over another stout hill, high to the top and over, through a residential area with homes on either side, then past the little green fence, a hard right past the little signs that read Sonas House and Fairway Cottages then the turquoise green sign that said Tobermory Golf Course Pay and Play.

"The sign is misspelled Callum; it should say pray and play because that's what you need on this field of battle. Ready yourself for whatever we find on the course today. Gird your loins and your mind, steady your psyche, your patience, your fortitude, for today could be the finest day of golf ever played, or the end of the end and utter defeat."

They pulled up to the little clubhouse and

parked at the end of the lot. There were around twenty-five men milling about in front of the porch. They ranged in age from scruff-haired teenagers to silver-haired retirees. Most of them smiled when they saw Tom and Callum walking towards them. One of the gents with silver hair looked at his watch and shook his head in dismay.

"Twelve thirty," he said loudly. "Didn't think you were going to make it."

"The boat was touch and go. Barely made it across the channel." Tom shook hands down the line towards his tormentor. "You didn't think I would miss this for the world, did you? I was getting ready to commandeer a dingy and row here if needed. I was prepared to swim the firth with one hand while holding this four iron with the other.

He stopped and hugged one of the men, slapping him on the back before continuing down the line.

"Hello everyone, meet Callum, he'll be partnering up with me today, brought him here to show him how a real game of golf is played. Back in the stone age when real men walked this earth, they had but one club that they used for sport *and* for war. Maybe it was a battle ax, or a broad sword, or pike, and whilst walking from one skirmish to another hit a little round rolling stone, or maybe the head of their vanquished enemy on the ground to pass the time and that was the beginning of golf. Some might say that the word itself, golf was derived from a Scotsman being tortured on the rack in the Tower of London. The word flog was on the wall and the pool of tears that he wept formed a mirror that spelled the word backwards. Pretty much sums up the gist of our little passion."

Callum followed behind, shaking hands as he went and stopped next to Tom and reached out his hand to the two men standing in front of him.

"Looks like you brought a ringer from Argyll Tom. What's your handicap lad?" asked the younger of the two.

"I don't have one," said Callum.

"He's a scratch golfer," said Tom. "Hits the ball, then scratches a body part."

Tom motioned to the men in front of him with true dignity and respect. He nearly bowed but held himself in check.

"This is Neil. Lord of the Isles, and his playing partner Derek, poet, editor, inn keeper, and philosopher extraneous."

"Watch it," said Derek with a warning face, then smiled and shook Callum's hand. "I'm not really here for the golf as much as the craic."

Callum looked at him with a quizzical face. "What's craic?"

Derek chuckled as he recognized the accent.

"From the states, are you? Ah, we're a' met thegither here tae sit an tae crack wi oor glesses in oor hands. That's from David Shaw lad, The Wark o The Weavers."

"Always quotin' the classics are ya?" said Tom. "Showing off is what you're doing. Craic is loud bragging talk Callum, and you'll not hear one bit of that from me on this day. I didn't travel all this way across the grey and treacherous sea, and along the long and winding road from Craignure for talking. I'm only here for the action. I'll let my four iron do the talking."

"The only thing grey and treacherous is the hair on top your head, and the only thing long and winding is the diatribe coming from your lips," said Neil, then he opened the palm of his hand and held it out graciously towards the first tee. "The honor sir is yours."

"Drams on the tee?" asked Tom with a whisper out of the side of his mouth.

Neil winked and patted the little backpack slung over one shoulder and they all started walking towards the tee box. Neil took out a long smoke colored bottle, twisted the metal cap off with a snap and handed it to Tom.

"Slàinte Mhath," said Tom and took a drink then handed it to Derek who repeated the toast, took a sip then handed it towards Callum. Tom held up his hand. "Not a drop for this lad, he's my designated driver. Don't worry about the excess, I'll handle his share."

"He's not in on the betting then," said Neil. "Can't 'ave a ringer from Oban cashing in on us poor old men. Pound per hole, one tie all tie?"

Tom nodded. "The usual." Then he teed up his ball, took a couple of practice swings to warm up, set his feet square, waggled the clubface twice, then paused, pulled the club back slowly in a wide arc, and swung with the greatest of ease down and through, the ball barely making a sound as it left the clubface and flew straight two hundred yards through the air landing softly high up on the hill in the middle of the fairway next to the black and white striped pole marking the center. The crowd on the back of the tee cheered. Tom winked at Callum. "Straight is good."

Callum was up next and he felt a little nervous on that first tee in front of a small crowd of people he'd never seen before, then blocked out any thought of them, teed up the ball, took one warm up swing, looked down the fairway and picked a target. Straight is good he thought to himself as he brought the club back over his shoulders in a high arc, then keeping his head steady, eyes squarely on the top of the ball, cranked the club down and through it, flushed it, pure adrenaline and speed, power twisting his torso, whipping the iron through the tee, the ball disappearing like a rocket launch reaching its apex high over the spot where Tom's ball was resting then sailing far past it, the inertia finally spent it settled fifty yards past. A two hundred fifty yard shot with a six iron. The crowd was stunned and let out a collective yell, shouting while the ball was in the air.

"I knew it," said Neil, shaking his head. "A ringer."

Derek lined a drive with a three iron just short of Toms, and then Neil, also with a four-iron lofted one that landed just a few yards past Tom's and they were off walking down the fairway and up over the hill while Neil asked Tom how far past his ball did he think his went.

"I don't know how I can consistently hit the ball farther than you, when I'm a few days older."

"Early ripe, early rotten," said Tom after Neil won the first hole.

By the fourth hole, each of the three competitors had won a hole, Tom chipped it in from off the green on number two to some type of cursing from Neil that Callum had never heard before, and guessed it might be Scots Gaelic, strange words half gargled, half shouted, grunted and garbled. Derek won the third hole with a long winding putt that clanged against the flag and dropped in with a backdrop of whining.

On the fourth tee and another dram for good luck they started singing.

Tom started them off with the first lines and the others joined in with loud off-key voices that echoed over the fairways:

"By yon bonnie banks and by yon bonny braes. Where the sun shines bright on Loch Lomond. For me and my true love will never meet againnnnn."

They held the last word in a high-pitched refrain till the last bit of breath whispered from their lips, then wiped imaginary tears from their eyes.

By the time they reached the ninth tee Callum was afraid he was going to have to carry all three of them on his back the rest of way.

Back on the eighth fairway Tom missed the ball twice while loudly arguing that they were practice swings while in the background Neil was shouting 'Three, four!".

On the edge of the green on the eighth hole after putting out, they all laid down with the empty bottle between them, goofy smiles on their faces, and it was only someone yelling 'FORE' loudly in the fairway behind them that got them up and moving again.

The match between them was all knotted up with each player winning two holes, number seven and eight were ties, leaving number nine as the deciding hole, a three-hole carry-over.

Someone was going to walk away with six extra pounds in their pocket even if they had to have a putt-off on the practice green next to the clubhouse.

Tom sent his tee shot a hundred yards to the right out of bounds to joyous laughter from Neil and Derek, with both of them nearly falling down in the process. Then, when Neil hit his tee ball out of bounds on the left it was all up to Derek, who plunked it straight down the middle and Callum began to suspect that Derek was not taking full drams on the tee, but perhaps only pretending to take sips and waiting till the last hole to pounce on the unsuspecting victims. And then when Tom and Neil both hit their next tee shots out of bounds again it was all but over. Even if they could get the ball in the fairway on their next attempts, they'd be laying five where Derek was laying one. They conceded the match, each of them handing over three sterling pounds, and the empty bottle. They watched as Callum hit his last tee shot down the middle.

"Show-off," said Neil.

Derek picked up his ball along the way, no sense adding fuel to the bonfire, and they watched Callum hit his approach shot to the green, two putt for par, then trudged to the clubhouse singing Auld Lang Syne.

For his part during the round Callum stayed above the fray. He realized quickly that this really was all about the craic for them. Some of the banter was pretty funny, top notch gutter humor, and they'd obviously been around the block a few times together. He deduced by listening that the three of them all went to Tobermory High School.

The other three were so involved in their match play that they seemed to forget that he was even there. It was after all a competition and he could see by the other golfers around the course that most of them were taking it pretty serious and grinding away at their shots.

Callum ended up with two over par and took third place. Not bad for his first time on the course and taking into account his playing partners and their rambunctiousness wreaking havoc on his concentration, yelling expletives at each other during his backswing. In many ways it was a great training experience learning how to maneuver a golf ball around a strange course with just one club in hand.

Hot steaming soup and fresh bread was the fare after the round, and then with time running short the two men bade farewell.

Promises on future matches in Oban, against the pagan crew in Craigmore, as well as a few bits of worldly wisdom in parting and they were on their way, Callum driving and Tom strapped safely into the passenger seat, setting his head against the window and soon he was fast asleep, snoring loudly as they navigated back to Craignure and the fishing boat waiting faithfully at the dock.

Tom slept the whole way across the firth, and only rustled from his slumber when they docked and Callum practically had to carry him to the car.

"Blast that Neil," he mumbled, then fell asleep again till they pulled up to his house long after the last light of day had departed for the evening, the cold black night surrounding them.

Still grasping his one club, the four iron, using it like a walking cane in one hand while Callum kept him steady, wrapping his arm around his other shoulder, they made their way to the front door. Golden light poured out from the entrance in a welcoming glow.

With hands planted firmly on hips, Mrs. Gillam feigned dismay and hid a smile as she gently scolded her husband for his foolhardy behavior.

"Saints in heaven, Thomas Gillam, you should be ashamed of yourself. Such abhorrent deeds in front of young Callum."

He slurred his objection.

"The only abhorrent deed today was losing the match to that blasted Neanderthal who resides in my beloved Tobermory. Usurper on the throne of my forefathers, and blatant renegade. I am an outcast, a vagabond in exile, a pariah, and a lost soul. And yet there still is hope as long as I have me trusty four iron in hand. By all that's right and good in this world I will return for revenge someday. But for now I need to lie down."

Callum let him go and Tom put his hand against the wall to guide himself into the house.

"Thank you for driving home Callum," he said without turning around. "Fare well."

They watched him wobble down the hallway.

"Would you like some dinner?" asked Colleen shaking her head with a wry smile. "Or a ride home?"

"I'm fine," said Callum. "They had a nice soup and fresh bread at the course. That was quite a time we had. So, Tom and Neil eh?"

"Quite a pair those two. Put them together and watch the fireworks. They've been friends since diaper days, so what is that sixty-seven years now? Always up for a battle on the links and they've always got to try and one up the other. Most of us just stand well on the side and watch the show. Probably a good thing they live on opposite sides of the firth."

Callum saluted her, turned and started walking home through the dark night with the six iron.

19.

On Sunday, January 14, Tom drove up to Callum's house at five in the morning. There was candlelight on in the kitchen, and when the car settled to a stop, the front door cracked open and Callum stuck his face out to see who was driving.

Tom wrapped his jacket up around his neck as he made his way up the steps and went inside the house.

"Surprised to see you up so early," said Tom.

"I however am not surprised to see you up," said Callum. "I couldn't sleep."

"Bad dreams? Banshee's chasing you through the bog? Did you three putt from half a foot?"

"You're not supposed to tell people about your dreams. Might make them come true."

"Ahh, baloney. I had a dream one night that I one putted every green, told everyone that would listen, and it still hasn't happened."

"Yeah, but that's a good dream."

"It'd be a bad dream for me competitors. Let's go for a ride, I'll take you back over to

Mull."

"Another one club challenge at Tobermory?"

"No golf today. Leave the bag. I'm going to take you over there to see some of your history lad. You talk about Scottish roots. Well let's go see some actual living roots and take a little tour of some relics."

They headed down to the dock at Oban as the grey light of day was lighting up the sky to the east. There was a northwest wind blowing through the Hebrides, and the boat captain was going to make the call whether to go across within the hour.

The trip across was rougher than two weeks ago, and they stayed inside.

They rolled off the ferry at half past ten in the morning took a left turn and headed south, past Arlene's Coffee Shop, then a wooded stretch before seeing more buildings, whitewashed with grey roofs, passed by a small empty church with a sign outside that read; 'The Church of Scotland, Torosay and Kinlochspelve'. Tom slowed a bit as he drove by on the other side of the highway.

"Built in seventeen eighty-three by the Duke of Argyll. In eighteen twenty-eight it was struck by lightning and burned half the roof. Some people said it was because a Maclean and a MacQuarrie were in the parish at the same time. My parents were married there, bless their souls, in nineteen hundred and fifty-one. He was Presbyterian and she a Catholic."

They continued on down the highway, then through a long wooded stretch that lasted nearly a mile, the road itself down in a vee with forty foot hills on either side and towering pines on the left side and another type of tree on the right. Low scrub bushes, the rounded hills made of crushed rock as though a bulldozer had plowed through here at some point in time and threw the rubble to the side.

Then the sign said single track road, use passing places to permit overtaking. Past a low rock wall and a gate to a small house on an estate, a little red mailbox set into an arch on the wall, a shallow lake, another half mile of wooded roadway, then an open field on the left and a sign that read; Duart Castle 200 yards, Open to Visitors. Past the sign to Kilpatrick and left onto a narrow road just about wide enough for one car, the woods now closing in tight, up over a small hill, turning left then right, and stretching off to left now the watery straights of the Hebrides. Tom stopped the car for a moment and on the lonely point to the east stood a castle on the point.

"There she is lad. Duart Castle."

Off in the misty distance behind the dim structure set on the headland, stretched the Isle of Lismore, the shores of Eignaig, and the Loch Linnhe that separated them.

The road opened up now, low grassy flat lands leading down to mud flats along the shore, as though the salt air mowed the trees down leaving only the hardy grasses. Across a cattle guard, tires rumbling on the metal gates set into the ground. The entire right side barbed wire fenced now with no cattle in sight.

The castle disappeared behind a small hill, then over and the road heading straight for it, disappearing again behind a hedge of trees bordered by a low running rock wall that seemingly traveled from the sea, with large round boulders set on top, like sentinels in a line, bunched together side by side, guards of the past, over another cattle guard in the gate between the rock wall that ran to the sea on the left and off into the hills and bushes, disappearing to the right, then as they came around the corner there it was, a thick stern castle with rounded parapets on the corners, windowless, ominous walls built with boulders the size of small cars, edges filled with mortar, the red tile roof line in the center, inaccessible, high pitched with staggered chimneys. The backdrop grey misty clouds draped over the Highlands behind Oban far in the distance.

"Take note, Callum Maclean, sire of the Americas. Here is a bit of your past. And mine too. As well as Margaret MacQuarrie, her father, and half of Scotland as well. There's around eighteen hundred castles in Scotland alone, six hundred in Wales, and around fifteen hundred in England, and built for good reason. They kept you safe when bands of marauding thugs, dirty bastards went on rampages. Things were a bit wild for a few hundred years around here. Invading armies from France, England, and even clans from over the hill banding together and battlin' one and another. When you look back at history it seemed like a constant seething battle for land and power.

Every ten or twenty years some new ballyhoo was brewing. People barely had time to catch their breath, replenish their stores, their families when another disaster would happen. Castle building went on for around five hundred years from the time William the Conqueror swept in from France and brought the practice with him. Castle building, fortresses of stone and mortar was a successful way to survive attack. Until gunpowder came around in the seventeenth century and cannons could destroy walls. Until then, castles were the ticket to survival and they're all over the place. This is the one that concerns us now."

"You didn't mention Ireland. How many castles do they have?"

"Well, that's a bit of a pickle. Some reports are there's thirty thousand but I don't believe it for a moment. The Irish can be a little exaggeratin' at times. A couple of rocks on the side of the hill might a castle to them. But not to a Scotsman." Tom chuckled and whispered out the side of his mouth. "Don't tell Sean McGinnis I said that."

They parked in the lot alongside two buses and walked down the sidewalk towards the giant structure. The sign at the front said Museum.

"We're going to the museum?" asked Callum.

"Not yet lad, we'll save that for later. Follow me."

He led the way to the left around the corner.

"See this corner stone? Set your hand on it."

Callum did as he was told. It was cold and covered with a fine layer of moss.

"This stone and most all the lowest ones surrounding us were set here with mortar nearly a thousand years ago by people just like us. I think this is the beginning of the castle, and though it's not the actual foundation, which is below the soil, it's the first rock above it, facing northeast towards Inverness."

I believe this first stone was laid sometime around 1336. John of Irsay, otherwise known as John MacDonald, Eòin Mac Dòmhnuill, was the Dominus Insularum, Lord of the Isles and would have been around sixteen years old. Descended from Somerled, Somairle mac Gilla Brigte, himself a descendant of Norse Gaelic Vikings who settled in Ireland and Scotland and intermarried with the Gaels and created the Kingdom of Argyll and the Isles in the twelfth century, then perished at the Battle of Renfrew, six miles west of Glasgow in 1164 when he got a little overzealous and tried to invade the Scottish mainland with forces from Man and Ireland. When Somerled died, his vast kingdom disintegrated and the islands of the Hebrides for the most part was left to his sons. Sometime around 1365, Lachlan Lubanach Maclean, descendant of Gillean who fought against the Norsemen at the battle of Largs, fell in love with Mary MacDonald, daughter of the Lord of the Isles. The father refused the marriage. Do you see a pattern here, young Callum?"

Callum for his part frowned slightly. He was

listening intently, still keeping his hand on the moss covered stone, the quiet atmosphere of the castle standing over the ocean, and the history lesson magnifying his insignificance.

"The father refused, and somehow, Lachlan was able to kidnap him, and force him to accept the marriage. It was not a marriage of convenience or of patronage, but one of pure love."

"I'm not kidnapping Maggie's father."

"I'm not suggesting it. Officially that is and I'll deny it in a court of law, but I think it might be easier than trying to win The Open lad."

Callum shook his head. "You were saying? Something about the Macdonald's and the Macleans?"

"At any rate, the two were married, and one of the items of Mary's dowry was this fine castle that we're standing next to. It was probably not quite as large as it is now, and might have only been half built, but was a structure nonetheless. Lachlan became the first Laird, or landowner of Duart Castle.

Lachlan had five sons, Eachann, John, Lachlan, Neil, and Somerled. See where this is going? He married the descendant of Somerled and named his son after him. Eachann, the Red Hector the oldest boy and the heir, was a renowned sword fighter, and became so famous that knights from distant lands came to measure swords with him. One day a knight from Norway travelled to Mull and challenged Eachann to mortal combat. There's a green hill in the little town of Salen, near the shoreline in between Craignure and Tobermory where the knight from Norway is buried after Hector defeated him. Hector died at the battle of Harlaw in 1411 in the Aberdeenshire, all the way on the east coast on the other side of Scotland."

"For the next hundred and eighty years, each successive heir was either named Hector, or Somerled Maclean."

"In 1647 the castle was laid siege by Argyll government troops and the Clan Campbell but the invasion was forced off. In 1653 Cromwell sent six ships of war that anchored off Duart with the intent to bombard the walls into submission but on the thirteenth of September a storm blew in and sank three ships and scattered the rest."

"Sir John Maclean was born in 1670, inherited the castle and lands of the Maclean clan when he was but four years old and was assigned to his uncle's Lauchland and Lachland who managed the clan lands in Argyll and Bute. By all accounts they managed the holdings badly and ran up a huge monetary debt. When that debt was called to be paid the Macleans evaded payment for a time and threatened armed resistance."

"In 1678, troops led by Archibald Campbell, 9th Earl of Argyll successfully invaded Mull, and John was forced to flee. He was eight years old. Argyll got a commission to secure the Highlands and disarm all the Catholics, especially the Macleans and Macdonald's, but he was accused of treason and executed by guillotine at Edinburgh Castle on June 30, 1685. In 1691 when he was twenty-one years old, John Maclean relinquished Duart to the Campbells, specifically to Archibald Campbell, 1st Duke of Argyll, son of the decapitated Earl."

"Descendants of Archibald Campbell, sold the castle in 1801, to a MacQuarrie, who eventually sold it to Carter-Campbell of Possil who kept it as a ruin within the grounds of his own estate to the north, Torosay Castle. He later sold his Torosay Estate which now included the ruins of Castle Duart to A. C. Guthrie in 1865. On September 11, 1911, the ruin was separated from the rest of the Torosay Estate and was bought by Sir Fitzroy Donald Maclean, the 26th Chief of the Clan MacLean and restored to the clan two hundred and twenty years after it was surrendered."

"How do you know all this?" asked Callum.

Tom shrugged. "It's a hobby I guess, to know about a few things that went on around here. Pus I have a personal interest in this Castle and the Macleans, and the Campbells. My great, great grandmother on my mother's side was a Maclean, and my great, great, great grandfather, also on my mother's side was a Campbell. Imagine how that went when the in-laws came to visit."

"You've got a Maclean for an ancestor."

"Yes, young Callum, that is for sure. I'm a Maclean. That and two pounds will get me a cup of coffee in yonder gift shop in the Castle. You and I are distant cousins as well as the Macleans are concerned and probably other clans as well. You must understand that since all these people in the Highlands, and those in the Lowlands, and Wales, Ireland, and even Britain have been living together and battling for the past thousand plus years, our bloodlines have been mixed many times over, on the battlefield as well as the bedroom if truth be told. Thank God the fighting has ended for the most part, and now our battles are fought on the football and rugby pitch, and sometimes golf courses. We've been playing England in rugby since 1871, just about the time that the wars stopped. We beat the English one to nothing at Raeburn Place in Edinburgh in 1871, and I can guarantee there were a few bloody noses in that match. They called the matches an international friendly but you can bet there was nothing friendly going on in between the lines. Over the years we've traded wins. Since 1910 we trade venues every year, in Edinburgh, then London, then back to Edinburgh and so forth, and we've only stopped the match from 1939 to 1947 during World War two. We've whupped those bastards three times in a row now."

"You're my cousin."

Tom reached over and slapped Callum heartily on the back.

"And that's why I'm going to take care of you Callum. See that you get a good education on the intricacies of being a Scotsman. Take note of the rocks that make up these walls. The lightest ones weigh a few hundred pounds lad, and back when they were laid in place and mortared there were no bulldozers or forklifts. No motorized cranes to lift them, no trucks to deliver them from the seaside. Just hands and feet and muscle. And maybe that's a reason that the Scots and English, not to mention the Welsh and Irish were so crazy for a time during the castle building days. It built us into he-men."

Callum kept his hand on the large rough hewn rock set into the wall, and wondered if one of his ancestors rolled it into place and filled the side with mortar. Something about the place seemed familiar.

"This castle didn't build itself Callum. Sheer might and willpower built it. And now it's a struggle for the Maclean clan to keep it intact. There's no armies of men under the command of a chief anymore. And maybe that's a good thing."

Tom was quiet for a few moments as his words sank into both of them. A thousand years of battling for the Highlands, and now they stood next to an aging castle looking out over the straights towards Argyll.

"All those people who built these castles and battled over the land. They're all gone Callum. They took nothing with them when they went to the other side. They built empires and left empty handed."

"I know how that goes," said Callum.

"All they left us is this pile of rocks. And this," Tom patted his own chest then reached over and patted Callum's. "They left their spirit. And it runs deep in the both of us."

20.

Late one afternoon at the beginning of February towards sunset after hitting balls at the range for a few hours Callum decided to play a couple of holes until it was dark, then hobble home.

He was tired and worn out. Hitting driver off the first tee he sliced his shot into the woods on the right side up near the green and went to look for it. There was a south wind blowing and he could hear shouting and laughter coming from the rugby field next door and decided to have a look after finding his ball stuck in the mud under a tree. Toting his bag through the woods and over the creek he made his way to the clearing on the other side.

It was a large well maintained square field with lights on tall poles on the edges for night play, chalk lines around the perimeter and two goal posts on either end. In the middle of the circle at the midfield at that current moment was a scrum. Six players on each side, heads down, arms locked over backs, legs churning, battling, somewhere in the middle was the ball, with two rovers on the side, waiting.

The team on the right got momentum, turning the opponent from right to left, breaking their scrum and winding up with the ball, heading down field battling the whole way till that team scored. Breathless, they all made their way back to the center where one player remained on the ground holding his knee. They tried to help him to his feet but he declined attention, got up on his own and limped to the sidelines.

"Now what?" said one of the men.

"We'll play six a side," said another. "Nigel can ref."

"I don't want to ref, let Crosbie."

"I'm playing mate," said the bloke named Crosbie.

That's when they all spotted Callum standing in the woods near the sideline.

"Eh, who's the bloke over there?"

"Scared the piss out of me for a minute there. Thought it was a banshee coming out of the woods."

"Strange looking."

"Just a golfer lost his ball."

"There's our seven," said Nigel.

"He looks kind of skinny," said Crosbie.

"We'll put him at wing."

"Hey mate!" shouted Crosbie. "Fancy a bit of rugby do ya?"

Callum shrugged his shoulders, trudged out of the woods, set his golf bag on the side and joined them in the middle.

"Hey, I know you," said Crosbie. "You're the Yank who wants to marry Maggie MacQuarrie."

"Heard about you," said Nigel.

They all crowded around him. Everyone wanted to have a close look and they each had a word or two to say.

"Your poor old dad left you an old house and that's all."

"Sixty million to charity and none to his own son. It's a pity."

"So you're going to win The Open are ya?"

Callum looked at the gang of men surrounding him. They looked to be in their late twenties and early thirties. Probably businessmen in real life, but here in the pitch they were rugby warriors. Mostly tough looking, old mended flat broken noses, gaps in teeth, tousled hair, half beards, bruised arms, bloodied knuckles.

"I thought you called me over because you wanted to have a go at a bit of rugby," said Callum. "But if you want to talk about our personal life, we can go build a little campfire, roast some marshmallows, sing songs and go around in a circle and do some bonding."

Crosbie laughed and then they all laughed along with him.

"Good one mate. Have you played rugby before then?"

"Just a bit."

"You know the rules."

"You're playing sevens. Looks like you need a wing."

Crosbie nodded. "That's right, you're in." He whistled. "Rally up!"

The team Callum was with would receive the

kickoff. They plowed down the line ruck and a maul over and over, then the ball was in Callum's hands and he flew through the middle. Two of the bigger players tried to tackle him and wrestle him to the ground, then with a twist of his shoulders their hands slipped and it was off to the races. Two defenders on the side tried to catch him but it was no use, he got to the line and scored.

"Beginners luck," wheezed one of the players on the other team while Callum placed the ball on the tee on the sidelines and got ready to kick it through the goal post thirty yards at an angle.

He lined it up like he was going to knock in a putt, took five steps back, then three quick steps forward, leg snapping his shoe up at the ball and it flew in a high arc up and through the posts.

"Great shot!" yelled Crosbie. "You kick off now." And they lined up again and Callum kicked the ball up the field towards the opposing team who immediately started churning towards them, tossing the ball backwards as they went. The defenders tackling, ball on the ground, kicked backwards towards the next in line, mauling forwards, rucking, mauling, then Callum saw his chance as a halfback barreled towards him, he reached out to tackle the player then snatched the ball out of his hands and raced off down the field for another score. In all the commotion no one noticed how dark it had become, hands on knees, gasping for breath from the frantic running. Callum lay on his back, ball gripped close to his chest on the other side of the line with a smile on his face.

"Rugby," he whispered. He hadn't played the game since he'd been in Scotland, and it came back how much fun it was to score.

His team mates finally made it to him for the obligatory congratulations. The match was over. They shook hands with the other team with respect.

"So, you know how to play rugby 'just a bit', eh?" said Crosbie. "Where'd you learn, not America?"

"Tonga."

"Tonga?," he fairly shouted. "Bloody savages down there I reckon. That's rugby league down under, we play rugby union here. Bit of a difference you know."

Callum shrugged. "Tackle the guy with the ball right? From what I heard; rugby union is the 'gentleman's game'."

"Yeah," said a large man on the right. "The kind where you scrape the bottom of your cleats on the guy's face when he's pinned on the ground."

"Nigel and Liam here are from Australia, on contract with a construction company."

"Hey mate."

They both came forward to shake Callum's hand. Then Nigel made a fist and pumped it in the air. "Rugby league!"

The other players were quick and countered heartily shouting in unison.

"Rugby union!"

"Rugby league!" Nigel shouted again joined

this time by Liam, and it went back in forth a couple of times rugby union, rugby league, before they all got tired of it and laughed good naturedly.

"Nigel's from Queensland, and Liam here is from Sydney. Got a bit of a rivalry there eh?"

"Two teams with the most gawd offal mascots," said Liam while shaking his head. "Queensland is the cane toad, and New South Wales the cockroach,"

"State of origin series," said Nigel. "You play for the Australian state where you played your first senior rugby league game when you're sixteen. Queensland's got the better players but most of them go to Sydney to play in the pros. If they all got to play for Sydney we'd never win, but as it is, we dominate."

"Ah go stuff yourself," said Liam. "Queensland sucks."

"Cane toads, cane toads," Nigel goaded him with a fist.

"You ever play anywhere else?"

"Mostly in Tonga, I lived there for a year, but I also got a chance to play in Samoa, and Tahiti. I've been playing on a team from Kahuku, on Oahu."

"Tonga eh. You know that chant they do before the match?"

"The Sipi Ta?"

Callum got into a semi crouch and hit his hand on his thigh while making an angry warrior face.

"Mate ma'a Tonga! Hiii! Koe 'Otua mo Tonga ko hoku tofi'a!"

"You should be on our team," said the big man that Callum had plowed through for the score. He motioned to the other men surrounding them pointing to each in turn. "This is Grant, Twiggy, Banger, Scruff, Willie, Max, Cormer, Colin, Justice, Cannon, Mudder, Crosbie, Liam and Nigel."

"What's your name?" asked Callum.

""I'm Scott."

Callum motioned to the world around them. "So this is your land?"

Some of them chuckled pitifully. It was an old joke but one that took on a fresh sense of humor with a green horn saying it. Scotland.

"Aye," said Scott as he held out his hand. "And I'll be welcoming you to it. Looks like we have a new player gents."

21.

Tom introduced Callum to his nephew Jackie who was a sophomore in high school and a pretty good player. Since Jackie was related to Tom, he was also related to Callum somewhere in the distant past. They hit it off great. Jackie was sprouting like a weed at sixteen years old and offered to caddie for Callum if he made it to The Open.

They started playing late afternoon rounds at Glencruitten. Callum talked him into match play fifty pence per hole which is half a pound. He'd give Jackie a stroke per hole to make things more even.

"The most you could lose is four and half pounds," said Callum. "And you'd have to be playing pretty bad to lose by a stroke per hole. Are you a player, or aren't you?" Goading him into the bet.

The first match they had started out level enough with carryover ties for the first five holes. Then when Callum birdied the last four holes and pocketed the four and a half pounds, he had to up the ante to one and a half strokes per hole.

Towards the middle of February, it came to pass in Tom's mind that after a full grueling month and a half of practicing on the range and playing most of his rounds either on his own, or with Jackie and some of the locals around town that the time had come to up the ante.

Callum's game had improved to the point where he could almost go as low as he wanted, but he was getting stagnant, bored. Motivation for an event that was still nearly half a year away was a tough incentive.

He needed some stiffer competition than the old guys around the club, so Tom set up a few matches at some of the neighboring courses.

For money.

"I've got a plan," said Tom.

"What's that?"

"I've been thinking about it. The nuts and bolts of it all. The regional qualifying tournaments are scheduled for the last week of June. You have four months to get ready. You must deliver your application to the R&A no later than one minute before midnight on June the first. You must either be a bona fide professional golfer, or an amateur with a handicap of no more than point four, a scratch golfer. The qualifying tournaments are being held at a few courses nearby and you need to choose one as your primary choice and a couple more as alternates in case the docket fills up, or they need to move the venue for some other reason. Two courses, and I'll recommend Goswick, and Kilmarnock. You'll need to get used to playing those courses and quickly. Some of the competitors, the other blokes trying for a spot in the Open have been playing on those runs all their lives and know every inch and cranny, every blade of grass. We don't have time for that and need to have an accelerated learning curve, and the best way I know to accelerate a curve is to put some money on the line."

"I'm going to play for money?"

"We'll each put up half the cash," said Tom. "A hundred pounds each."

"What?" Callum's face turned red. "I don't know Tom. That's a lot of money for me right now. I lose I don't eat."

"Perfect," said Tom.

"Did you hear what I said? I don't win I don't eat."

"I've got enough confidence in your game that I could put up the whole wad, but you need to have some skin in the game. You need to start competing as though your life depended on it."

22.

Their first victim, as Tom put it was a semi-pro that played at Kilmarnock on a regular basis. Grant Larrabee, thirty-two years old, and a scrappy competitor.

"Is he a good player?" asked Callum.

"One of the best."

"Why'd you pick him for the first one? Why not get someone who's kind of good for the first round?"

"No sense in treading lightly Callum. Might as well find out quick if you've got the stomach for it. Competition in golf is no different from getting in the boxing ring. Saying you want to win, that you have to win, and actually going out and winning are two different things. When that bell rings you'd better be on your toes and ready, and the best way I think is to get in the ring with one of the finest players around and mix it up. Better yet if you get a bloody nose and can still come out swinging. No sense dilly dallying around."

"How do you know this guy?"

"Remember the grumpy fella in the picture

with me holding the card with fifty-nine on it?"

"Yeah?"

"It's his son."

Kilmarnock was a hundred and eighteen miles south, near Glasgow and took two and half hours to drive there.

Tom picked up Callum at five am sharp and they got to the golf course at seven thirty, just before daybreak. Sitting in a car for nearly three hours was not the most ideal way to show up for a match while your competitor was rolling out of bed and practically strolling to the course.

Callum recognized Barnaby Larrabee right off the bat as they waited by the clubhouse. It was almost as if the scowl from the picture that day was etched onto his face from that day forward. As it turned out he was a jovial sort and smiled when he saw them. Perhaps he was smiling at the prospect of winning some money from his old adversary, using his son as a proxy.

Tom and Barnaby shook hands and then Tom put him in a bear hug patting him on the back.

"Barnaby and Grant, I'd like to meet Callum Maclean."

"Maclean eh?" said Barnaby. "Got us a ringer from Mull?"

"Hardly a ringer," said Tom. "He's just starting out playing the game. I'll be honest with you, he got it in his mind to try and qualify for The Open."

"The Open?" scoffed Grant. "Fat chance at

that."

Callum smiled, he liked it when guys were overly confident and boisterous. It usually meant they were reckless, unfocused. It was always better to act and feel as though you were the underdog.

"It's just a pipe dream," said Callum. "Tom here said it might be a good idea to test it out against one of the best in the game."

Buttering him up, throwing him off-guard.

But it was all for naught.

Right out of the gate Grant jumped up by two strokes on the first hole when he birdied it with a long winding twenty-foot putt from the fringe, and Callum bogeyed from the sand.

From there it was a beatdown. He was up by seven at the turn, up by nine on the thirteenth hole, and even though Callum rallied with three straight birdies on the final holes, Grant won by six, cruising to the finish line with worry free tap in pars while Callum was sweating miracle chips and long putts.

"Nice doing business with you gents," said Grant as he grabbed the two hundred pounds, then slowly and methodically counted out the bills, and handed half to his father. The scowl on his dad's face was still a scowl but now had a bit of a smile wrapped around the edges.

Tom was magnanimous in defeat and shook both their hands graciously and asked hopefully.

"Great round Grant. Perhaps we can do this again?"

"Why anytime. How about tomorrow or the

next day?"

Rubbing it in.

"No, no," said Tom. "I've got a busy schedule and can't get down here, and Callum here doesn't have a car. Maybe in a couple of weeks?"

"You don't expect to have strokes given do you?" said Grant. Rubbing it in farther.

"No, no, let's keep it straight up. We'll try to give you a better challenge next time. Well, we'd better be off."

On the long ride back to Oban, Callum was sullen, while Tom was whimsical.

"Well, you finally woke up on the last three holes, that's encouraging."

"It sucks," said Callum. "It sucks to lose to a prick like Grant, and it sucks to lose a hundred pounds. I'm actually not sure which is worse though. Either one is bad enough but put them together and this is one of the worst days I've ever had."

"Hold onto that feeling Callum. Remember it on our ride home and tonight when you're tossing and turning and having nightmares handing over your money because of a few missed shots. You got taken out of your game right off the bat."

"I went in the bunker and he had a miracle birdie. Two strokes down on the first hole."

Tom nodded. There it was.

"And that's where you lost it. The whole match boiled down to that very first hole Callum, didn't it? Think about it now. You tightened up, and he knew it. You lost faith on one lousy hole. You lost the magic and you didn't get it back until the final three holes but it was much too late by then, wasn't it?"

Callum was silent. There was nothing he could say to take away the sting. In his mind he could still see Grant gleefully counting the money. His money.

They stopped along the way at a little inn and Tom bought a light dinner for the both of them. Callum still had a bad taste in his mouth and had the waitress box up the leftovers.

"Well," said Tom as he stopped in front of Callum's stone house. "Get a good night's rest and get the bad dreams out of the way, we have another match tomorrow morning."

"Tomorrow?!" said Callum. "Another hundred pounds from my pocket?"

Tom looked at him with serious eyes while shaking his head.

"Don't forget for a moment that you're a Maclean. Protector of Argyll. Don't let that hundred leave your pocket without a fight this time. As well as my hundred."

23.

"How'd you sleep?" asked Tom cheerfully as Callum tossed his clubs in the back seat and sat up front.

"Just peachy," Callum replied, with a wry look in his eyes as he strapped in his seatbelt and the car lurched down the bumpy road. "I forgot to ask you last night who our next victim is going to be, and even what golf course we're going to play on. But then I realized that it doesn't really matter who the other player is, or for that matter what golf course we're battling it out on. Because I'm not even battling the other guy *or* the golf course."

"Oh yeah?" asked Tom. "What are you doing then?"

"I'm going for the magic," smiled Callum. "From the first shot to the last and every single one in between. I'm going for all the cliches you can think of, from the beginning of the round till the end, that invisible realm that's just outside of our understanding, outside the grasp of our senses. I've got to just let it go, trust in the magic, grip it and rip it, think about what shot I want to hit and completely immerse myself in it, from the moment I set my feet to the micro moment when that ball stops rolling and just enjoy each and every second of it, bring the whole universe and every blade of grass on the course into play."

Tom looked over him with a grimace.

"You haven't been hitting the bottle have you? Or smoking some of that wacky tabacky? You check the expiration dates on the perishables in your fridge?"

"I had a cup of coffee, a hard-boiled egg and a donut. How long till we get to the course?"

"Hour and a half. We're going to..."

Callum put up his hand to stop Tom from uttering another word, then leaned against the side of the passenger window and went to sleep.

They headed north and pulled into the club parking lot at seven thirty-five and met their competitor at the practice range. He was a small bloke, about five foot three with a short compact swing, and was hitting a mid-iron onto a green about a hundred fifty yards away.

Every shot looked like a mirror image of the one before it, as if he was a robot with a pre-programmed swing.

"Don't let his size fool you," said Tom. "He can hit it a mile and putt like a demon. Plus, he's known as a bit of a hot head. He might try to draw you into a squabble to throw you off your game. Best to be on your toes."

Callum, however, was in no mood for niceties. He was still fuming from losing a hundred pounds just a few hours ago and the only way not to blow his top was to vent steam.

"I couldn't care less how he plays," said Callum. "All I care about is how I play. And I sure as hell don't give a rat's ass about his demeanor. Try to pull me into a squabble will he?"

They shook hands politely.

"Alex Cardin, I'm a Welsh transplant working for an aggregate company, systems analyst. I heard you're from America, what do you do for a living?"

Callum had a feeling that 'ol Alex, the systems analyst knew exactly what he did for a living and was trying to get an early edge on things by making him say something he might be ashamed of.

"It's true, I'm an ex-pat, a Yank, and I cook fish down by the docks in Oban. I make so much money at it that I only have to work one or two days a week."

Alex's left eye hardened.

"Sweet. I heard you challenged Grant Larrabee down at Kilmarnock yesterday. How'd the course play?"

Word got around fast. How'd the course play, he asked.

Another craic.

This was like a rugby match where you needed to smash the other guy in the face, and run with the ball, before he did the same to you.

"The course was great; I however was not. Grant beat me by six strokes if you want to know the final dirty details. Now are we going to sit here on the driving range and chit chat, or are we going to play a competitive round of golf? If you'd prefer, you can ask me how the weather is down south and I can ask you what you had for breakfast, what's your favorite color, and do you like cats or dogs, or both? Maybe we should just forget about golf and hold hands and go skipping down the lane singing songs?"

Now both of Alex's eyes were hardened.

"You don't have to be a dick about it. I don't like your attitude."

Callum turned to Tom. "I didn't know you brought me to a popularity contest. I thought it was a golf match."

"Alright tough guy," said Alex, eyes flashing. "Let's increase the bet. Three hundred pounds."

"Make it four," said Callum and put out his hand to seal the deal.

"Make it five," said Alex, but he did not put his hand out in return.

"Five it is," said Callum, and left his hand out. Alex turned on his heels and grabbed his golf bag from the stand and stormed off.

"See you on the first tee," he bellowed over his shoulder.

And that's the last time either of them spoke another word to each other during the match.

"What are you doing?" asked Tom as they walked towards the first tee.

"Putting some skin in the game, isn't that what you told me to do?"

"I only have a hundred pounds on me."

"Well, I've got four, the last money I have in

the world. Looks like it's time for me to put up or shut up, right?"

"You sure have a way of stirring up a fight."

"Why Thomas Gillam I'm surprised at that accusation. I'm not here to stir up a fight, I'm just here to play a round of golf and feel the magic."

Tom chuckled. It was funny in a way. The little man on wheels, Alex Cardin with a reputation as a master of manipulation just got pummeled before they even got to the first tee.

Maybe the lad was onto something.

Tom, as an observer tossed a tee in the air and it pointed mostly at Alex, giving him the honor to hit first.

He teed up his ball, set his feet and hit a bomb, up over a sand bunker into the middle of the fairway and they all watched as it continued to roll and roll and roll well out of sight. And that was the last great shot he hit all day.

Callum set up square, and also hit a giant tee shot, calmly, effortlessly, without hitting a single warm up shot on the driving range, as Alex was well aware, and when they finally got to their balls, Callum was twenty yards past Alex, who was stuck in a divot.

"Blasted," he muttered as he surveyed his situation. Granted, it was just the first shot of the match, but not only was it in a divot, but it was nestled against the front edge, the worst possible break. He clunked it, hit it fat and the ball ended up well short of the green.

"Magic," said Callum, loud enough for all to hear as he admired his ball sitting fine on the flat grass, a hundred yards to the pin. He pulled out the old wedge. With one hop he nearly holed out his wedge shot, and it one hopped like a little bunny and stopped a foot from the cup for an easy birdie.

Alex, on the other hand sitting two, well off the green, hit a low bump 'n run that got a little hot and went ten feet by the cup. He missed that putt, let out a muffled curse, and that was the end of him.

Callum was three up at the turn and ended up with a four under par sixty-eight. A nifty score with five birdies and one bogey.

Alex, on his home course against a fish frying Yank had but one birdie against five bogeys and ended up with seventy-six. Eight shots behind.

Still, he took his hat off and shook Callum's hand, then counted a wad of cash and put it in his hand.

"Nice round," he said, then turned and walked away.

"That's how you do it," said Tom. "This is after all a gentlemen's game. Talk all you want in good nature before, during and after the match. But if you lose, take it like a man, and never wish an opposing player ill will, for that is the cardinal sin. Wishing bad luck on someone else whether in golf or life, is the same as wishing it upon yourself. Even the great ones will tell you that they may have had a rival or two that bordered on being enemies on the course, but were in essence kindred spirits, striving for the same thing, to win. You may find yourself pitted against someone like that in the future, and you may be able to push each other to great heights."

Over the next few weeks, they played a few more matches against some of the top players in the area, then Tom set up Callum in a tournament with prize money. Callum put on his application that he was playing as a professional, took third place honors with a hundred pounds in winnings, and that was all it took. Now he would enter the Regional Qualifying for The Open as a professional.

Over the first part of March, he played in a few more tournaments as a pro, but failed to win any money, and the first prize money that he won seemed like an anomaly and dwindled to zero. He was a sharp player, but in tournaments with more than one competitor, he faltered. Tom began to get worried about their little project and put him back on the feathery for a week to set him straight. At the very next tournament after the feathery adjustment, he took tenth place, and at least re-couped his entry fee.

24.

On Friday the fifteenth, the Ides of March, Tom drove up to Callum's house at three thirty in the wee morning hours.

The crescent moon was rising in the east ahead of the coming sunrise, which was still three hours away.

The temperature was forecast to be ten degrees Celsius, a balmy fifty degrees Fahrenheit, and with a clear sky and no rain in the forecast it was shaping up to be an epic day for golf.

Tom strode carefully up the cobblestones, intent on keeping his feet under him on the uneven pavers. He knocked lightly on the front door listening intently for movement inside, then hearing nary a footstep or groaning complaint knocked louder this time as though he was the constable getting ready to break down the door and arrest the villain.

"Crimeny!" came a shout from inside, then shuffled footsteps across the wooden floor and the door cracked open. "What now?" whispered Callum with a raspy voice.

"Grab your clubs, we're going on an

adventure."

"It's four in the morning for crying out loud."

"Come on now, enough of yer belly achin', I've got your coffee and breakfast in the car. We've got a ways to go."

"Couldn't you at least give me a minute to use the loo?"

"Fine, I'll grab your clubs, get yourself straightened up and out to the car with you. I've got a surprise."

Callum winced. Tom's surprises could be painful and they were usually precipitated by a loud knock on the door in the cold dark night long before sunrise. Not only did Tom enjoy surprises, he seemed to thoroughly appreciate springing them on an unsuspecting, soundly sleeping Callum.

Hiking to the top of Ben Nevis, the tallest mountain in Scotland at the break of dawn, one and half miles seemingly straight up into the clouds to build his legs and stamina.

Sheep shearing at MacGregor's farm outside the town of Glenmore to build his wrist strength. A couple of sheep would've been no problem, but three hundred from the dark of dawn till lunch.

Then there were the Highlands games which were actually quite fun but left him bruised for days after. Tossing the caber, a hundred-pound twenty-foot pine log that he had to manhandle, hammer throw, shot put, weight over the bar, with one hand throwing a twenty-five-pound anvil with steel ring on it over a bar ten feet high, tug of war with twenty burly Scots on either side trying to pull the others into a mud pit. They won that contest but got into a bit of a rugby scrum brawl afterwards.

Tom set the clubs into the boot of the car and sat at the wheel, engine running, heater on while he waited for Callum who shuffled out the door and down the cobblestones, hot breath forming clouds of steam as he went like a locomotive going down the tracks. He went around the car and sat in the passenger seat, throwing his backpack into the rear seat.

"So what fine adventure do you have planned today good sir?"

"Well now that's the attitude," said Tom handing Callum a hot lidded mug of coffee in one hand and a donut in the other, put the car in drive, down the dirt driveway and out onto the pavement, heading south.

"South is it?" said Callum, still waiting for the announcement of the destination.

"Aye," said Tom. "Down around the craggy glen, and south it is we'll go. By bush or bright or dead of night, by foot or fowl we'll fight or flight, a gallus errand to the scrap, with a nary a thought to the pit or the plight, and buckets of gold at the end."

Callum nodded appreciatively.

"Is that an old Scottish rhyme?"

"Naw, I just made it up." He turned to Callum with a proud face. "A true Scotsman can make up a rhyme on the go, it's in our blood man."

"South," said Callum again, trying to prompt

the old man into telling him where in the heck they were going without actually asking the question. "Well, we've got the clubs in the car, so I'm assuming we're going somewhere to play golf."

Tom looked over at the young man with astounded eyebrows raised.

"You, young Callum continue to amaze me with the astute clarity with which you take the smallest of clues and solve the case. I believe someday you might even find a position at Scotland Yard working with the finest detectives on the planet, cracking the most difficult crimes in the land. With your bright mind you may even deduce the hiding place of the Loch Ness monster and finally put that mystery to rest."

Oh brother, thought Callum, shaking his head imperceptibly, and taking a bite of the donut. It was much too early, and he was still too sleepy to try and keep up with the old man's wit. He took another bite of the donut and thought hard while looking at his watch. It was three thirty in the morning. Sunrise was at six thirty. They were travelling at around sixty five miles an hour on an uncrowded road. They could travel nearly two hundred miles before sunrise.

"Are we going to Glasgow?" There he finally asked the question.

"Bah. A fine city for ballroom dancing and shopping for the women, but not for golf. We're heading for Royal Troon. We'll go past Glasgow as fast as we can, through Paisley, and

Barrhead, and Newton Mearns, take the right fork at Kilmarnock, then head for the sea. South of Barrassie on the shores of Troon is the one of the finest golf courses ever devised by man."

"Why there?"

"Why there, good grief man, that's where The Open is being played this year, your precious Open, four months from now in fact. We're going there to test your game at the old course. It's an expensive run, three hundred pounds per player."

"Gad," winced Callum. "I don't have that kind of money."

"Nor do I," said Tom. "Plus, it's usually booked solid and you can nae just show up and play. But I know a guy."

They turned into the entrance at a quarter to six, still over half an hour till dawn, drove past the clubhouse and into a little parking lot next to a cart barn. A tall man was standing next to a utility vehicle waiting for them. He looked down at his watch and shook his head as though sorely disappointed.

"Grab the bag," said Tom. "I was trying to get here a little earlier so he wouldn't be waiting for us. I told him we'd be here at six and even though we're fifteen minutes early he's always got to show me up."

"Friend of yours?" asked Callum.

"You'll see soon enough."

The tall man was tapping his foot as they walked towards him, the clubs in Callum's bag clinking as they went.

"Callum Maclean, I'd like you meet Nathan Pickett, he's the most handsome greenskeeper south of Argyll, and here at Royal Troon a master horticulturist, one of the best in all Scotland, second only to yours truly."

The tall man smiled at Callum and gave him a good handshake, then patted him on the shoulder.

"Sure, now he's telling me to my face that I'm handsome, but I'll bet on the ride down here he was telling you I was a minger who fell out of the ugly tree at birth and hit every branch on the way down."

Then he turned his attention to Tom.

"So, this is your project, eh? He's the one who's gonna put you back in the game?"

"I never left the game you old cricket. I could still whoop you like a yardstick at the bally."

Nathan laughed wholeheartedly at that.

"You're in good hands here lad. Well, you seem sturdy enough, I'll bet you can hit the ball a kilometer on the carry."

"I do okay," said Callum warily.

"But can you putt?" said Nathan.

Both Tom and Nathan chuckled when Callum didn't answer right away.

"That's okay lad," said Nathan. "None of us can if truth be told, and if anyone ever says they can then they're liars and jinxed themselves in the process. The heck with long drives, it's the wee game that wins the match, and don't let anyone tell you otherwise, it's the four-foot putt that's the devilish shot, and the one that wins the match."

"They have a motto at this club Callum," said Tom. "As much by skill as by strength."

Callum looked closer at Nathan and nodded his head. "I've seen you before, not in person but in a picture. You're on Tom's wall, he's holding a trophy and a scorecard with a fifty-nine on it."

"So, he's got it on his wall, does he?" said Nathan as he looked at Tom, shaking his head with mock disdain. "Is it in a special frame that he built, with wood from the rowan tree? Is there a garland of sparkly lights around the perimeter, and does he wave a holy tin of burning incense while chanting in Gaelic?"

"You've seen the picture man; you've been to me house!"

"Sure, but that doesn't mean you might've amended it over the years. Maybe you've made that single picture into a sacred shrine that you hang all your gilded laurels around and have a little blanket and pillow so you can sleep under it."

"Don't listen to him Callum, he's just jealous that he's had nary a sixty-one in him, let alone a fifty-nine."

"Aye, I've had sixty-twos a plenty, quite a few of them in my time, and some of them on the championship course you're about to set foot on young Callum. Ask old Tom over here how low a score he's shot on this course."

"Bah," said Tom.

"Well?" pressed Nathan.

"Sixty-four and you know it," muttered Tom. "It was a lucky putt you had and you know that too. I was in the clubhouse with a sixty-four on the final round, Callum. I was up by a stroke. The cup was mine. He made a hundred-foot putt from off the green on number eighteen for birdie and the win."

Nathan smiled at last. "Aw good memories, I'm glad you remember. And it was a lucky putt. Ones of that length always are and never let anyone tell you otherwise. The four-footer is the key though. They're the ones of all out grinding skill and determination. Maybe after the round or on another day you can come to my house Callum, and I'll show you the picture of that day, me with the trophy and old Tom here scowling on the side."

"Bah," said Tom. "I never would have brought him here if I knew we'd be taking a bath in hogwash before the first tee. I'd at least 'ave brought a towel and change of clothes, and maybe a bar of soap as well."

Callum for his part, shook his head and chuckled, realizing that these two friends seemed to enjoy the back and forth bashing as much as breathing.

Nathan leaned over towards Callum, speaking low in a conspiratorial tone.

"Has he told you yet about his super-secret scientific method for playing golf?"

"He's given me a few tips, some pointers."

"Yes, but has he given you *the* most precise, technical process on the mechanics of hitting the ball?"

"I don't know," said Callum and they both looked at Tom who shook his head.

"I was saving that one for last," said Tom with a frown. "I've got the lad shaping the ball, right or left, straight, high, low, top-spin, back-spin, side spin, you name it, thinking about where he wants the ball to land, to roll out. I guess he's about ready for the final lesson."

Tom winked at Nathan.

"Aye, it's as though I've taken every excellent shot ever made in the game of golf from the beginning of time, rolled them all into a liquid orb of greatness, then boiled it, condensed it, refined it, distilled it into one single drop, one pure technical thought that everyone from a Neanderthal to the great Jack Nicklaus can use to perfect their swing and propel a little round golf ball with the greatest of ease. I should have won the Nobel Prize."

"Aye, you should've won it," said Nathan. "The Nobel Prize for science."

Callum looked from one old man to the other, but neither of them continued. They just looked at each other and nodded knowingly.

"Well?" said Callum. "What's the tip, what's the great scientific method?"

"You think he's ready for it?" asked Nathan one more time.

"He's ready," Tom nodded, and he looked at Callum. "The super scientific method to playing golf at the highest level known to mankind is; see ball, hit ball."

They both watched him while he digested the words.

"That's it?" said Callum, exasperated.

"I thought you said he was ready for it,"

frowned Nathan.

"He is, but he hasn't tried it yet. Today might be the best time of all, on the great Troon course."

"See ball, hit ball," said Callum shaking his head.

"It works," said Nathan. "In any action sport, your mind can get in your way, slow you down, you must rely nearly one hundred percent on instinct, whether it's rugby, basketball, cricket, tennis. Golfers tend to get a little too technical, keep your left arm straight, cock your wrist at the top, swing inside out..."

"You forgot the full body turn," said Tom.

"Yes, that and rotate your hips at the target. You're standing there with all these thoughts swirling around in your brain, trying to do everything on the list and in sequence, and you forget the most fundamental thing of all..."

"See ball, hit ball," said Tom matter of factly.

"All there is to it," said Nathan. "In fact, that's the method that old Tom here told me one day, and I used it to whoop up on him with my hundred-foot putt and a finishing sixty-two."

"Ya had to shoehorn that in there one more time did ya?" said Tom.

"It's the truth," said Nathan. Then he looked down at his watch again, all business. "We've got about thirty-five minutes till the actual sunrise, we'd best get you to the first tee. Play at your own pace, take your time with your shots. You've got a good caddie here and he can show you the trouble spots, the places to avoid and the places to attack. You'll probably be on the fifth or sixth hole by the time the first paying group goes out so you'll have plenty of spacing."

Tom reached out and tried to place a piece of paper in Nathan's hand, who scowled and pushed it away.

"What's this?"

"You know what it is, just a small thank you to take the little lady out to lunch or something."

"Yer money's no good here you crusted old scallywag. Put it away now."

Tom grumbling stuffed the money back in his front pocket.

"Payment enough will be to see young Callum here in The Open. I know it's a long shot but we need all the help we can get. With all the Yanks and Brits and Euros coming here to try and win our championship I'll do whatever I can to get you a leg up. I know you're officially a Yank at the moment, but Tom told me your story. You've applied for citizenship; you're trying a marry a Scottish girl, *and* you're Scottish at heart and that's good enough for me."

They jumped in the jitney, with Tom up front with Nathan and Callum in the back for the bumpy ride along the dirt path that lined the ocean towards the first tee.

Nathan parked the jitney to the right of the tee and they all climbed out. With the headlights suddenly off they were plunged into darkness till their eyes adjusted to the dim light. It was eerie with the lack of wind, the ocean churning onto a rocky shore to their right, the imminent sunrise and the faint glow of lights from Glasgow twenty miles to the northeast. Facing nearly straight south, an imperceptible ghostly land seemingly flat laid out in front of them. Nathan and Tom both turned on flashlights to help them navigate the path to the tee box, no sense in tripping on an errant stone or divot which at their age would ruin their day. When they were all safely on the level perfect turf of the tee box, they turned off their lights to adjust their eyes and absorb the mystic surroundings. Off in the distance they could hear machines, giant man driven lawn mowers grooming the fairways and greens for the busy day ahead. Hidden by short hills somewhere up ahead on the course, headlights shone through the salt mist in the air, dull beacons crisscrossing on the horizon.

"They've finished the first couple of holes and are moving down the course," said Nathan. "You'll have a crisp untrod surface from tee to green. Should be a fine day for golf. Wish I could play hooky and join you, but duty calls."

Callum put the bag down and surveyed the dull grey surroundings, waiting patiently for instructions. He noticed a sentence written on the wall under Royal Troon:

Tam Arte Quam Marte.

"What does it mean?"

"It's from Latin," said Nathan. "As much by skill as by strength. It's our motto. You can nae overpower this golf course with a driver off the tee. It takes precise iron play.

"Hole number one," said Tom. "It's called Seal, and later in the day we'll have a few dozen seals laying about on the rocks down by the beach causing a fuss, but we'll be long gone by then. The business side of it is this; the hole itself is three hundred seventy yards to the pin, the fairway itself is wide, maybe fifty yards with deep rough all along the left and patches of the deep stuff on the right along the wall that borders the beach. There's two pot bunkers on the left and two on the right. The front edge of the ones on the left are right at two hundred fifty yards, two seventy carry. The sensible play is to take a long iron and put your shot right in the middle of the fairway and in between them."

"Aye," said Tom. "That's the sensible play."

"You can nae win a golf tournament by playing sensible all the time," said Tom. "This golf course is designed for risk reward, and this is one of those times to attack if you have the game to do it. Right here on the first hole. Nathan?"

"Aye aye, "said Nathan. "There's many places around this course where you can choose to be bold and leapfrog in front of the competition, and this is definitely one of them. Keep your drive straight and slightly left of center and you'll have seventy yards to a slightly elevated green with birdie or better lighting up your imagination with dreams of magnificent glory. But fall short, and into one of the bunkers with edges eight feet high, and double bogey or worse is the guarantee."

"Two fifty on the left, two seventy on the right," said Tom. "With a good four iron you can fly it two twenty, two thirty. I've seen it, like clockwork. We have a bit of a north breeze, not much but a wee bit to help. Can you see the outline of that mansion way down on the horizon?"

"Yes," said Callum.

"That's your target. The pot bunkers on the left are right in line with it. I want you to hit the tee shot just to the right at that roofline. Right above the window with light on the third floor. Just a basic mid-high tee shot. You can nae see the bunkers I know, but if you put the ball on that line you'll be right in the middle right of the fairway with a short iron to the green."

Callum was amazed. Strategically analyzing the first shot and where you wanted it to go, even though they had just drummed into him that it was only as simple as see ball hit ball. It was almost as though both old men were living vicariously through him to hit the ball as they used to be able to when they were young and firing rounds the low sixties at will.

"I'll watch the first two shots if you don't mind," said Nathan. "I'd like to see him on the green in two, and then I'll be off to work."

The sun couldn't rise fast enough for Callum and he began to get anxious, bone jarring nervous for the first time. It was almost as though he were actually teeing it up on the first hole of the first day at The Open, and the butterflies were churning in the pit of his stomach.

"Where am I going?" he asked.

Tom shone the flashlight down the fairway, it made a perfectly straight beam of light exactly perpendicular to the tee markers.

"Straight away lad. Two twenty carry, with another twenty roll out and you're in business."

Callum placed the ball in the nook of the tee and plugged both into the perfect sod, took a step back, swung the club a few times to loosen up and looked back down where the ball had been.

"I can barely see the ball."

Tom shone the light down on the back of the ball until Callum set up, feet square, he pointed the light straight down the fairway, then back at the white ball on the tee.

"It's a leap of faith Callum."

"See ball, hit ball," whispered Callum and set his feet firm, cleared his mind of all thought, brought the club back high over and behind his head, then with a mighty heave body thrust lag delay at the point of impact, full follow through, head and eyes still watching where the ball once was a split second ago, leap of faith following through, club, shaft, grip leading his hands arms, shoulders hips through the powerful arc and finally bringing his head swiveling up eyes peering into the sky, dawns dusk on the edges, flashlight beacon tracing up and tracking the little white ball in a high arch fading fast into the distance.

Nathan whistled. "I think he's got it."

Callum remembered to breathe, the

adrenaline rush of hitting the tee shot nearly caused him to pull the ball to the left, but he was able to control his emotions, and follow down and through, and just hit the ball. He exhaled deeply and both old men looked at him and smiled.

"Pretty fun eh?" laughed Tom. "Playing a round of golf at Royal Troon. And that was only the first shot."

"I'll go find the ball," said Nathan and headed to the jitney, while Callum shouldered the bag and joined Tom walking down the short grass pathway, close clipped from the tee box that led to the fairway. The light from the sunrise was incrementally increasing now, and Tom put the flashlight in a side pocket of the bag as they walked.

"You and Tom seem to have known each other for a long time," said Callum.

"Aye, we grew up together in a way. Back in the day, junior golf and rugby, two of the most diametrically opposed sports on the planet that you could ever find. We were always on separate teams being from different towns. He broke my nose in a rugby match when I was thirteen, and I think I might have accidentally broken the little toe on his foot in a scrum for the ball a year later. He claimed it was on purpose but I'll dispute that at the gates of heaven. I would say that we were arch enemies at first through our early teens. But then we got thrown together in a couple of team golf matches. Scottish amateur events, we were both tops in our age division, and the powers that be put us together. Best ball matches against the British and Irish teams. Suddenly we were not only teammates, but comrades in an army brigade in some ways, in battle against the enemy, and we became fast friends.

Nathan had the cart parked in the center of the fairway and he was standing next to the ball that was very close to the pot bunker on the right, just about five feet from the edge.

"Came a little too close to the bunker," said Nathan shaking his head.

"Aye," said Tom whistling. "I've been in this bunker, Nathan too. No fun on the first shot of the round and one that could test your mettle that's for sure."

"One twenty to the center of the green," said Nathan. "The pins on the left today so you want to land the ball to the right of center, can you see the pin?"

"Yes," said Callum squinting in the dim light.

"Good, I had the crew put all the pins in the championship position for you. Give you a good test right out of the gate. One ten on the fly, high an arc as you can muster, you want that ball to land soft and roll forward just a bit, no back spin, that'll kill you, you'll roll back off the green and maybe into one of the greenside bunkers, and they're the monsters you dream of at night. One ten on the fly, soft forward bounce. You got that shot?"

Callum just nodded and pulled out the old hickory shafted wedge, taking a couple of practice swings, bouncing it off the turf. Tom pulled the bag farther away and held it upright, whispering silently to himself, hoping that the practicing with the old clubs and the featheries would make a difference. Sometimes the beginning of a round, even the first two shots could define a golfer, shape them like clay in the maker's hands, confidence was a funny thing, ethereal and wispy, able to overwhelm a person with nagging doubt, sagging at their sinews, or carry them through with sublime confidence buoying their motions.

With an ultra-smooth swing, Callum brought the club back in an arc over his shoulders and down through the ball, keeping his head down and eyes on the ball long after contact, watching the dirt settle into the divot while the two other men watched the ball high in flight disappear into the dim light and they could all hear the light gentle thump as it landed somewhere up on the green.

"I think you're on the green Callum," said Nathan. "Now there's something I'd like you do before we move on. Tom give me a ball please."

Tom pulled one out of the bag and handed it to Nathan who tossed it into the pot bunker to their left.

"You probably haven't seen too many of these on the courses you've been playing up north. These are the killers and they're designed to destroy even the most skilled golfers on the planet. They are to be avoided like the plague. If you get a little fancy and try to fly over them on the drive or hit an errant shot pulling it right or left and find yourself in one, you mustn't panic. Just find the quickest safest way out, and sometimes lad the best route is backwards and back onto the fairway."

It was a test.

"Golf is like life in a way," said Tom. "Sometimes you have to go backwards to go forwards."

Wasn't that true thought Callum as he looked at the ball in the deep bunker. It was nearly perfectly round in shape, except the front edge was much higher than the back. He grabbed a sand wedge and stepped down into the pit. The front edge was higher than his head while the sides tapered down and the back edge facing towards the tee was about three feet high, still high enough to make any shot out a challenge. Trying to go up and over the front offered no advantage and was out of the question. To the side was also no great option. Backwards and into the fairway was the key. He set his feet, digging them into the sand for leverage and thumped the ball out of the bunker, backwards ten yards.

"Now you've got one thirty to the center of the green," said Nathan. "Not a big deal, except now you're laying two and you've got to get up and down in two shots to save par. Let's see what you've got."

One twenty on the fly. Callum grabbed the old wedge again, he'd just hit it a little harder, give it another ten yards. Set up, studied his line for a moment, couple of thumping practice swings, then one smooth swing down through the ball that flew high into the air, higher this time with the stronger thump, now in the increasing light they could all see it land on the green, and this time with the high ball flight increased spin, when it bounced on the green it stopped abruptly and rolled backwards off the green and into one the bunkers at the front.

"Now you're lying three in another bunker and need to make that shot to make par."

"Why can't I just take my first shot?" said Callum, exasperated at this predicament.

"You can lad," laughed Nathan. "I just wanted you to get a little bit of a bad taste in your mouth about these bunkers. They're world destroyers and best to be avoided at all cost. You might hit one or two drivers on this course all day, maybe five woods off the tee all told, two drivers and three metal woods. Accuracy is the key. I've been in just about every bunker on this course, as has Tom here."

"I'd rather not think about it," said Tom shuddering. "Gives me nightmares."

"Maybe someday, if you get along in your game and think you might have a legitimate shot at getting into The Open, we'll have you play a practice round and only hit it out of the bunkers all around the course, every single one of them. Just in case you wind up in one and won't need to wonder what to do about it."

When they got up to the greenside bunker, they could see that he had a good lie. The ball had rolled about five feet away from the high front edge next to the fringe. Callum grabbed the sand wedge and stepped down into the bunker.

Imagining to himself that the tournament was on the line, he had to get up and down in two shots to win. Hitting it backwards was not an option in that situation. He had to get it on the green to give himself a chance to make the putt. If he took the easy shot backwards, then he'd have to make a chip shot over the bunker and hole it out. In this case going forward was the only option. The front side of the bunker was at eye level and he could see his other ball close to the hole. That was his target. Get it at least that close to have a shot. He set his feet digging them sideways into the crusty sand, opened the face of the club, opened his stance, he was going to thump the club two inches behind the ball and like a surgeon lift the ball out of the sand and onto the green, and that's where his eyes focused, two inches behind the ball. With a smooth swing, pausing at the top, then down and through the club made a thumping sound, wedging under the ball, an explosion of sand lifting the ball up, up and at the last second hit the side of the bunker and rolled back in.

"SON OF A BITCH!" Callum yelled, then spurted out more words that were barely understandable, his face red, spittle flying till he ran out of air and had to calm down and take a breath. "I'll take my shot that's on the green," he said then picked up the ball from the sand, put it in his pocket, reached over to grab the rake on the edge and calmly raked out the divot and his footprints as he made his way back to the edge and stepped up onto the grass.

Nathan had a wry smile on his face, but Tom was wearing a bit of a frown.

"I'm sorry, I lost my temper," said Callum.

"Is that what you call it," chuckled Nathan. "Why I've never heard such swearing in all my days. Not on a golf course or down at the dock full of rough neck sailors' home from a year at sea. I have to tell you the truth though, I used to thoroughly enjoy seeing my competitors lose their cool. More often than not it meant the beginning of the end for them."

"Golf," said Tom calmly. "Is more than a game of controlling how you hit the little white ball. It's a game of controlling your emotions."

"I'd like to watch the putt," said Tom. "Then I'll be on my way."

Deep orange hues lit the mountains to the east as Callum lined up the putt that was about fifteen feet from the cup. It was fairly straight with a little left to right break. It rolled right up towards the cup then at the end broke hard to the right and stopped less than a foot away. He walked up, disappointed, but reserved and tapped the putt in and heard the resonant clunk as it hit the bottom of the cup.

"Well," said Nathan as he clapped his hands heartily. "You're even par on the first hole. Many a golfer following behind you today would be glad to trade places with you. Good luck, keep it in the fairway and out of the bunkers and I'll see you on the last hole in a few hours."

As they came to the eighteenth tee, looking north towards the clubhouse it was nearly nine o'clock and Callum was five over par on his first jaunt around the Old Course.

"Five over par's not bad," said Tom. "Considering this is your first look at this course. Now here's a puzzle for you. This hole is called Craigend and is named after the farm that used to be here. We've got a south wind at our back coming down the stretch, and a wicked bunker on the right that comes into play with a long iron. I think you might be able to get over it with driver, but if you go in, it might be double bogey or worse."

"And if I get over it?"

"Brings birdie into play."

"This is a practice round," said Callum. "I think I should go for it."

"This is your first round," said Tom. "And sometimes first impressions have a lasting effect."

Callum pulled the driver, teed the ball high and stepped back to survey the scene once more. The sun now peeking through thin cirrus clouds riding high in the sky, a quarter mile away was the clubhouse and the eighteenth green, and more than halfway between them lay a large bunker. A couple of practice swings to loosen up, and he laid into the ball like he was digging a trench behind the house. With a swift whoosh and a crack, it flew off the tee like a rocket, climbing like a jet straight for the bunker then reached its apex over the sand and landed on the other side.

"Nice shot," said Tom. "I think you went three fifty at least with this helping wind."

His second shot from a hundred fifteen was with the old hickory wedge, lofted high towards the front of the green, rolling up to fifteen feet, and he missed the birdie putt, it rolled just to the right side over the edge.

Nathan was on the side of the green watching with interest.

"Bit of a tester at the end there. This green is firm and fast and we keep it that way on purpose. How'd you do?"

"Five over," said Tom as Callum went back to try the putt again. "Had a chance for a seventy-five, but seventy six will have to do for today."

"Come down and play this course anytime you want. We'll get you out before dawn. You can stay at our home; we have a guest house out back.

Callum shook his hand. "Thank you sir."

"I think you'll do fine," said Nathan. "Just stick with Tom here, he'll steer you straight.

25.

Over the next few months Callum played in every weekend tournament he could find. During the week would take a bus down to Troon or catch a ride with Tom, stay in Nathan's guest cottage, do work around the house in trade, and play Royal Troon at dawn.

On the last day of practice before the regional qualifying event, Callum opted to play Royal Troon. He felt comfortable playing there and wanted to keep that comfort level high.

Plus, he didn't want to see the other competitors who were undoubtedly practicing at the designated course, trying to get their last licks on the tricky fairways and greens.

It was a nice, early morning round at Troon, he teed off at around five in the morning, before dawn as usual, hitting the ball down the fairway on the first hole in semi-darkness, trusting his swing through all eighteen holes, flowing through on the chips and putts.

It was an easy round and he played as though each shot was being hit with the feathery on the ground, each crack of club head on ball needed to be precise and square.

Cranking drives as though digging a ditch with a four iron, lofting pitches with smooth measured pace. Putts lined up and unhurried, following through with confidence on each swing of the club.

He was finished with the round by nine in the morning, practiced his putting and chipping on the range till noon then packed his clubs and bags for the ride north.

26.

On the last Monday of June under cloudy skies and cool winds from the southwest at less than ten miles per hour, regional qualifying day arrived for eighteen hundred players at courses scattered around the U.K. It was perfect golf weather all across the country. Eighteen holes, stroke play. A hundred forty-two spots were available for the Final Qualifying events in a week.

The practice tee and putting green at Callum's course was packed with players and caddie's. A hundred and fifteen players were scheduled to tee off.

As fate would have it, Callum was paired up with three of the best players statistically in the field, two were golfers from America, one a top amateur player in college, and the other a semi-pro who played on the mini tour. The third player in the foursome was Grant Larrabee who was hitting short pitch shots on the practice tee, every one of them bouncing around the pin. After every shot he'd look around the area at the other competitors as though searching for someone.

As soon as he saw Callum he smiled broadly and walked over.

"Back for another whooping I see. Couldn't believe my luck at getting paired with you. My footing's a lot more solid while I'm standing on your neck."

Callum shook his head in disappointment while setting his bag on a stand. Of all the people in the world to be paired with.

"Well, well, well. Look who we have here. The big banana. You're surely the best player in this field Grant. Why, I'm surprised you even *need* to qualify. You shouldn't have to prove your worth by mixing it up with the rest of us unwashed heathens. They should just award you a spot in The Open on your reputation alone. For running your mouth."

Grant's smile faded quickly.

"I'm going to make mincemeat out of you just like I did the last time."

Callum took his hand off his golf bag and got closer to Grant. A quick uppercut should do the trick and no one would even know.

"Hey, hey, hey," said Tom walking quickly from the side getting in between them and spreading them apart with the two palms of his hands. "This is a gentleman's game. No boxing allowed. Wait till after the match."

"He started it dad," said Callum with a wry smile.

Grant's face was livid, pointing his finger.

"And I'm going to finish it." Walked back to his bag and pulled out the driver, teed up a ball and hammered it three hundred yards.

"Making friends again I see," said Tom.

At the end of the day, Callum took third place to earn a trip to final qualifying, Grant was in fifteenth place and out.

The next week, the first Monday of July was Final Qualifying at four different courses, with four spots into The Open at each venue. This was a one day, thirty-six-hole event, stroke play, under a cloudy windswept day throughout the country that tested the nerves and mettle of all who were entered. The winds were out of the southwest again but fifteen to twenty knots mixed with light rain from time to time. Callum was two over par through his morning round, well off the pace, then teed off for his afternoon round a little after eleven o'clock and turned on the afterburners, birdied the first five holes, bogeyed six and seven, parred holes eight through sixteen, squeaking into the final two holes by the skin of his teeth with a birdie/birdie finish and five under par to take the final spot by one.

It was a solemn moment for Callum, and for Tom as well as they stood under an awning watching the final players finish the last hole in miserable conditions. Perhaps if the weather had been more accommodating, the results would be different. Holding a golf club that was slippery wet was never an easy task, but that was golf in Scotland at times.

The other three players who made the cut were ecstatic, cheers and fist pumps, taking photos while holding pieces of paper that said simply: The 152nd Open – Royal Troon.

For Callum, he was silent, reserved. Tom could sense a change in the young man when he first met him, from cocky arrogance and anger to humble confidence, and maybe a bit of wariness, or fear. It was hard to tell which.

"I injured my wrist on the last hole," said Callum, so quietly that Tom could barely hear it. "My back foot slipped and I clipped the ground on my pitch shot. I couldn't hit another putt if my life depended on it."

Tom nodded. That explained the sullen attitude. One errant shot could make all the difference in the world, and here it was.

"That was the worst shot you had all day," said Tom. "And it couldn't have come at a better time. Don't let on to anyone around here that you're injured. We'll get some ice on it in the car."

27.

On the morning of Saturday July 13, Callum and Maggie caught the first ferry to Mull. It was exactly five days till The Open, and with Tom's advice Callum needed a short physical and spiritual break. Two days to rest and reflect. No golf, no swinging a club, no sweating over putts. The slight injury he acquired at the thirty-six-hole final qualifying event was nearly healed, just a little bit of pain was left in the edge where the outside of his wrist met arm bone, and at the top of the elbow, both tendinitis. Nagging injuries that could knock the toughest of the tough out of competition unless you were careful.

"Walk ten miles a day," said Tom. "To keep up your stamina, your wind. But don't so much as grip a pint in that hand. In fact, no drinking at all. Don't talk about golf, don't even think about it. Relax your mind and when you come back on Monday we'll get right to work."

They booked a room at a bed and breakfast near the harbor, left their bags on the bed, got a coffee and donut at Arlene's, and walked south through the town. The first stop was Torosay

Church of Scotland. They sat on the bench outside and watched the world go by while they finished the coffee, the donuts were long gone.

"Have you ever been inside this church?" asked Callum.

"I've never been to Mull," she said, and he looked at her with surprise.

"Ever?"

"Never wanted to, until you asked me."

Callum was silent while she continued.

"There's a few things I never told you about me, about my family, and I guess now would be a good time."

Callum figured he should let her know what he knew, right now, so she wouldn't have to say it.

"Listen Maggie, Tom told me about your mother, about the short break-up with Malcolm, the Yank, and the boat capsizing. He also told me that she was an incredibly beautiful woman, both inside and out, and that the whole town took it hard."

She nodded and wiped a small tear from the corner of her eye.

"I figured someone would fill you in on the details. And I'm glad it was Tom since he was right in the middle of it and saw everything happen. I didn't know all the facts till I was about ten years old. They sort of swept all the bad stuff under the rug to protect me, which I guess was the right thing to do. I've always been a little bit afraid of this island. In a way this is where my mother disappeared."

Callum put his arm around her shoulder and

pulled her head against his and held it tight for a quiet moment.

"Tom told me that a bolt of lightning hit this church in eighteen twenty-eight and burned half the roof. He said some people claimed it was because a Maclean and a MacQuarrie were in the parish at the same time."

He looked at her and tilted his head.

"Well here we are again. Care to test fate and walk inside?"

She smiled.

"Okay."

They sat inside next to each other on a well-worn wooden pew for a quarter of an hour without saying a word, just watching the colorful pane glass window at the back of the altar, listening to the magnified sounds in the eaves, until another couple opened the door and came in to sit down nearby, and Maggie put her hand in Callum's and they went back outside.

They hiked to the top of a peak where the radio and TV transmission tower stood and looked out over the sea towards Oban. Then back down and along the shore to Duart castle, back to Craignure and a light dinner.

The next day, Sunday, they took a bus ride out to the west side of the island, to Fionnphort, caught the ferry to Ilona and hiked along the shore to the Abbey and Nunnery, then sat for a few quiet moments in Saint Oran's chapel and listened to the wind swirling over the roof.

It was a forlorn, windswept part of the island

with low running hills covered in mottled rocks and grass, a one lane road bordered by waist high rock walls and dozens of walking tourists scattered all along the path from the ferry to the Abbey and back.

Monday morning, they took the first ferry back to Oban. Halfway across the straight they made a pact. Maggie would watch the event from afar but would not interact with Callum at all. He was on his own, for that's how he seemed to play his best golf, with no distractions, and the simple sight of her was bound to take his attention away from the job at hand which was to play every shot at the highest level.

Tom was waiting at the dock with Callum's clubs and bag packed in the car.

"See you Sunday afternoon," said Maggie simply. "Get on with you now." Kissed him on the cheek and watched as they drove away.

28.

The large black banner stretched across the grandstand said simply: The Open.

"Are you ready?" asked Tom as Callum walked off the practice green. The wrist injury was gone, he had a steady stride and a determined glint in his eyes, but Tom could tell there was still something not quite right.

Callum put the putter in the bag that was standing upright in a caddie rack and looked straight at Tom and whispered.

"I'm scared to death."

He put out his hand and grabbed the old man's forearm, his hand was trembling.

"Hey now, wait a minute lad, don't be worried." Tom put his other hand on top of Callum's wrist to stop the shaking. "This is normal. Happens to the best of the best. Why, some of the greatest champions in history were ready to pee in their pants right before they conquered the world."

He thought hard and quick.

"You're from America so you've probably heard of Bill Russell who was one of the greatest basketball players of all time. He played for the Boston Celtics, and we followed that team. Celtics, right? That's *our* team. Anyways, before every big game he would vomit before they took the court. It was like clockwork, and Red Auerbach wouldn't let the team leave the dressing room until he was done. The greatest basketball player of all time, six foot ten, two hundred fifteen pounds of pure muscle, his nickname was Bill the Hill and the Stuffer. He destroyed other teams, and every player on them. He played thirteen seasons and won eleven NBA titles in that span and there he was, nervous as a nelly, puking in the sink before the game. The greatest player in NBA history. You don't feel like puking do you, because if you need to, we'll get you to the loo right away."

Callum took a deep breath; his hand was steady again and he took off his hat and smoothed his hair.

"I've never seen so many people in one place at the same time. There's cameras everywhere."

Tom chuckled and grinned knowingly from ear to ear. "Don't worry about that lad. No one's here to watch you anyways, and that's the beauty of it. No one cares about you; they don't even know who you are. You're flying under the radar. Sure, and there's five thousand people here, but they're here to watch the top ten or twenty golfers in the world. They're here to watch Rory, Jordan, Scottie. Not to mention Tiger. You ever heard of that guy? You think all these people would rather watch you, or Tiger? You have got to remember there's a hundred and fifty-six golfers in this tournament and you're number one fifty-six on the list of people that anybody wants to see."

Callum nodded. Tom decided to derail his thinking a little more, get his mind on the game.

"How many clubs do you have in the bag?"

"How many clubs? Fourteen."

"You sure?"

"Yeah, I counted them before we left the room."

"Count 'em again."

Callum frowned but did as he was told, quickly putting his index finger on each club in turn.

"Fifteen, what the hell."

"That's a two-stroke penalty per hole for each hole up to four strokes total."

Callum pulled out the errant club, it stood out like a sore thumb. It was one of Tom's old irons.

"You trying to sabotage me?"

"Trying to keep you up on your toe's lad. It wouldn't be the first time someone put their club in the wrong bag. Your bag was just sitting here all on its own."

"Jackie had to use the loo."

"Wouldn't matter to the rules official. That's four strokes and you're out of the game. Make sure you check your bag before you hit the first shot on the first tee, and make sure your caddie's hand doesn't leave this bag unless one of you is standing next to it."

"Sounds like you might have some

experience with that particular penalty? Did it happen to you?"

"Once. And it will never happen again."

They saw Jackie trotting from the clubhouse towards them. Tom reached out and grabbed Callum's hand. It was steady as a rock.

"See? Once you get out there and hit that little white golf ball you're going to be right as rain. What's your first shot going to be on the first hole? Your tee shot."

"Four iron, just to the right of center and short of the bunker."

"And then after that?"

Callum smiled.

"See ball, hit ball."

"Good, from there you're on your own, I've given you all the help I can and no coaching is allowed from the sidelines, but luckily, you've played enough golf on these links that you could find your way around on the darkest dreadest moonless night while being chased by the banshees.

Callum looked at the crowds of people standing around the first tee watching the next set of golfers teeing off, and then halfway down the fairway on the left side he saw the familiar shape of a head just above a black jacket, her neck draped with a scarf colored with red, green, and blue squares, yellow and white lines, the Maclean tartan. Maggie. She smiled at him then turned and disappeared into the crowd.

She didn't want to disturb him, she said, but in a way it did the opposite.

Callum felt as though he was walking not on

a cloud, but inside it, floating on air as he approached the first tee with Jackie next to him. He pulled the four iron from the bag, checked the number on the bottom, and out of his pocket a tee and ball. He counted the clubs again, and it calmed him down. Thirteen in the bag and one in his hand. He was in the eleven thirty-six am pairing with two other golfers, one a hot shot from Spain and the other from the Netherlands that no one had ever heard of.

None of them had ever met before and they shook hands politely on the side of the tee as they went about their business getting ready for the test of their lives. You could cut the tension with a butter knife. It was the eleven thirty-six am pairing, the worst tee time of the lot said Tom on the practice tee so if you want to dig it out of the dirt like the great ones, then you're a lucky bastard and that's the time you want.

They spaced the tee times eleven minutes apart and the next group was huddled on the sidelines while the other two golfers hit their tee shots, then the announcer triggered the sound system for the third and final player from this group.

"Now on the tee from Oban, Scotland, Callum Maclean."

There was a smattering of polite applause from the crowd of dozens. Most of the patrons were out on the course following Tiger and Jordan and Scottie, or milling about the practice area watching the other top golfers who were getting ready. It was eleven forty in the morning on the dot as he put the tee in the ground, set the ball on top, stepped back, took a couple of loose practice swings, settled his feet, and looked once more at his target two hundred yards down the fairway.

'See ball, hit ball', he whispered to himself and without another thought, all instinct and pure adrenaline bliss pulled the club back in a wide arc behind his head, slight pause at the apex, hip, knee, shoulder turn whipping, torquing his body forward, keeping his eyes straight down on top of the ball until the club face rocketed crisply through the round shape that quickly disappeared, holding his head steady, rotating through and up into the follow through, finally lifting his eyes to where the ball must be flying and there it was fifty feet in the air, a piercing low shot that floated at the end of its travels, landing softly with a puff of dust at the one ninety mark and rolled another twenty, just short and to the left of the bunker on the right.

Another smattering of polite applause from the gallery and a couple of good shot remarks.

He handed the club to Jackie and they were off walking steadily down the fairway side by side.

Callum felt as though he were walking in a tunnel, as though he was the only person on the golf course, all peripheral vision blurred out, his only focus his golf ball in the distance and the next shot that looked to be about a hundred and twenty to the pin. The wind was at his back and he visualized the shot the whole way while walking to the ball. He wanted to land it on the one ten mark and let it release and roll ten to the cup. One ten and ten, no more no less. His playing partner hit a longer drive, a longer more dangerous drive and was perilously close to the left side bunker though closer to the hole. The other one from Spain was right in the middle and long. Callum would hit first. He pulled out the pitching wedge, visualized the shot one more time, set his feet, one look at the target, then pure bliss, clubface crisp through the ball that took a high arc, up and over the edge of the bunker, landing softly in the middle of the green and rolled up and stopped twenty feet short of the cup.

Callum was pissed, his cheeks turning a fiery red, eyes blazing, and he held his anger in check. The player from the Netherlands was ready, and quickly hit his second shot to the front edge of the green. The player from Spain in the middle of the fairway took his sweet time, having a hard decision to make on what club to take, what line to make, he went back and forth with his caddie, pulled a club, put it back, pulled another, put that one back, and this was just his second shot of the day. Callum had never played with this guy and already he didn't like his pace of play, so decided to ignore him. He looked back at the tee and the next group getting ready to tee off. It might be a while the way things were going. He counted the clubs in his bag again, then looked up at the sky, the clouds high in the jet stream rolling from west to east. Then mercifully he heard the crisp sound of club on ball and an immediate curse, so he looked up to see the ball flying low in the air, too low to get over the green side bunker and in it went, hitting the top edge and rolling back into the sandy pit. More cursing in the colorful foreign language. Callum closed his ears and concentrated on walking forward.

Marching like a single solitary soldier on a mission to save the world. Feeling his spirit rise with every step, the essence of the golf course seeping up and through him. He'd walked these links fifty times in the past few months and it was familiar territory. He recognized bumps and flat areas, landmarks along the way to the pin.

They were allies, the golf course and him one and the same. Kindred spirits intermingling, the life of the grass and the air above it a tonic elixir, exhilarating, enrapturing, intoxicating, brilliant, intense, and then he was at the edge of the green with flat stick in hand lining up the putt in his mind while still walking towards it and carefully placing the Indian head nickel behind it before lifting the ball and handing it to Jackie.

He'd had this exact putt before, at least a dozen times or more. It wasn't the one he wanted to start the round, but it was the one that he ended up with after all. It was makeable, but frisky and needed finesse, it always ran a bit to the left at the end. You could take some of the break out of it with a forceful stroke, but too much and you'd leave yourself a knee knocker coming back.

The Spaniard hacked it out of the sand

miraculously up and over the lip of the deep pot bunker and ended up just outside of Callum's ball and he smiled slightly. He'd have two reads, one from the guy on the edge of the green and the guy who hit out of the bunker.

The long putt from the edge sailed past the two markers, curved to the left and stopped just short of the cup and he tapped in for par.

The Spaniard cursed as his ball also curved to the left and stopped short, and he tapped in for bogey.

Callum wasted no time. It was a simple putt. He knew the line from previous rounds and just had it verified with the other two puts.

Over think it and run the risk of tensing up. He set his feet, lined up the putter square behind the ball, took one steady breath in, exhaled slowly while making smooth contact and watched as the ball rolled steadily, curved slightly left and into the cup with a distinct 'tok' for a birdie. And just like that he was tied for the lead. The polite applause that they received on the tee was amplified, and the glee of the small crowd at the birdie was appreciative. It was a brilliant birdie.

The second and third holes were uneventful for all three golfers, the first tee jitters had melted away in the heat of the first few shots and now they were focused on keeping the ball in the middle of the fairway and keeping it on the green.

The fourth hole gave them fits, all three hitting right of the fairway into the rough, Callum being the leader of the pack with the birdie still owning the first shot off the tee, and the other two followed his ball as though in a slip stream. Even the golfer from the Netherlands gave out a bit of a curse, but Callum remained silent and being the shortest off the tee hit his second shot back into the fairway and back into play.

The fifth hole turned out to be one of the early keys for Callum. He'd always seemed to be attracted to it. The undulations, the curves and views with the ocean to the right. It was all carry. Leave your shot short and it was gone in the gorse forever. There was a neatly trimmed walkway from tee to green eight feet wide, and you could hear the faint whispers of ancient ghosts as you walked. Golfers who were lost in the past, lost in the gorse.

Greenan.

Named after the old castle ruins south of Ayr, and aptly named as it left many a golfer in ruins while playing it.

Treacherous.

A par three, two hundred ten yards on the fly with danger all the way to the edge of the green. One deep pot bunker on the front right and three at the front left, with the wind from the sea trying to push you into them.

For some reason it fit Callum's eye. He liked it from the first moment he saw it on the first day with Tom so many months ago. Sure, he'd been in all four of the bunkers a few times each, and in the gorse once or twice, but for the most part the majority of his time spent on this hole was ecstasy. His cut shot, the fade from left to right fit the shape of the green, land it on the front left and let it run a bit to the cup. Over the past few months he'd birdied it just as much as pars or worse. It was a fifty-fifty split. And he had one ace.

There was something about it.

The sharp salt smell of the ocean mixed with the heather on the shore. The view down the coast unfettered by fairways obstructing your vision. It was just you, the tee box, and the green sitting up on a slight plateau, beckoning you to land a golf ball high and soft.

Callum still had the honors and got ready to hit first. Stood with feet square behind his ball for a moment, visualizing the shot shape, the flight path, the landing area. Then set up, squared the clubface, tapped his left heel twice, inhaled then exhaled slowly, halfway through the breath, bringing the club back in a high arc over and behind his head, arms, wrists, shoulders, hips, knees not separate links moving separately, but all as one, down and through the ball he kept his eyes planted on the ball, then the divot exploding dirt, grass and sand, watching intently the perfect scoop of sod, then his pivoting arms lifting his head reluctantly skyward from the strike through the dirt, ball halfway to the hole before he caught sight of it. Murmurs from the crowd around the tee box as he and they, and his fellow competitors all watched it like spectators at a rocket launch at Cape Canaveral, heads swiveling as one, the ball reached the apex just before the first bunker on the left, curving slightly right held up against the wind, landing softly halfway to the hole and rolled straight down into it, bouncing slightly against the flagstick as it dropped in.

The sound turned deafening instantly, for here was something spectacular and the crowd erupted in a frenzy. Two hundred people can make a lot of noise if they're all yelling at the top of their lungs at the same time, and suddenly everyone else on the course nearby knew that something great had just happened.

Normal people, especially Scots reserved even in the presence of great shots rarely yelled that fervently. His fellow competitors gave him the congratulatory handshake, caddie's offered fist bumps, but Callum remained calm. Sure, he just aced the hole and was three under par, but it was just the fifth hole.

Then came the eighth hole. Originally called Ailsa because of the view from the tee, the name was changed around 1909 when Willie Parket Jr., who won the Open twice, wrote that the green was the size of a postage stamp and the name stuck. One of the most famous holes in golf.

On paper it was the easiest and ranked eighteenth hardest on the course. A hundred and twenty-three yards to the center of the green, downhill, flanked by five bunkers.

The green was narrow, forty yards long and fourteen wide shaped a bit like an hourglass.

On the left and long sat a narrow bunker the shape of a coffin and was the final resting place of many a golfer's dreams over the years. About ten yards long, four yard wide, and five feet deep if you were unlucky enough to get stuck in that bunker you would have to dig yourself out.

When you were standing on the tee facing the flag on the green and looked in a ninety-degree angle to your left over your shoulder you had a perfect view of Ailsa Craig Island, about twenty-eight miles southwest poking out of the sea like the top of a giant head.

Callum still had the honors after acing the fifth hole. The wind was slightly out of the southeast now, blowing straight towards the hole.

"One twenty-five to the pin," said Jackie. "Take ten for the helping breeze. One fifteen, maybe one thirteen."

Callum wasted no time reaching for the old wedge with the hickory shaft, and it was the first time anyone in their group had seen it.

Whispers on the edges of the crowd, and his playing partners and caddie's took notice. It looked like a relic, slightly rusted, obviously a wooden shaft.

"One thirteen," whispered Callum, "on the dot." Then thought to himself; Hit it to the left just a tad and spin it right in. Envisioned the shot coming off the clubface, soaring in the air.

Closed his eyes for a brief moment, set his feet, looked once more at the target, back at the ball, cleared his mind of all thought, brought the club back and swept clean through it, head down all the way through impact, when he looked up he couldn't see the ball at first and then he spotted it as the crowd murmured, halfway to the green, at its apex, dropping now out of the sky, landing softly next to the pin, took one hop then rolled two short feet and rested against the pin for a moment before dropping down into the cup. His second ace in the last four holes. The crowd, which had suddenly doubled in size since the fifth hole went wild from tee to green.

By the time they reached the eighteenth tee Callum was five under par and two shots in the lead.

The mob following their group had swelled from a few dozen to a few hundred as word spread around the course. In the last one hundred and twenty-four years only two Scotsmen had won the Open, and the last time was twenty-five years ago when Paul Lawrie won at Carnoustie in a playoff. That was also the last time as far as anyone could remember that a Scotsman had been in the lead.

It was the eighteenth that he hadn't been able to figure out. For some reason it had Callum's number.

Craigend. Named after the farm that used to sit where now there was a fairway. It was rated the second easiest hole on the course, but not as far as Callum was concerned. During his practice rounds over the past few months he tried all types of shots off the tee. It was absolutely necessary to hit the ball in the center of the fairway and avoid the bunkers on the right and left. It was tempting to try and fly it over the bunkers and take them right out of play but it was risky, you had to flush the ball off the clubface and hope a gust of wind coming off the firth of Clyde didn't push it to the right and into the deep bunker.

Sometimes when he tried to lay it up short, it just kept rolling and went right into the bunker on the right. Always the right one with the eight-foot face that was impossible to get out of. When he made absolutely certain it was short of the bunker, it was too short and the second shot, a long iron was tough to get close to the pin. Over the back of the green was out of bounds. Two bunkers guarded the front of the green, and you had to send your ball to the front of the green with a high soft shot so it wouldn't roll past the pin and out of bounds.

It was an unfortunate mystery. Over the past few months when he used driver off the tee, he could carry the ball over the bunker on the right, then have a short iron to the green and would make birdie about half the time.

The only problem was that he went in the bunker half the time he used the driver, and then would end up with double bogey or worse.

It was a dilemma.

He had a twenty five percent chance of making birdie with the driver, a twenty five percent chance of making par, and a fifty percent chance of double bogey or worse.

He was in the lead.

At The Open.

No sense in getting greedy. He pulled out the five iron and hit a nice easy straight shot down the center of the fairway and kept the ball thirty yards short of the bunker on the right.

Now he could hit the five iron again and get it on the green as fast as he could, make par and get in the clubhouse with the lead.

His second shot came up short, on the fringe and did not release. It hit a pitch mark and bounced to the left side of the green and rolled off perilously close to the bunker. He'd have to stand on the edge of that bunker with his heels hanging over it to hit his third shot and try to get it close to the pin.

The end of the round, any round of golf, but especially in a tournament situation, was magnified by being a championship event, the last couple of shots were in some ways the hardest of all.

You could see the finish line staring you in the face, all you had to do was cross it, but it wasn't a simple race. In golf you had a dilemma, this little problem of a shot that needed to be made with all the intent and purpose you could muster. The concentration and worry spent on every shot over the past eighteen holes had usually worn down even the most ardent focused player and the intensity needed at the end had to be conjured up like a spirit at a séance.

Callum lined up the putt, analyzed the angle and the break, then stood with heels over the sand filled pit, crowded against his ball just a few inches from his toes. It was awkward, he had to hit the ball over the little ridge of rough grass that curved down towards him with just enough force to make it up and over onto the green, then high lining it towards the hole that broke off to the right.

The crowd that had grown to hundreds was silent, then as he struck the ball with the putter and it crept over the hill a collective sigh mixed with groans filled the air.

It was woefully short and trickled meekly down below the hole and came to rest still over ten feet away.

Although no said it, and the words did not need being said out loud, those three dreaded words seemed to be whispered in Callum's ears.

'You're still away.'

He took his time, put a coin behind the ball then used the little line on top pointing it straight towards the cup while Jackie took the flag out and stood to the side.

A ten-footer, slightly uphill, no break, the easiest putt in the world to make and he missed it to the right. The ball stopped one inch to the right of the hole and seemed to sit there mocking him. A lousy ten-foot putt and he missed it.

The crowd groaned at first and then erupted in applause as he tapped it in for bogey. Still one shot in the lead.

The other two golfers made their putts for par and handshakes all around. Someone shouted from the edge of the crowd.

"Drinks on the house Callum?"

Half the crowd roared with delight.

"Make that a double!" someone else shouted.

They made their way through the crowd and Callum was a sensation, everyone wanted to either shake his hand or pat him on the back.

Two holes in one at The Open. It had never been done before and was the only reason that he was in the lead for the moment.

He signed his card and then two officials approached him. They wanted to inspect his clubs. Especially the old nine iron. The masher/niblick with the hickory shaft.

"Go ahead," said Callum and pulled it out of the bag for them.

They studied the club and measured the length from tip to toe, and width of the metal head.

They studied the grip and the grooves in the face of the club, and they studied the initials etched into the hosel, T.M. rubbing their fingers over them as though trying to pull out some of the magic.

"Looks fine to me," said one of the men and the other concurred.

"Nice club."

29.

On the other side of the globe, six thousand eight hundred miles away, and eleven hours behind, on the island of Oahu at eight o'clock on that Thursday morning, the sun was peeking through the trade wind clouds while Tavita Kava sipped his morning coffee and scrolled through the news on his computer. Not just any news, the sporting news. Tavita was a sports junkie. Any kind of sports, he followed them all. Football, baseball, rugby, tennis, basketball, volleyball, cricket, pickleball, any and every sport with competition involving a ball that needed to be carried, hit or thrown.

It started when he was about five years old growing up in Kahuku on the east side of Oahu.

Football was huge for the boys in high school that was dominated by the Samoans and Tongans who immigrated there over the years to work on the sugar plantations.

They were a physical people, and success in sport meant success in life, and losing meant disgrace. Sport was battle and they prepared themselves for games by doing the siva tau, the war dance.

Kahuku was a small seaside town, small in size but big in spirit. Kamehameha highway was a two-lane highway, the only road both in and out of town, and opposing team's buses and cars were pelted with rocks and coral from the younger crowd hiding in the bushes after games. It was a rough town, with a great team, but they could never get by Saint Louis, the powerhouse private high school from over the pali, over the cliffs in Honolulu.

Saint Louis stacked their teams with talent. They recruited the best players from around the state providing free tuition to the high-priced school and they rarely lost the title game. From nineteen eighty-six to nineteen ninety-nine they won the championship fourteen times in a row, taking out Kahuku on six of those occasions.

Until finally in the year two thousand, the turn of the century, turn of the millennium, turn of the tide, the universe, when Kahuku finally prevailed at the championship game at Aloha Stadium.

A giant line of cars and buses clogged the highway back to Kahuku after the game and the bus with the players stopped at every small town on the way, got out and did the siva tau to cheering crowds.

Tavita was five at the time and it lit a fire in his belly, a competitive bonfire that burned to this day even though he was nearing thirty. Too old for football, his main outlet now was rugby.

He usually had half an hour in the morning to scour the sports pages, then it was off to work at the power station.

Rugby was in full swing down under in Australia and there were a few interesting matches. Baseball was heating up and there were two no-hitters on the same day.

Wimbledon had been running for two weeks and just finished today. Even golf was on the front page. Mostly because Tiger was in the event. Even the title of the story had his name as the lead-in:

Tiger in the hunt, three shots back at the British Open.

Tavita shook his head.

Idiots.

Everyone knew it was The Open, not The *British* Open.

He skimmed through the story and looked at the leaderboard, scrolling down the list. The usual suspects, Rory, Jordan, Scottie, Wyndam and sure enough, there was Tiger -1.

Ten names down on the list and yet leading the story line. He was minus one with five other golfers also at one under. It was the name sitting two lines above Tiger's that made Tavita squint and draw in a sharp breath.

Callum Maclean. -4

"Pulu māʻoniʻoní," he whispered in Tongan, then repeated it in English. "Holy cow."

Then he smiled wide, laughing while shaking his head. "No can be brah. Gotta be another Callum Maclean."

That bugger disappeared six months ago and no one had heard from him. Not a peep. His phone was disconnected and there was no forwarding address. Like he dropped off the face of the earth.

He punched into the search engine 'Callum Maclean The Open Royal Troon' and pushed the enter button.

Ten stories popped up. All links to British newspapers and one for the Glasgow Times. He clicked on the Glasgow Times and the headline read:

Scottish American golfer in the lead at The Open

Underneath the headline was a picture of Callum standing with a caddie on the tee. And not just any Callum, but *their* Callum.

He briefly led by three strokes at one point, the story went on, until two bogies on the back nine derailed him, one at the eleventh hole called The Railway, and the other at the eighteenth hole called Craigend.

The story further went on to say that he was given citizenship the week before the event, and he was the first Scottish player to lead The Open at any point in the tournament although briefly since Paul Lawrie won it in nineteen ninety-nine. Twenty-five years ago.

Rumor had it that he promised to win The Open to gain some unknown father's permission to wed his daughter.

Then the story went on to tell how he was also a rugby player on a local Oban team, and the whole team was travelling south to rally him.

That made Tavita a little angry at first. His eyes narrowed, and he gritted his teeth.

His *Oban* rugby team was travelling south to rally him. Nothing about his *Kahuku* teammates.

Then he remembered vividly that Callum Maclean, *their* Callum never asked anyone for anything.

Never.

He just went out and did things. On his own. He went out and did things and never even told anyone that he did it. Like the day he went surfing at Third Reef Pipeline on an out-of-control stormy day, and never told anyone that he caught a wave till someone saw it in the on-line magazine. 'Unknown surfer catches giant wave' with Callum riding a monster wave five times his height.

One time he broke his leg at a rugby match and hid it from everyone because he didn't want sympathy. Said it was a pulled hamstring and he couldn't walk. Sat on the sidelines till the game was over. Drove himself to the hospital with a broken fibula. Still never told anyone till Tavita spotted him with a cast and crutches hobbling to the store for food.

Stubborn as a mule.

Tavita nodded, his face stoic now, determined. He picked up the phone and called his older sister in Honolulu at her travel office.

"Hey sis, I gotta get to Glasgow quick."

"Quick, as you mean in two days?"

"How about getting me there by tomorrow."

"By tomorrow," she said with a tinge of sarcasm.

He could almost see her face, her eyes and

mouth in that stupid, mocking, 'oh really' look.

"Okay, even if I could line up the flights, you have to realize it's six hours to California, another seven to the east coast, then another seven to Glasgow. Add it up. Twenty hours in the air, not counting layovers. Twenty-four hours maybe and that's non-stop either travelling or waiting in the airport for the next flight."

"Okay line it up. We're wasting time."

"Why do you want to go to Glasgow anyways?"

"Callum's in The Open."

"*Our* Callum?"

"Yes, our Callum, get snapping on the flights, I gotta make some more calls and I'll get right back to you, we'll need at least eight maybe ten tickets, so get ready. Better make that fifteen."

She whistled.

"You're looking at around five thousand dollars per person round trip for airfare," she said. "Not including hotel, transportation, and food. Fifteen people would be seventy-five thousand in airfare. A hundred thousand all in."

"Sounds fair," he said without breaking stride. "We'll rent a bus and live in it for a couple of days. Coolers and barbecues."

"I'll waive my commission so it'll be around forty-five hundred for airfare per person."

"Fine, fine," he said, impatient. "I'll call you right back with a head count."

After he hung up his sister looked at the

screen for a moment and around the office that seemed bleak and meaningless.

On the wall was a travel poster of Scotland, bagpiper and all next to a mountain with a waterfall.

"Well, I'm going too then," she said and started searching for flights.

30.

If word spread quickly on the golf course after his round, it spread like wildfire around the country, and it wasn't without controversy either.

Callum Maclean, so the reports said, from Oban, Scotland was leading The Open.

Heated arguments in bars and pubs around the country from Gills in the far north to Gretna in the south and every small town along the way, and especially in opinionated Glasgow and Edinburgh. Heated arguments that in some instances turned into ferocious all-out brawls that spilled out into the cobble lined streets. A Scotsman was in the lead with spectacular play, but not everyone was in agreement that Callum Maclean was indeed a true Scotsman or could even claim to be as such.

In the interview after his first round, the reporter from the BBC asked him bluntly about his heritage and Callum was as forthright as he could be with Tom and Jackie standing steadily beside him for support.

"It's true I was not born and raised here on

Scottish soil. I ran barefoot buck naked as a child on other shores and other lands before settling here just a few months ago. My ancestral namesake is from the Isle of Mull, the Macleans from the castle Duart, and my father was born and raised here in this country. Born in a little house on the outskirts of Oban and emigrated to the States with his family when he was a child. The law is clear as far as laws can be clear. I have indeed claimed citizenship as is my right, and I do claim it as far as this championship is concerned. I'll play as a Scotsman and with the blue and white flag on my bag. But I do not claim to be a Scotsman to the people of this country in any way shape or form, because that is not something that an outsider, which I am, can claim, it can only be given."

That interview was played over and over in the pubs and the mob was split fifty-fifty. By all that is holy, claimed the fifty percent that were for, his family home is in Oban, and he can trace his lineage to the Macleans who fought with Robert the Bruce at the Battle of Bannockburn in thirteen fourteen.

That's a lot of rubbish and the hell with that, said the other fifty percent. Unless you were born on this soil and ran barefoot over it, skinning your knees on the rowan tree and farming the land in toil during the endless winter months, you'll never be true Scots.

Even though the half that were bitterly against giving Callum his right secretly wished that he would be able to win as Scotsman, their stubborn nature prevented them from admitting it and even increased their fervent oppose, then throw in a pint or two or three and it was on.

Callum went with Tom and Jackie to stay with Nathan at his house just outside Troon.

They'd have a simple meal with potatoes, green beans, and mutton that Nathan's wife prepared. Then a quiet sunset on the porch.

"Best to lay low," advised Nathan. "No television, no radio. As far as you're concerned, you're in last place with a long road up a steep hill to the top. Get some rest, eat some food and get back at it tomorrow. You had quite a round, that's for sure. How do you feel lad?"

Callum for his part was physically exhausted and yet inside his mind was swirling, racing. Playing each shot over again as though he was watching a newsreel. And yet in some ways it was a blur. The round, although taking nearly five hours, seemed at the end to have only lasted a few minutes, so intense was his concentration that he could not remember a single word spoken by anyone around him. He couldn't remember seeing a single person on the edges after the first shot off the first tee box.

He knew he gave an interview after the round but couldn't remember a single word that he said. He could vividly remember seeing Maggie in the beginning before he teed off on the first hole, and that was it. True to her word she disappeared into the crowd as her vow not to be a distraction.

They sat at the table after dinner, Tom and Nathan and Jackie.

"The weather's supposed to take a bit of a turn tomorrow morning," said Tom.

"And what's new about that?" asked Nathan.

"Nothing new, just stating the obvious."

"Winds will be from the northwest in the morning, then turn south in the afternoon. Couldn't be more favorable for a morning start."

"Aye lad," said Tom. "With an eight thirty start you'll have the wind at your back most of the day if all goes well."

"You'll just have to be careful not to get too greedy. For every ten knots take one less club. Do nae go over the green lad. Not on any hole. Not one."

Tom saw the look in Callum's eyes. They were turning dull and it was time to turn in, enough talking about golf.

31.

The next day was a rough one from the get-go for Callum. He couldn't sleep from midnight till just before dawn. Tossing and turning, mind racing. It was a battle of wills with himself but he just could not force himself to go to sleep. Then just about ten minutes before the alarm went off he finally dozed off into the most precious deep sleep he'd ever experienced, mind numbing bliss, only to be rudely awakened by the most awful blood curdling buzzing sound in the world.

Breakfast was hard to swallow, his throat seemed constricted. There was a twitch in his left eyelid.

He had a pain in his stomach at the very top right where his ribcage met his liver.

"Nerves," he told himself and tried to shake it off.

The half hour before the first tee time was hectic. Giant crowds of people packed at the gates trying to get in. The type of people who had never been to a golf tournament in their lives and most didn't even know how to hold a club. They knew how to yell though, even at seven in the morning, probably with drams and coffee.

Off in the distance as he putted on the practice green he could hear competing rugby clubs singing their team songs.

A golfer walked by with a smirk on his face, complaining to his caddie and manager.

"What is this, a golf tournament or a rugby match?"

That simple statement should have settled Callum down. His people were here to back him up. Didn't matter. The lack of sleep, the tossing and turning transformed his smooth swing into a tight wound hack. He bogeyed the first three holes, and his erratic play even seemed to affect his playing partners, and especially Diego, the Spaniard who he was paired with again.

Sometimes when things are going bad, they spread to those around you. Poor shots are contagious in golf. Callum's first three drives were short and he was first to hit each time, and each time he went into a greenside bunker and had to scramble for bogey. Callum would go into a left side bunker and Diego would go into the right side. Callum went into the right bunker and Diego went in the left. Under or overcompensating on distance each time. But where Diego was hot headed and would curse loudly, Callum stayed calm on the outside, letting the heat dissipate into the soles of his feet.

On the fourth tee as they were waiting for the group in front of them to clear the fairway,

Callum heard Diego's caddie talking to him in Spanish.

"Don't watch the Scotsman anymore."

"He was playing so good yesterday. I felt like I was being pulled along in his tailwind."

"Today he's pulling you into the bunkers. Stop watching."

Callum got a little ticked off hearing the caddie talk about him, so he walked closer and spoke to them in fluent Spanish which completely surprised both of them.

"My apologies for pulling you into the bunkers Diego. That was not my intention. I'd like to make it up to you."

"How?"

"I'll bet you a hundred pounds sterling that for the rest of this round I hit it closer than you on every approach shot."

"It's against the rules to bet money," said his caddie angrily. "You trying to get us in trouble?"

"Okay, no money, how about the loser sings the praises of the winner to the press after the round."

The caddie still frowned, but Diego smiled.

"That's a bet I'll take. I don't think it crosses the line. It's a bet on pride, machismo. The bet is for words, and words are not against any rules. So, you speak Spanish. You must have heard me cursing you yesterday."

Callum nodded. "Yesterday you were cursing my good fortune. Today you're cursing my bad. I'd like to get back to how it was."

"So would I," said Diego. "So would I. Okay

amigo, you're on."

"Do you speak Gaelic?" asked Callum.

"No."

"Tiugainn."

"Is that a swear word?"

"It means, let's go. The fairway is clear." Callum motioned to the tee box. "You have the honor."

The fourth hole. Dunure. Named after the village and the castle south of Troon. A par five.

Five hundred fifty-five yards long, a slight dog leg to the right, and the fourth hardest hole on the course. Diego popped his drive two ninety down the middle, power fade to the right, and Callum followed suit. With two sixty-five left to the hole and the green protected by two deep bunkers on the right and one on the left they both laid up. Diego left his second shot eighty-five yards from the hole, and Callum ninety-five. When Callum got to his ball, he wasted no time and pulled the old nine iron.

"There's that club," said Diego from the side to his caddie. Then watched with great interest as Callum casually lofted the ball high into the air onto the two-tier green, it bounced around the hole a few times, then settled three feet from the hole. Diego set his feet square, looked once at the pin then lofted his pitch shot higher into the air, seemingly hovering over the pin, landing past it then with backspin rolling backwards past the hole, past Callum's ball and ending up four feet from the hole.

Game on.

It's funny how a round of golf sometimes

seems to be controlled by an invisible switch.

It's a mental game of controlling your emotions as much as hitting a little ball. But one of those emotions is an instinct that can't be controlled. Can't be defined or labeled. For every individual it's different, their own trigger.

For Diego he played better when people around him were playing well.

For Callum it was a simple little bet. On that fourth tee box, a switch was turned on, and Callum and Diego's little side bet pulled them back towards the lead.

For the next ten holes it was like they were in their own little world. Callum was closer to the hole on each of the ten, but not by much and they each had five birdies and five pars.

They left the third player in the dust, and he was an afterthought as they battled each other down the stretch.

And then they came to the fifteenth hole.

Crosbie.

Named after the castle on the Fullarton estate nearby. A long and difficult five hundred two-yard par four, and the third hardest hole on the course. Both players bombed their drives three hundred yards and still had two hundred to the hole. Callum was first to hit his second shot and it began to drift left while in the air, with a little too much draw action, hit the front of the green on the upslope and spun sideways and backwards into the deep bunker on the left side.

"Thu bastard," he whispered.

"Get that shot out of your mind," said

Diego's caddie. "It's a one eighty-five shot to the front of the green. One eighty-five and fifteen roll out."

Diego nodded. Time to put the gringo out of his misery. He settled his feet over the ball, took one slow look at the pin and fired away with a high fading shot. His ball also caught the right to left wind and started drifting towards the left side of the green. Both he and his caddie talked to the ball.

"Ve a la derecha. Go right, go right!"

It caught the left side of the green, but with the fading left to right spin rolled towards the center, ending up twenty feet from the cup. Diego looked at Callum with a calm face and tipped his cap towards him.

Callum wanted to slam his club into the ground and break it in half but took a deep breath and shrugged his shoulders. It was a good run, and he'd been in this bunker quite a few times over the past few months. The leading face of the bunker was about four feet high. It wasn't as deep as the bunker on the right, but deep enough to make you hit out towards the side, and to the front, the fringe of the green, no way you wanted to take a chance at going straight at the pin and risk catching the face of the bunker and rolling back in.

Front of the green and he still had a long shot forty-foot chance at par. From the looks of the sand spread out on the grass bordering the bunker he wasn't the first one today to face splashing it out.

With his heels and back pockets wedged up

against the vertical face of the bunker, three feet from the side which in itself was three feet high, Callum opened the face of the sand wedge, focused his eyes on a spot two inches behind the ball and swept the club down and through that spot splashing a bucket of sand mixed with a golf ball riding on top of the geyser back onto terra-firma, green grass.

Lying three now. A low easy pitch shot straight at the pin breaking a bit right to left, it caught the top edge with too much speed and lipped out and around the hole as the crowd shouted at first thinking it was going in, then gasped and groaned.

Diego nuzzled his putt up to the hole and tapped in for par, while Callum sweated over a two-footer and watched as it trickled in, catching the left edge, holding his breath the whole way.

Their little bet was over, Callum had lost but there were three important holes left to go.

They walked together and there on the scoreboard up ahead could see that they were leading by one stroke, both of them nine under.

"Double or nothing?" asked Callum.

"What are you talking about?" asked Diego.

"I get it closer on the approach shot the next three holes and we're square on our bet. You get it closer on even one hole and I talk about how great you are, *and* how great a caddie you have."

"You're loco, you know that?" Diego shook his head and looked at the scoreboard again. One shot ahead was nothing. "Okay, tiugainn," he said in Gaelic. "Lets go."

Number sixteen. Wall. A five hundred fifty-three-yard par five, the eighth toughest hole on the course. Both men drilled their tee shots down the middle and their second shots to a hundred yards. Callum pulled out the old wedge and Diego shook his head as he watched it settle three feet from the pin. His wedge flew over the pin again, but did not release back to the cup leaving him fifteen feet for birdie which he made, pumping his fist as it went in.

Callum had a ho-hum semi tap-in uphill putt that went straight into the bottom of the cup.

Number seventeen. Rabbit. The furry creatures still loved this particular area, just not when there were thousands of people trampling around. A two hundred eighteen-yard par three, and the thirteenth hardest hole on the course. Diego still had the honors and hit a low punchy shot that caught the front of the green and rolled to within ten feet. A great shot and the crowd acknowledged it with solid applause.

A great shot but not great enough.

Callum hit a shot that climbed higher in the air, reached its apex as it approached the front edge of the green and settled five feet from the pin.

Number eighteen. Craigend. A four hundred sixty-two-yard par four and the second easiest hole on the course. Diego still had the honors and hit a monster drive that started in the middle of the fairway, then began to fade towards the bunker on the right, hit the ground rolling, rolling and stopped right at the top edge, Diego and his caddie's eyes wide as saucers as they watched in terror, then sighs of relief as the ball came to a stop in safe territory.

Callum tapped his chin as he pondered the situation. The wind was blowing just a bit from left to right and from behind them. He might be able to pop it down the middle and squeak by the bunker, or even crank it over it.

That bunker on the right though, was death.

He reached for the four iron and didn't think twice about it. Ball teed up, nice smooth swing, and it rolled out ending up only thirty yards behind Diego's ball, but safe. The difference, however, between a hundred eighty-five-yard approach shot, and a hundred fifty is immense.

Callum's second shot with a seven iron, with the low trajectory, hit the fringe, took a weird bounce in a divot and pinwheeled to the left and almost off the green, forty feet from the flag.

Diego, with nine iron in hand, hit a high soft approach that rolled to within fifteen feet.

Callum nuzzled his forty-footer to a few inches and tapped in, while Diego just missed the birdie putt and also tapped in.

Both men made par and for the moment were in the lead.

The press surrounded Callum and Diego as they left the green, walking together and they stopped near the clubhouse before going into the scorer's room to certify their cards.

"How do you describe your round, Callum?" asked a reporter excitedly.

"Well, first of all," said Callum. "I'd like to acknowledge the incredible skill that my playing partner, Diego over here displayed. Truly phenomenal. And his caddie was incredible. I mean, as far as caddie's go, he's one of the best I've ever seen."

Diego and his caddie were on the side grinning, while Jackie frowned and the reporter had a strange look on her face.

"Yes, Diego's caddie had a great round, but how was your round?"

"It was okay I guess. Got in trouble the first three holes then turned it around. Went into the bunker on Crosbie which is never a good thing, and then turned it around again, till this last hole. I'm not going to dwell on it though. I just can't get over how great of a round Diego's caddie had. Thank you."

Callum walked away and the dumbfounded reporter turned to Diego and his caddie and tried to clear her mind to ask them a question.

Tom walked with Callum towards the scorer's room.

"Looks like you both turned it around after the third hole. What was the bet?"

"Closet to the hole for the rest of the round."

"Crosbie got you?"

"Yep."

At Nathan's house that night, Tom was upbeat but Callum was sullen. Three strokes back of the leader. The players that finished behind them put on a clinic.

There was a soft knock on the front door and Nathan got up to answer it.

"Who in the 'el could it be now."

Standing in the door frame and mostly filling it was a sizeable man bundled in a jacket, long pants and boots. He looked cold and out of place. His face was large and very tan, dark brown, hair neatly trimmed on the sides, flat black hair on top.

"Excuse me sir," he said in perfect English which seemed out of place for such a ferocious Polynesian looking man. "I'm looking for Nathan Pickett."

"That's me lad. You have quite the accent. Where are you from, London? New Zealand maybe?"

"No sir, I'm from Kahuku, on Oahu, but my family is from Tonga, maybe that's the accent."

Around the corner in the dining room Callum sat up straight, his eyes brightened. He knew that voice.

"Tavita," he murmured, slid out of the chair walked quickly to the doorway and there was his archrival and ally, best friend, they embraced for a moment, Tavita slapping Callum on the back.

"Sorry we're late, we heard you were in a big match, so we came to give you some support."

"What do you mean we?"

Tavita's large frame hid the scene behind him and he stepped to the side. It was the Kahuku rugby team, the entire squad, twenty men, and a bunch of women behind them, and they all cheered when they saw Callum.

"What? Pulu mā'oni'oní !" he shouted. "How did you all get here? No one told me."

Nathan was worried. How was he going to fit all of them into this little house. Tavita laughed as he recognized the look on his face.

"Don't worry uncle. We're not staying here, we just came by to say hello and give a cheer to Callum. He is our brother."

He stepped back a few steps to merge with the crowd of men behind them and started the chant, slapping his thigh.

Teu to ki he tupe!1
Ko e 'aho!
Ko e 'aho mavava mo e tangi!
Teu mate maa Tonga!
Hii!

Tonga 'e!
Ta ke hu ki ai!
Katoa pe!
Taha!
Mo e to kotoa!
Teu fetau folau!

Hii! Haa!
Mo e peje!
Mo e lea!
'Otua ke tau!

Tau malohi!
'Ai Malohi!
Tau Fefeka!
'Ai Fefeka!

Tau ki Tonga!

To'o mo e hii!
Tau mo tangi!
'I 'olunga moihulo!
Feinga te tau 'ikuna!
'Ikuna kotoa!
Hii!

Then each and every one of them came forward and shook Callum's, Nathan's, Tom's and Jackie's hands and filed off into the night singing the national anthem of Tonga.

"There's something else I should tell you," said Tom. "The Oban rugby club is also on their way down here to cheer you on. I got the word earlier today. I just hope these blokes don't get into a scrum with them on the sidelines. Might be distracting."

Callum shook his head and smiled. "Not sure which team I'd pick to win that match. Don't worry, I'm not going to get distracted by anything."

32.

As luck would have it, Callum and Diego finished the second day tied for fourth and were paired again for the third round. The weather was cold and windy, and both men were wearing insulated vests.

They shook hands politely on the first tee and got ready for the announcer.

"Same bet?" asked Diego.

"Why don't we mix it up. Let's make it lowest score," said Callum.

"Embellish the player and caddie?"

"Player, caddie, and..." Callum looked around. "And that big Tongan standing over there." He pointed to Tavita who stood head and shoulders above everyone around him, wearing a giant coral necklace, wild hair, tattooed bulging arms.

After their round, the reporter from the BBC had them cornered..

"So, Callum. You left your tee shot on number eighteen well short of the bunker on the right three days in a row, and you made bogey two out of those three days. Are you afraid of going in that particular bunker?"

Callum frowned with a smile.

"Not afraid of any bunker, I've been in most

of them on practice rounds here and there. I don't know anyone who likes being in any bunker around this course. They're pretty deep, just like your questioning."

The reporter pressed.

"What if you're in contention on the last hole come tomorrow afternoon. Would you do anything different?"

Callum shrugged.

"Like I've said, I play against the course not the person, but I'm not a robot. If it comes down to the last hole, with one or two shots left to play, I don't know. It's going to be a game time decision. But I like how you're thinking. I would love to be in contention on the last hole. Right now, I'm only one shot ahead and there's eighteen left against the best players in the world. I'm only planning for one hole at a time and hitting one shot at a time from tee to green."

Diego was up next and Callum waited on the side with a slight grin as the Spaniard spoke slowly into the microphone.

"First of all, what a great round by Callum over there. I tried to keep up but fell behind early and had to scramble just to get to one shot back. His caddie Jackie was incredible, the club selection was impeccable, the putt reads some of the best I've ever witnessed. But I would say that the difference maker for this third round was the big Tongan standing over there."

He pointed to Tavita.

"I don't know his name, but every time

Callum came up with a spectacular shot, that guy was yelling at the top of his lungs. I'm telling you it was loud. That Tongan had a great round."

"Yes," said the reporter with a wry tone of voice. "The big Tongan had a great round."

As Diego and Callum walked away with their caddie's the reporter turned to the camera.

"Well, there you have it from the current leaders of the tournament. Neither man wants to take full credit for their achievements. Back to you Ross."

33.

As they stood on the first tee, waiting for the fairway to clear both men stood near each other with their caddie's.

"You ever been in the final pairing at The Open?" asked Callum.

"Never been in the final pairing anywhere."

"Me neither."

Both men were trying their best to keep their composure with thousands of people watching their every little move. TV cameras pointed at their faces with millions more studying their close-ups. A beehive hum of conversations from all directions.

Neither of them did well standing around, they needed action.

"I guess we could make a side wager. Closest to the pin, lowest score."

"We've done those already. I don't think we need a side bet today," said Diego.

"Maybe you're right," said Callum. "I've already got enough riding on the line to motivate me. I'm going to go out there and do everything I can to win this thing. Right now."

"As will I," said Diego."

"I guess the only side bet we need is the loser

has to watch the winner hoist the Claret Jug," said Callum.

"There's no guarantee either one of us is going to do that, have you seen the leader board? We're not in the lead anymore."

And those were the last words either player said to each other until the final hole.

By the time they actually put their tees in the ground, they were two shots out of the lead with a couple of groups ahead of them having hot rounds. They traded pars on the first three holes, and then on the fourth hole, Dunure, the par five, they got hot themselves, both men landing their third shots within a few feet of the pin for birdies.

They parred Greenan, the two hundred yard par three, then came to Turnberry, the six hundred yard par five and birdied that as well, climbing up the leaderboard again.

The seventh hole Tel-El-Kebir, a four hundred five yard par four was nearly a disaster with both players finding the bunker next to the green on the left and both were lucky to get up and down for sandy pars.

They both parred Postage Stamp, the eighth hole, and the ninth hole, The Monk. On the tenth hole, Sandhills with gorse on the right and a gulley on the left they sweated out pars.

Then the eleventh hole, The Railway, the toughest hole on the course, four hundred eighty-three yards with gorse along the left.

Diego blasted his driver three hundred yards down the middle and it rolled another fifty giving him a short hundred twenty-yard pitch to five feet and birdie.

Callum matched him with a drive of only two ninety that caught a bad bounce in a divot with no roll out, but a spectacular four iron from one ninety that skipped onto the green and settled just outside Diego for a matching birdie.

Both players as though playing inside their own little bubble, not a word to each other or anyone in the crowd. Sparse interaction with their caddie's. What's the yardage to the pin, what yardage to land it, shot shape, wind direction, club selection, settle over ball and strike it. Neither one of them took a drink of water or ate a snack, every motion, every thought was geared towards getting the golf ball moving forward, get it close to the cup and get it in. The level of intensity rising with every shot. The crowd was swept along in the drama, collective cheers and shouts sweeping over the golf course.

The twelfth hole The Fox, thirteenth hole Burmah, fourteenth hole Alton, fifteenth hole Crosbie, sixteenth hole Wall, like a heavyweight prize fight, each man oblivious to the surroundings, in the ring throwing haymakers and landing every punch. Birdie, par, birdie, par, birdie, trading the lead back and forth. The crowd frothing.

As they walked up to Rabbit, the two hundred eighteen yard par three seventeenth tee they were all square. Both men fifteen under and two strokes clear of the field for now. There was still one group on the eighteenth tee and one on the eighteenth green and anything could happen.

The Spaniard still had the honors and studied the tabletop green up ahead, talking calmly with his caddie. They looked at the sky, pointed to landmarks, picked grass from the side and tossed it in the air, watched the motion as the bits of thin leaves swirled in the air. It was going to be an eight iron, no, an easy nine.

They watched the wind again, tossed more bits of grass in the air then decided on the eight iron. They pointed at objects near the back of the green, there was a sign that was the target line. Just to the right of the sign, said the caddie. That's the line, with a baby fade. He was sure, absolutely positively sure and then a little gust of wind ruffled the flag, lifting it from left to right, and they changed their mind again and pulled out a seven iron.

Callum didn't watch the routine, he only looked over when it seemed as though the shot was actually about to be hit to make sure nothing went awry.

Diego's shot sailed high to the left of the flag then faded every so gently to the right, landed softly on the front of the green and rolled to within four feet of the cup.

Callum didn't need to think about what club to hit or throw grass in the air, he'd hit this same shot over a hundred times in all types of conditions, rain, squalls, south wind, north wind, no wind. The wind was out of the west at about eight miles an hour, which was perfect for a high arcing shot. Seven iron, hit it straight as an arrow and hold it up against that wind and drop it in front of the cup. He didn't care how close the other guy's ball was, or that there were two holes to play, the only pressure was his grip on the golf club, his feet settled into the ground, gravity pulling him towards the center of the earth, and the intense mental awareness that seemed to overwhelm him. Time slowed down, and all he cared about at that singular moment was this one perfect shot that was sitting in the palm of his hands. As he teed it up the crowd got quiet, even the rugby squads halfway down the fairway settled down, all eyes on him while his eyes were squarely set on the ball.

Smooth, smooth, smooth, he told himself as he brought the club back over his head, rotating counterclockwise, hands high over his head, dig, dig, dig his mind whispered as he lag stopped at the top then whipped down into a vicious strike on the ball, his eyes never wavering as the club flew through ball and tee, iron face barely clipping the grass where both had been, head still down till his arms up over his left shoulder now lifted his head and he looked for the ball sailing in the air towards the green, he could see everyone's head rotating from the tee, all along the fairway and near the green, thousands of spotters, pointers leading the way to the flight of the little white ball that arched high over the greenside bunkers, landed on the green and rolled a few feet from the edge towards the cup ending twenty feet from the pin.

Some groans, and polite clapping from the crowd. Not a complete disaster, but not quite the outcome most people were hoping for.

Callum and Diego walked even paced ten feet apart down the fairway towards the green.

In some ways kindred spirits, both of them way out of their realm, seemingly feeding off each other's shots, finding a rhythm with the crowd, which was overwhelmingly rooting for the Scotsman, and yet throughout the round Callum protected Diego, raising his hands for quiet when he was about to hit, tipping his hat on great shots.

It was all Callum could do to keep up with the young phenom., and now down to the wire twenty feet farther away he circled the hole twice looking for the elusive break. It was half a foot from right to left, he'd seen this putt in past rounds and knew he had to make it over the small ridge and feed it to the hole.

Finally satisfied, he placed the ball back and picked up the coin, settled his feet, struck the ball with the flatstick, the crowd at first silent, then as it started rolling a crescendo of shouts, go in the hole, go in the hole, but go in the hole it did not. It rolled by the edge and stopped two feet past.

Callum did not wince or frown or throw his hands in the air in disappointment, his face was complete stoicism as he went straight to the ball to finish up. As with all short putts, he took his time, put the coin behind the ball, set the line on the ball straight for the middle of the cup and just a hair to the left, stepped up and made it. Polite applause, the crowd sensed what was coming next. Diego stepped up to the four-foot putt without even giving it a read and drilled it into the back of the cup. The ball bounced off the wall and down into the cup with a sound that everyone surrounding the green, and everyone watching on TV could hear, it was the sound of impending doom.

One shot in the lead with one to go, Diego hustled to the eighteenth tee while Callum lingered, looking back at the green and the subtle break that he missed. He was in shock.

In the back of his mind, he could hear Tom telling him how the golf course was a single living breathing entity, interconnected, every blade of grass, every root intermingling, communicating.

Jackie pulled on his elbow and Callum broke free from his trance, remembered suddenly where he was. Headed to the dreaded eighteenth hole, the elusive one.

Diego was ready to hit when Callum finally made it to the tee, he stood quietly to the side with Jackie and watched the practice swings with the driver. Diego was going with driver and why not, he'd birdied this hole every day and with a one shot lead you had to keep the pedal to the metal.

With a mighty back swing and perfect tempo Diego's ball blasted off the tee, all eyes following it as it sailed through the air three hundred yards on the fly and landed in the center of the fairway in between the bunkers.

Safe. As Diego swirled the club in his fingers

and picked up his spent tee all eyes turned to Callum.

It was the ninth inning, two outs and no one on base. The fourth quarter with fifteen seconds left and the entire football field to march with no time outs. One shot behind on the last hole at the Open Championship that you'd played safe and bogeyed twice in the past three days.

Three hundred ten yards to the front of the bunker on the right. The correct shot was three hundred yards, leaving it short of the trouble then you'd have a hundred fifty-four yards to the hole. Callum had been hitting it two eighty leaving a hundred seventy, a little out of his range for a close shot.

One down with one to go. For the past four days Callum played it one shot at a time, but now at the end everything changed. There was no denying that he was in a match play situation. He needed to win the hole to extend the tournament. Tie or lose the hole, and he lost.

The problem was the wind blowing slightly against them from the northwest. If only it was at their back like the very first morning that he played this course there wouldn't be moment's indecision.

It was driver, he took a deep breath, and as the head cover came off and he pulled the big club the crowd applauded.

"You got this shot," said Jackie. "You've been starving this little puppy all week on this hole, and now it's time to let the big dog eat."

A silly cliché and he said it to calm Callum down, but he could see the hands trembling a bit and he put his hand on Callum's chest to stop him for a moment until their eyes locked.

"You got this shot. Nice and smooth, lean on it with everything you got, straight down the middle."

Callum nodded, eyes steady. He placed the ball on the tee in the palm of his hand, then plugged the end of the little green stick in the ground, the tips of his fingers brushing the blades of grass. One entity. Feet steady, crowd silent, you could hear the breeze through the rough nearby. Smooth backswing, lag at the top, vicious down stroke, club through ball, head steady at the top of an uncoiling boomerang as the ball rocketed through the air, the strike was so intense and the situation so dire that hardly anyone shouted, all attention was on the ball that looked like it was going to fly over Diego's ball in the center of the fairway, high in the air, too high, when it started veering to the right, a gust of wind, a spin of the ball off the tee, a combo of both, or simply a smack down from the golf gods, the ball went straight into the bunker and plugged into the middle.

Groans of sympathy filled the fairway. The game was over. End of match. Diego did not even want to *look* at his competitor and walked straight down the fairway with his caddie without glancing back.

Callum was calm on the outside holding onto the club for a moment too long before handing it to Jackie. Calm on the outside, yet on the inside his ears were ringing from the rush of adrenaline pumping veins in his head.

It was over. Still, he walked with his head held high down the fairway, not looking at anyone, not acknowledging the cascading shouted words of encouragement. He never took his eyes off the ball stuck in the middle of the sand bunker, and the flag at the green so far away.

If only he was a few yards farther back in the bunker he might have a miracle shot at getting to the green, but the way the bunker wall towered over the ball it was impossible.

"Sometimes you have to go backwards to go forwards," Tom's voice in his head appeared.

Even going backwards in this situation was going to be nearly impossible.

"It's not over yet," said Jackie. "You put it back in play and you'll have about one seventy to the pin. Don't forget that first hole in one at Greenan on the first day. That was two ten.

And he was right. If he could get the ball back on the fairway he'd have a long shot and even if he didn't hole it out, a par would still leave him one stroke back, and this was golf. Anything could happen. Diego could go over the green and out of bounds or find a bunker of his own.

Callum stood in the bottom of the bunker, envisioning a shot, then climbed out and pulled the old nine iron, the niblick. He needed a little magic on the ball and this was the most trusted club in the bag.

Strange, as he scrunched his feet into the

sand holding the heavy old club, a déjà vu moment, as though this golf club was in this exact situation long ago.

The ball was sitting on a smooth level sand surface, he had to hit it both sideways and backwards to get it on the fairway.

Smooth, smooth, then dig, dig. The club scooped under the ball, touching only sand and about a bucket of it, lifting the ball in an explosion of white, terminal velocity the little golf ball settled into the center of the fairway where he should have been on the tee shot.

It was a clean lie in the middle of the fairway, and it was just about the position he was in the past three days, except now he was lying two and hitting three from a hundred seventy-five. Fifty yards behind the leader who was knocking pitching wedges close all day.

It was a gut choice. They'd gone over it the night before over dinner. If he was in this position on the last hole with a chance to win, then pull an extra club. He'd been hitting eight iron every day trying to keep the out of bounds past the hole out of play. Keep it short and let his putting do the rest, but he'd missed each time and three putted each time. The hell with playing it safe, that option was long gone when he hit it in the bunker.

He pulled the seven iron and Jackie stepped well to the side to give him room. The crowd was restless, some shouting his name. He was almost certain he heard Tavita yelling in Tongan.

See ball, hit ball. He hadn't been nervous

over any shot since the beginning of the tournament till this moment. He visualized the shot, picked out a target line towards the grandstand, the pin on the green so far away. He stepped up to the ball, squared his feet, squared his mind, got ready to hit the ball, then his eye twitched slightly and he stepped back.

Murmurs from the crowd, Jackie came back over with the clubs and set them next to his feet, this was normal in tournament play for a caddie to come back over in case the player wanted to pick a different club, normal except for Callum. He looked down at the bag, put the seven iron back and pulled the six iron. Two clubs more than what he'd been using. Took a couple of practice swings to feel the weight, then searched the crowd for Maggie's face. It was a sea of humanity all blended into one, thousands pressed together, time was running out, he had to hit the shot. See ball, hit ball. He took a deep breath, shrugged his shoulders to relax the tension.

"Dig it out of the dirt," he whispered to himself. "Like a true Scotsman on the shores of Troon." He made a promise and now it was time to pay up.

Smooth, smooth, smooth, his mind whispered as the club slowly came back high over his head, then dig, dig, the flash of metal through the little ball suddenly gone from sight, head pulled up by twisting torso, thousands of heads following the flight high up into the air, straight for the green, over the green side bunkers, over the fringe, still in the air, then settling softly ten feet from the cup, rolling now, thousands screaming now as it rolled and rolled, slowing down slightly but still moving forward straight up to the sharp edge of the cup.

And stopped.

From their angle it looked like it was right on the edge. The wind changed, swirled from the southwest, picked up with a gust, lifting the flag at an angle, fluttering on the end of the pin.

The crowd went wild. Someone started stomping and soon a few thousand people were stomping their feet on the grandstands, trying to force the ball into the hole. That stupid horn blaring, bagpipes squealing, as Callum and Jackie walked forward down the fairway.

The Spaniard was ready to hit, he was only a hundred and thirty yards from the hole and either had a wedge or nine iron. He looked at his caddie for help, the noise was deafening.

Callum held up his hands and motioned downwards in the universal appeal for quiet and the crowd settled down. The Spaniard nodded to Callum in appreciation, then went through his short routine again, listening to his caddie point along the target line, give one more verbal affirmation, then stepped back with the bag and watched as his player squared the clubface, settled his feet, looked once more at the green, then smashed the ball high into the air floating over the fringe, then landed and stopped twenty feet short of the pin.

Callum caught up to him and was silent as they walked side by side. The other man looked at him and said, "Nice shot."

Then the yelling and stomping started again, a deafening thunderous roar, horns, bagpipes, someone set off a firecracker in the parking lot, a mini cannon went off in the distance.

Callum looked over at Diego.

"If that ball goes in because of the noise, I'll pull it right back out and putt it."

"No you won't. That would be a penalty."

"How would that be a penalty?"

"You can't just hit another shot because you don't like the outcome."

"I don't want to tie *or* win like this."

"It doesn't matter what you want. It only matters what the rule is."

The noise doubled suddenly in volume, and when the two competitors looked back at the pin the ball was gone. Everyone in the stands was on their feet jumping, arms in the air, going crazy, a frenzied sea of humanity gone wild.

Callum's face was red hot with anger as the two men and their caddie's got to the edge of the green, he motioned for the head judge to meet them in the middle. Two other judges met with them and the seven men discussed it.

In the background by the scoreboard was a giant TV monitor and it kept showing the ball rolling into the cup, over and over again with the crowd jumping in the background.

"I'm going to pull that ball out and putt it," said Callum to the official. "There's no way it rolled in on its own."

"We watched it the whole way Callum," said

the official with his hands out in a defensive position. "No one touched it or came near it. It looked like it was being held up by a single blade of grass that finally wilted under the weight." He pointed to the giant TV. The camera zoomed in and the ball sitting on green grass and the white edge of the cup filled the screen, they could clearly see all the dimples and the logo. Half the ball was over the edge, and it looked strange that it didn't fall in, until it finally did. Over and over and again. The camera zoomed in even further till you could see the tiny stiff blades of grass only a handful at most, holding up the ball, then slowly bending over as though commanded by the other grass around them.

"I can't believe I'm saying this Callum, but I'm sorry that ball went in on its own. You birdied this hole."

Callum was still shaking his head.

"I'm not accepting it."

Diego smiled and made a motion with his hand to the crowd, the universal sign of a slam dunk, then patted Callum on the shoulder.

"That's the ruling Callum. That ball is good. No one will ever think otherwise." He paused for a moment to make sure Callum was looking directly into his eyes. "Don't worry, I'll make my putt."

"You damn well better," said Callum, narrowing his suddenly bloodshot eyes. He walked over to the cup making sure he stayed a few feet away, looked back at Diego's ball where it was sitting on the green, then stepped to the left of the hole, bent down with two fingers, lifted the ball out of the cup and held it high for everyone to see.

Bedlam.

Rolling thunder for a few more moments that slowly quieted down to polite applause as the crowd seemed overwhelmed and out of breath after yelling for the past five minutes.

Callum walked over to the edge of the crowd and saw a young boy around three years old wearing a Scottish flag pin on his shirt standing shyly with his mother, and he handed the ball to him.

The raucous behavior of the crowd swelled and Callum held up his arms, palms spread, waving down like a swan's wings pleading for quiet.

Then all eyes were on the Spaniard. The arena for the past few minutes, like the tarmac of an airport with a jumbo jet taking off overhead, was now so silent you could hear the proverbial pin drop. It was almost too quiet, and eerie. You could hear the waves on the shoreline nearby, gulls squawking, wind barely whistling, the flags gently flapping on the grandstands as the Spaniard and his caddie lined up the putt.

One man was left to finish, and that man with grim determined face paced around the flag pin searching for an answer to the eternal question on which way the putt would break. Which way it would break and by how much.

He counseled with his caddie and they crouched and motioned as though conjuring spirits with hands, whispering to each other on the pace and direction needed.

Callum for the first time that day as he stood on the sidelines waiting for either utter destruction, or a reprieve and a playoff actually looked at the crowd around them and wondered at the outcome, it had all come down to this, a four-day marathon, a hundred and sixty golfers, thousands of epic shots and it came down to this one single putt.

One putt to win, two putts to tie. Three putt from twenty feet on this slippery green was not out of the question, he knew that as a personal fact.

And yet he steeled himself for the worst, that this one putt would sink into the hole and sink him as well.

Be absolutely ready, he told himself, for either outcome. Be gracious, be humble. You had your chance.

The giant scoreboard behind the green had his name on top and he'd finished the tournament at fifteen under par. He searched the crowd for Maggie, but it was a frothing sea of faces, and hundreds of people waving Scottish flags.

Diego was finally done lining up the putt and he stood one final time behind the ball, adjusted the target line a microscopic amount, then picked up the coin, stood steadily over the ball and with a smooth confident stroke, started the ball towards the hole. The crowd of thousands as one seemed to hold their breath in a hush, all eyes on the ball as it bumped and rolled forward, turning slightly left as it got closer to the hole, gasps and shouts, crying, yelling, screaming both to go in and to stay out, while the ball hung on the lip for a short excruciating moment and then dropped over the abyss and into the cup.

No one was watching it more intently than Callum, and when it dropped into the cup he suddenly saw his father in his mind's eye, his ears were ringing, every inch of his skin was buzzing while his heart no matter how hard he tried to prevent it was sinking into his stomach, tears welling in his eyes, he blinked them out quickly, not wanting anyone to see them, he couldn't wipe at them, when suddenly he lost all control of his leg muscles and fell crouching onto the ground in complete destruction, his world in one split second come to an utter, complete and bitter end, he held onto the earth with the palm of his right hand stretched over its surface, and in his depleted state couldn't tell if he was holding up the world, or it was holding him up, and it was the grass that brought him back to life, the feel of the thin soft blades on his fingertips and at the center of his palm.

He stood up quickly, brushed off his pants, took off his hat and walked to shake hands with Diego, who took his hand gladly then put Callum in a bear hug that lasted a few moments. He whispered three Gaelic words in Callum's ear:

"Bha mi fortanach."

I was lucky.

Callum shook his head.

"It's only lucky if it's a fifty-foot putt. That was only half that and all skill."

"Not what I meant," said Diego. "I was lucky to beat you today. We'll see each other again I hope."

Then he raised Callum's arm next to his for the crowd to witness, and the scene turned to anarchy.

Hundreds of revelers stormed the green, rugby players, golfers, housewives, kids, ruffians with blue and white face paint, young girls, businessmen in collared shirts and ties, old ladies and old men, a couple of Tongans, even some caddie's and players joined in, swarming Callum, mobbing him, shouting and singing they lifted him onto their shoulders for a moment to carry him towards the center of the green, until he broke free and ranged in the middle of the swarm. Like an errant piece of flotsam on the edge of a roaring sea, Diego was pushed to the edges.

Off on the side, at a safe distance, Tom stood next to Nathan.

"Well, he came close," said Tom, shaking his head and sighing.

"Aye, if only he could have kept it out of the bunker on eighteen. Might have had a chance at it."

"What are you talking about?" said Tom. "That shot just now was the shot of the tournament."

"Even better than the ace on the postage stamp?"

"That was the first day with miles and miles of golf ahead of them all. That shot from one seventy-five just now was made with everything in the world on the line. Everything. And he almost pulled it off. It was only epic because he went into the bunker in the first place."

Maggie pushed through the crowd and when Callum finally saw her he frowned and shrugged while she threw her arms around him. She had tears in her eyes.

"Ya big oof."

"I got a dang B on the seventeenth hole," he whispered.

"What?"

"I'll tell you someday."

Maggie's father made his way through the crowd and stood in front of the old greenskeepers.

"Well," said Tom to him, while nodding his head towards the mob surrounding Callum. "There he is, the hero of Scotland and he only came in second place. Imagine if he would have won."

"Michelangelo would be floating down from the gates of heaven at this very moment," said Nathan. "To carve his image in pure marble right here on the eighteenth green. That's what would happen."

"That and a winged unicorn would fly down out of Argyll and carry him off on its back to Edinburgh Castle, and land him on the throne." Tom frowned at Maggie's father. "So, are you going to hold onto that bet, that promise of yours?"

"What are promises good for then? If not to keep?"

"I've got half a mind to..." started Tom.

"Oh, hold on to yourself. I'm not as hardheaded and cold-hearted as you might think Thomas Gillam. C'mon both of you. Follow me."

The mob was slowly moving with Callum and Maggie in the midst of it towards the edge of the green. When Callum saw Tom, Nathan, and Malcolm walking towards them he pushed their way, Maggie holding tight and they stopped in front of the trio. The mob was still shouting, most of them, a roiling tumult of heads and hands bouncing in the air, then a slow calm swept over them as they watched and realized that something momentous was about to happen. All eyes and ears were on Malcolm who pulled himself up, puffed out his chest with head high and spoke loud enough for everyone to hear.

"Well, a promise is a promise and what good is a man if he doesn't keep it. Now, I promised to give my blessing to a marriage if you won the Open and I was doubly surprised as anyone when you took me up on it. *No one* thought you could do it and rightly so as the results clearly show. You did nae win the Open son, so that wager is finished."

The crowd was impatient and angry and started to boo and hiss their displeasure peppered with a few colorful words.

Malcolm held up his hands.

"Let me finish. It was an impossible task, yet you still took it on, and by the looks of it gave it everything you had. That shows the type of courage and fortitude that we hold dear in this country. By the looks of it you weren't trying to win the tournament for fame and fortune as much as to win Maggie's hand in marriage. And that's the type of spirit and strength I was looking for."

He was silent for a moment as the entire crowd leaned forward, hovering on every word and waiting for the finale so they could start yelling again.

"I've decided to make a new promise, and that's to give my blessing to the marriage..."

The crowd was about to erupt in a frenzy but Malcolm held up his hands and shouted loudly.

"... ON ONE CONDITION."

The crowd groaned as one and waited like a balloon that was ready to explode then suddenly deflating.

"On one condition," he said again until all was quiet again.

He studied the couple, weighing their resolve, and then seeing that they were waiting for him to speak, continued, talking slowly and methodically.

"I'll approve of the marriage on one condition. That the marriage be a proper one at a church in Oban."

Bedlam again, the entire crowd cheering as one. Tom reached over a pile of shoulders, and ruffled Malcolm's hair then stood back at a safe distance, out of punching range.

Callum grabbed Maggie in his arms, embracing her with a kiss while boiling turmoil surrounded them.

Tavita stood at the front of the crowd and held up his hand respectfully asking for recognition and shouted loudly. "Excuse me sir! EXCUSE ME!"

The crowd turned silent again at the sight of Tavita, bare chested with giant chest and biceps covered with tattoos, hanging coral necklace, war crown, grass kilt.

Malcolm furrowed his brow, irritated at the interruption, and nodded to the large Tongan. "Yes, yes, what is it?"

"Our plane flight is tomorrow morning sir. Could they have the wedding tonight?"

"Tonight?!" Malcolm shouted. "How are we going to manage that? We need a church; we need a priest..."

A man wearing a suit and tie stepped out from the crowd.

"I'm Father Callahan from Saint Ninian's Church, and it's available if you want. It's just about two blocks away. I'd be more than happy to preside over the ceremony."

All eyes turned back to Malcolm, ruffled hair and all.

"Well," he muttered, suddenly out of words. "I guess that would be okay..."

He could barely get the last word out, the ay from okay drowned out as the crowd erupted in a frenzy, horns blowing, bagpipes squeaking, the mob jumping up and down and sideways.

Malcolm was pushed to the outside edge by

the jostling crowd, nearly tumbling to the ground, while Callum and Maggie embraced again in the center of the tumult.

The Spaniard whistled loudly from the side, and one of the officials put his hand on Callum's shoulder.

"Excuse me Callum, but we need you to sign your card so we can certify the scores and declare the winner. We have duties yet to perform."

Callum pulled himself away from Maggie and whispered in her ear. "Don't you move, I'll be right back."

Twenty minutes later, on the eighteenth green in the early evening, surrounded by grandstands full to the brim, after giving accolades to the thousands of volunteers, golf course staff, patrons, sponsors, and players, and after presenting the silver medal to the leading amateur, the official said simply into the loudspeaker:

"With a score of two hundred sixty-eight, the winner of the gold medal and the champion golfer of the year, is Diego Sanchez."

There was a rousing round of applause and cheers as the champion walked from the side to lift the Claret Jug in triumph, but half the crowd as they clapped and cheered was also wondering what could have been.

Mobs of people gathered around Callum and Maggie as the ceremony slowly wound down.

Their hands got weary from all the handshaking, backs sore from the shoulder slapping, and Callum signed hundreds of hats and shirts and body parts from the rowdy crowd. Tavita was his bodyguard and kept the rowdiest of them at arm's length. The Scottish battle horn blared far off in the distance, and dueling bagpipes left the arena, their mournful sounds slowly fading.

It took another half an hour for the crowd to thin out and with a long drawn-out dull thud all the excitement came to an end.

34.

Malcolm sat on a plastic chair next to the eighteenth green and watched the workers clean up the area and begin the enormous task of breaking down the event. Bleachers and tents, chairs and tables, trash and recycle cans, porta potties, flags, banners, scoreboards, giant TV monitors, and miles of cable.

The sun was beginning its descent into the west over the Firth of Clyde, the actual sunset still hours away, yet the colors slowly turning from blue grey to reddish orange.

Stragglers walked all over the place, up and down the fairways along the old course, some mesmerized, seemingly in a daze from the spectacular finish, as though in a trance Perhaps a mass hypnosis of the crowd had somehow occurred thought Malcolm.

It had been quite a day.

He chuckled and shook his head. Everything had turned out as planned. From the moment he laid down the gauntlet on Christmas morning a few months ago, till the ending of the tournament, his plot worked nearly to perfection. If Callum had actually won The

Open it might have been too good to be true. It was the effort that he made that was the most important part of the whole equation.

It was a test that needed to be applied, a necessary trial, and the lad rose to the occasion as a true Scotsman would. The fact that he did not win was immaterial. We rarely win events, thought Malcolm, large or small, any of us, as we live throughout our lives, and it's the determination, the will to succeed that is the ultimate achievement in the end.

If his daughter was going to marry someone, he had to make sure the young man would follow through, not give up and walk away.

He reached into his coat pocket and pulled out a worn golf ball. There was a date and a time written on it. June 21, 1999 – 5PM Royal Troon #8. His one and only hole in one. His lucky golf ball, and he brought it specifically to this final round hoping that it brought them all the luck that they needed.

'I guess it brought us enough luck after all,' he thought to himself and tossed the ball high in the air with his right hand and caught it deftly with his left.

An attractive woman was walking nearby and she clapped appreciatively.

"Nice catch."

She looked to be around thirty-five years old if Malcolm could make a guess, dressed smartly, curves in all the right places, with long brown hair and a friendly smile.

"Why thank you," he said, rising politely, taking off his hat while placing the golf ball in his pocket, and looked around to see who she was with. There wasn't another person within fifty feet of them.

"Are you a player?" she asked. "Do you play golf?"

"Me? No, not really, not anymore. I used to. A long time ago. And you?"

"Oh yes. It's a passion actually. I play every chance I get. Coming to The Open has been a dream of mine for quite some time."

Malcolm noticed her accent.

"You're from the States are you?"

"Yes, I'm from Montana. And you?"

"I live a few miles north, in Oban."

She smiled. "That's in the Highlands."

He shrugged. "It's Scotland."

"Oban's on my list of places to visit on my trip."

"On holiday are you?"

"Reminiscing, like a lot of us do I suppose."

"What do you mean by that?"

"Retracing heritage. My great grandparents lived a few miles east of here, in Dundonald. My granddad used to joke that we owned the castle, but it was too hard to keep up the stone walls and the weather was too harsh in the winter. So, they moved to Montana where you have ten feet of snow and it's twenty below zero three months out of the year. Granddad had a sense of humor. This is my first trip to Scotland." She reached out her hand gently. "My name is Katie Stewart."

"Malcolm McQuarrie," he said while bowing slightly at the waist, and took her hand for a moment. It was soft to the touch and took quite a bit of effort for him to let go after an appropriate amount of time. He noticed in the corner of his eye without looking that there was no ring on her left hand but that didn't always mean a thing. He squinted one eye and tilted his head just a tad as though he was an inspector from Scotland Yard, then asked.

"What's your maiden name Katie, or rather, what name did your great grandparents go by. Maybe I know a few of them still."

She smiled at his questioning, a roundabout method to find out if she was married.

"My great grandparents name is Stewart," she said. "Which is also my maiden name."

He tried to hold it back, but the slight crack of a smile edged his face.

"You're unmarried then?"

"Aye," she said in a forced Scottish brogue, with a twinkle in her eyes. "And you?"

His face began to turn a shade of red as his overall confident demeanor faded. He tried to talk but in his heightened state of emotion took a few split seconds to get the words out. In this moment, they had to be the truth. Nothing less.

"I was married once, a very long time ago, nearly sixteen years she's been gone."

She reached out her soft hand and put it on his arm.

"I'm so sorry."

The twinkle in her eye had vanished, replaced by compassion. He guessed in that instant that she might be a nurse or a doctor able to heal with a simple look. His composure returned. Peace and a strange sense of destiny swept over him.

"I have a wedding to attend, my only daughter is tying the knot in about half an hour from now, here at a church in Troon. Would you care to join me?" he asked hopefully.

She was silent for a moment, contemplating, and he continued with optimistic confidence.

"Afterwards I can take you to dinner. I think we may have a lot to talk about."

She waited a moment longer before answering, studying the man and the nature of his face, his brooding eyes, hulking physique, holding his hat in his hand with patience and respect. A simple man by all outer appearances, and just maybe she thought, she found what she'd been looking for, a true Scotsman from the Highlands, and she nodded serenely.

"I'd like that."

The relief in his face was overwhelming, not a smile of joy, but pure thankful bliss.

"It's been quite a day," he said with a sigh. "Quite a day."

She put her hand into the nook of his elbow as they walked northeast past the clubhouse, still bustling with activity, across Craigend Road, then up narrow South Beach Lane bordered by red brick walls towards Saint Ninian's Church two blocks away, it's bells ringing gently through the cool evening air, the warm glow of golden lights beginning to fill the homes of Troon.

An Deireadh   (The End).

Royal Troon
Tam Arte Quam Marte
Established 1878
Par 71 - 7,208 yards

1	Seal	370 yards	Par 4
2	Black Rock	391 yards	Par 4
3	Gyaws	379 yards	Par 4
4	Dunure	555 yards	Par 5
5	Greenan	210 yards	Par 3
6	Turnberry	601 yards	Par 5
7	Tel-El-Kebir	405 yards	Par 4
8	Postage Stamp	123 yards	Par 3
9	The Monk	422 yards	Par 4
10	Sandhills	452 yards	Par 4
11	The Railway	483 yards	Par 4
12	The Fox	429 yards	Par 4
13	Burmah	473 yards	Par 4
14	Alton	178 yards	Par 3
15	Crosbie	502 yards	Par 4
16	Wall	553 yards	Par 5
17	Rabbit	218 yards	Par 3
18	Craigend	464 yards	Par 4

Printed in Great Britain
by Amazon